"You're tresp... private property!"

Theron called out to the bag lady.

She turned, and, ludicrous as it seemed, Theron found himself staring at . . . a clown.

He opened his mouth to speak, then closed it again, staring at her with unmasked perplexity. What the hell did a man say to a woman sporting a putty nose, a ridiculous painted smile, blue freckles sprinkled on rosy cheeks, and eyelashes that fanned out in dainty black paint streaks?

She moved toward him, her hand thrust into the pocket of her patched plaid skirt.

"Welcome home, Mr. Donahue," she greeted him, holding out a bouquet of battered paper roses.

Theron gazed down at the flowers in his hand, astounded that he'd accepted them.

Then, as he looked back at the clown-woman, an incredible sense of déjà vu gripped him. . . .

Dear Reader,

Welcome to the Silhouette **Special Edition** experience! With your search for consistently satisfying reading in mind, every month the authors and editors of Silhouette **Special Edition** aim to offer you a stimulating blend of deep emotions and high romance.

The name Silhouette **Special Edition** and the distinctive arch on the cover represent a commitment—a commitment to bring you six sensitive, substantial novels each month. In the pages of a Silhouette **Special Edition**, compelling true-to-life characters face riveting emotional issues—and come out winners. Both celebrated authors and newcomers to the series strive for depth and dimension, vividness and warmth, in writing these stories of living and loving in today's world.

The result, we hope, is romance you can believe in. Deeply emotional, richly romantic, infinitely rewarding—that's the Silhouette **Special Edition** experience. Come share it with us—six times a month!

From all the authors and editors of Silhouette **Special Edition**,

Best wishes,

Leslie Kazanjian,
Senior Editor

CAROLE McELHANEY
The Perfect Clown

Silhouette Special Edition

Published by Silhouette Books New York

America's Publisher of Contemporary Romance

This book is dedicated with love to
my husband, my friend, my life
Jim
And to my dear friend
Sarah Elizabeth "Sally" Henley.

With special thanks to
Craig Ruben, who is Craiggles the Clown,
And to
JRS, Jr., whose beautiful property inspired the setting for
this story.

SILHOUETTE BOOKS
300 East 42nd St., New York, N.Y. 10017

Copyright © 1990 by Carole McElhaney

ISBN: 0-373-09581-3

First Silhouette Books printing February 1990

All the characters in this book are fictitious. Any
resemblance to actual persons, living or dead, is
purely coincidental.

®: Trademark used under license and
registered in the United States Patent and
Trademark Office and in other countries.

Printed in the U.S.A.

Books by Carole McElhaney

Silhouette Special Edition

A Slice of Heaven #332
The Perfect Clown #581

CAROLE McELHANEY

lives with her real-life "hero" on a small ranch near Corpus Christi, Texas. She and her husband have four children—all grown and out of the nest. An animal lover, Carole keeps dogs and horses. She is a full-time student and a full-time writer, which makes for busy days.

Since the age of seven, her three R's have been: reading, 'riting and riding. "Now to be doing them all, what more could anyone want?" says the author.

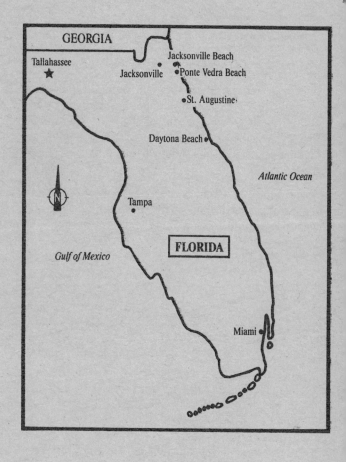

Prologue

*Nicole Ross's Farewell
Performance*

*Madison Square Garden
New York City*

Theron Donahue stood beside the owner of Circus Royale, Lawrence Westbrook. Lifelong friends, the two men talked, both alert to the activity surrounding them—the sights, the smells, the sounds of the circus offering a solid reminder of boyhood dreams come true.

All conversation abruptly stopped as the lights in Madison Square Garden dimmed until only a spotlight illuminated the trapeze rigging high above center ring. An expectant hush fell over the audience, just as it had before intermission when Nicole Ross had performed solo, awing them with her daring mastery of the Roman rings. Her breathtaking performance had caused even Theron's heart to thud heavily as, slipping her legs through the rings, she'd swung high, virtually launching herself toward the ceiling, then suddenly had let go of the ropes and plunged forward, her hair tumbling loose. There was no safety net below, and the illusion of a fall was terrifying. A captive audience breathed a collective sigh of relief as she caught the rings with her knees and floated like a vision high above, her honey-blond hair whipping around her, her smile wide and contagious.

And here she was again—the beautiful Nicole—looking dazzling in a white-and-emerald-green spangled costume. This time she climbed the web with her family, The Flying Rossinis. Stepping onto the pedestal and into the spotlight, she pivoted slowly, waving to the audience. This was her farewell performance. She was leaving the show.

High above center ring, her husband dropped a light kiss on her forehead. Below, thousands applauded and clutched the strings of green and white balloons, waiting for the finale, waiting to pay tribute to the sweethearts of Circus Royale.

The stentorian voice of the ringmaster echoed an introduction...and it began. Those spine-tingling, electrifying moments when all senses were bound to the beauty of perfectly controlled bodies flying and somersaulting. Hearts leaped—including Theron's. There were spins and flips, pirouettes and triple somersaults. Below, there was a net.

Then came the finale. The passing leap.

The silence of thousands was deafening. Theron held his breath as the catcher took his position. On cue, Nicole gripped the trapeze and whipped off the platform. Poised, her husband waited his signal, then leaped out, his body arched, his hands outstretched...

And it was over!

In one horrifying split second, it was *over*!

Bodies collided in the air and tumbled violently to the net in an uncontrolled fall. Nicole moved. Her husband was still. The spotlights dimmed, music blared, and while help scurried to center ring, in came the elephants and clowns, and the show went on.

His heart heavy with pain, his mind unwilling to accept what he'd seen, Theron ran with Lawrence to where Nicole lay on a gurney, tears on her cheeks. Irresistibly drawn to her, he gently rested his hand on her forehead, and as his gaze swept over her delicate features, her eyes fluttered open, raised to meet his, and his heart stopped.

Stunned, he stared into the most beautiful green eyes he'd ever seen. A weak smile of gratitude trembled on her lips, and when she was wheeled away a part of him unaccountably went with her.

"If there is anything I can do to help, Lawrence, let me know," Theron told his friend. Then turning away, he left the Garden, his mind on the woman who'd mesmerized him for those brief breath-catching moments when she'd soared.

Chapter One

Nicole Ross stood in the middle of the plush room, tightly clutching an oversize, tattered purse in her hands. The center of attention, she turned her gaze to the astonished faces gathered around her. No one uttered a sound. Rather, they sat spellbound as her eyes swept over them, touching each in turn.

She was an odd character, dressed in outlandish clothing. Her coat was too big—or was it just that the huge pockets and patches made it seem that way? Her blue-plaid skirt wasn't quite long or short enough, its hem barely touching the tops of bright red socks and high-top shoes. An old, at-one-time-fashionable hat was perched jauntily atop the riot of pale gold curls framing her exaggerated waiflike features. In the faded brown hatband, she'd secured a red paper rose.

Though out of place in the elegance of the sprawling beach house, she was perfectly at ease, her animated expression both happy and sad, her stance proud, yet somehow pathetic.

From somewhere in the room, a giggle erupted. Nicole sighed heavily, dropped her bag to the floor, and shed her worn gray coat. Enthralled, her audience inched forward, eyes round and watchful as she thrust a small hand into the pocket of her skirt. Leaning forward, she handed an enormous lollipop to the wide-eyed little girl sitting on the floor directly in front of her.

"Happy Birthday, Amanda! I'm Rossles the Clown!" she greeted brightly. "Are you having a good time today?"

"Uh-huh!" The child beamed, brown eyes dancing.

"Great!" Nicole squared her shoulders and tilted her head whimsically to address the twenty-two children sitting in a semicircle around Amanda. "Well, shall we get on with the party?"

The children giggled and nodded and squealed enthusiastically, and Nicole stepped back, her size-thirteen, custom-made clown shoes tangling in the straps of her purse, and she tumbled to the floor, executing a perfect pratfall. Her skirt hiked up, revealing hot pink pantaloons. Her mouth dropped open in mock horror. Her eyes widened and quickly, demurely, she pulled it down around her ankles. Laughter rippled around the room, and from that moment on, Rossles, the part august, part tramp clown, captured the hearts of her young audience.

During her act, Nicole gave her all to the children, delighting them with her antics, pulling them in to share her performance. They cheered wildly, laughed helplessly, and applauded with glee when finally she exchanged her outrageous shoes for worn ballet slippers and danced with surprising beauty and grace.

For the duration of her act, there were no problems in Nicole's life, no clouds on the horizon. There were only smiling faces and giggles, ballet shoes and buffoonery, balloons and lollipops. Then it was over, and she bowed low and felt the real world slip around her.

"Okay, kids! Everyone out to the patio! We'll have cake and ice cream in a few minutes!" Annabel Williams ushered the children out of the room and turned to her friend, a smile tugging her mouth. "I honestly don't know how you can do that routine day after day without killing yourself, Nicole."

Nicole rubbed her hips. "Believe me, I'll feel a couple of those falls tomorrow."

"Change your mind. Stay for cake and coffee. The kids would love it, and God knows, I need all the help I can get right about now," Annabel urged, rolling her eyes in desperation.

"I'd love to, but I can't, Annabel. I've got a ton of things to do this afternoon before your cousin gets in." Nicole shivered as she thought of the changes bearing down on her life. Sudden and somewhat disturbing changes, she reflected as she stuffed ballet slippers and clown shoes into her bag. Satisfied she'd collected all of her belongings, she glanced at Annabel. "Did all the kids get balloons?"

"Trust me, you'd know about it if they hadn't."

"Yeah. I guess I would at that."

"If you won't reconsider and stay for coffee, then how about having lunch at the Ocean Club next week?" Annabel suggested as they walked out the front door into the balmy Florida sunshine. "They've hired a new chef, and from all reports, his food is sinfully delicious."

"Umm-hmm." Nicole's mumbled reply was lost on the breeze as she ran lightly down the stairs and followed the sun-warmed sidewalk to the circular drive and her car.

Certain her friend hadn't heard a word she'd said, Annabel tested her theory. "He serves terrific braised sponge with wine sauce."

"Sounds great. It's one of my favorites," came the distracted reply.

"Oh, for Pete's sake, Nicole! What is bugging you? You've been preoccupied ever since you walked through the door today!" Brushing a strand of toast-brown hair out of her face, she narrowed gray eyes on her friend. "You can't be *that* worried about Theron and the kids moving down here!"

Nicole tossed her bag on the backseat and slid behind the steering wheel, peering up at Annabel through the open window. "It's a natural reaction, okay? I like living in the gatehouse. Tag and I have had the run of the estate for two years," she said, referring to the caretaker. "I don't have the slightest idea of what to expect from your cousin. I don't know what changes he's going to make or what his children are like or..." Nicole thought of the photographs in his study; photos of a tall, stern-looking, bespectacled man whose eyes reminded her of the sea on a bright summer day. "Or what he's like," she finished quietly.

"You're impossible." Annabel shook her head. "We've been through this a hundred times! Haven't you heard a word that I've said about them?"

"Yes, I've *heard*." Mentally, Nicole reviewed the ages and talents of the Donahue children. Fifteen-year-old Rusty was a musician—guitar and drums. Julie, thirteen, was an avid equestrian. And ten-year-old Jenny was talented in ballet and gymnastics and mischief. "I'm not worried about the children."

"Good, because they'll love you to death, and you'll adore them. So, that leaves Theron." Annabel studied Nicole thoughtfully. "He might be a bit on the stubborn side and he highly values his privacy, but he is *not* going to arbitrarily throw you out into the street.''

"You got that chipped in stone somewhere?" Nicole smiled wryly.

"Who offered you the cottage in the first place?" Annabel demanded. "And who called me after you moved in, asking that I meet you, take you under my wing, show you around, introduce you to people?" Silence met her. "Well?"

"Your cousin," Nicole conceded.

Annabel raised her hands, palms out. "I rest my case."

"That's not saying he won't bring his household staff down here with him and move them into the gatehouse."

"He won't do that. If anything, he'll hire a housekeeper once he's settled into the Palm Valley house. Someone local who already has a place to live," Annabel told her. "Why don't you try to relax? If Theron wanted you out of the gatehouse, he'd have already given you notice."

"You're probably right." Nicole managed a smile. "But I'd still feel better if I knew him."

"You do!"

"Meeting someone while lying half-conscious on a gurney in the middle of Madison Square Garden doesn't constitute a formal introduction," Nicole countered. "And you know, as well as I, that when he comes down here for a visit, it's on a whirlwind. He locks the gates behind him and leaves again almost before we know he's been here," she said, adding wistfully, "That beautiful house has been virtually deserted since he built it."

Annabel sobered. "I know. Jessica's death hit him pretty hard, Nicole. It changed him a lot. Even his writing has suffered. But...he's coming to terms with it, and quite frankly, I'm glad you're living on the estate." When Nicole looked up curiously, Annabel grinned. "Every eligible female within thirty miles of here is anxiously waiting for a chance to sink their claws into him. Unfortunately, for all the wrong reasons.''

Nicole didn't have to ask what those reasons were. Theron Donahue was one of the country's leading playwrights. A wealthy man. A widower. A supreme "catch."

She started her car, and felt suddenly chilled as she caught a glimpse of the box on the seat next to her. In the box was a manuscript. More precisely, it was an unfinished play written by Theron that Nicole had found stuffed in a corner of one of the many bookshelves in his study. She'd dusted it off, read it, and intrigued, she'd taken it to the gatehouse to read again. And again. Guilt flushed her cheeks with color. She had to return it quickly, before Theron arrived and discovered it missing.

"Hold your guest room open for a few days, all right?" she commented grimly. "I might be needing it."

"Rubbish." Annabel backed away from the car. "Gimme a call, and we'll go for lunch. And thanks for doing Amanda's party on such short notice."

"No problem." With a wave of her hand, Nicole eased out of the driveway and turned south on Ponte Vedra Boulevard, her mind whirling.

She *was* nervous about the Donahues' move to the estate. Because of the changes their arrival would initiate, yes, but there was something else. Something she couldn't quite put her finger on. Yet, it had gnawed at her from the moment Tag had made the casual announcement over coffee that morning: "Theron's due in late this afternoon." Her heart had pounded almost as hard then as it did now, and intuitively she knew it went far beyond her desperate need to return the manuscript. That could be accomplished easily enough, and no one would know that *Images* had ever left the house.

So... if not the manuscript, then what was turning her inside out? she wondered.

Tense, her hands clinging to the steering wheel, she drove, barely noticing the towering palms, the well-manicured lawns and sprawling homes, the golf courses and deep blue lagoons that dotted the landscape of the plush northern Florida resort community, Ponte Vedra Beach, that was situated close to the dunes and sandy beaches of the Atlantic.

Turning west, she crossed Highway A1A and sped along the narrow strip of asphalt winding through the rural community of Palm Valley.

It seemed like only yesterday that she'd driven this road for the first time. Her life had been shattered then. She'd lost all that she loved—her husband, their unborn child, her career as a trapeze artist. Circus Royale had pulled out for another season on the road, leaving the winter quarters south of Jacksonville nearly deserted. As the train had rumbled out of sight, taking away her family and friends, a deep-seated sense of loneliness gripped her. She desperately needed a change. A place to heal physically and emotionally.

Lawrence Westbrook's words rang out as clearly now as if she were hearing them for the first time rather than on that dismal day two years ago, and she rode with the memories.

"I know you want to move, Nikki. Go out and have a look at this place. It's a cottage on the Donahue estate." Smiling, Lawrence had shoved a piece of paper into her hand. "Theron and I used to hunt this property when we were kids. Long before he developed it. I've already talked to him. It's yours if you want it. Good luck, babe, and get that shoulder healed. We want you back in the show as soon as you're well enough," he'd said, then kissing her forehead, he boarded the train, giving her one last command. "Go look at the cottage."

Curious, she'd gone. She'd sped along this very road and driven over the wooden drawbridge that crossed the Intercoastal Waterway, and not far from the base of the bridge, she found the narrow lane that wound between a towering canyon of pines and palms for a good quarter of a mile.

Oh, how well she remembered the first glimpse of the Tudor cottage nestled in the trees! It was enchanting! Perfect!

She drank in the lovely sight of the stucco-and-wood structure, with its paned windows and window boxes. A brick wall enclosed the small yard in front and behind the house, the lawn rolled down to a creek that separated the gatehouse from the estate grounds. Beyond the creek, sheltered by trees, she saw the large Tudor mansion and outbuildings, all immaculate, all, much to her surprise, empty.

Precisely what she wanted, she'd climbed out of her car and walked through the wrought-iron gate toward the cottage.

"Hey! You lost or somethin'? This is private property!" The gruff voice startled her. Whirling around, she encountered a crusty, old man whom she guessed to be in his midsixties.

"I'm Nicole Ross." Holding out her hand, she received a reluctant but firm handshake. "I was told the gatehouse is for rent."

"I ain't heard nothin' 'bout it." The old man eyed her suspiciously.

"Is Mr. Donahue here?"

"Nope."

"When do you expect him?"

"Look, girl, I'm busy. You want to talk to Mr. Donahue, go to New York. Now, reckon you'd best be on your way." Dismissing her, he went back to work trimming the hedges.

Belligerent, old coot! she thought, stubbornly standing her ground. "I'd appreciate it if you'd at least hear me out," she persisted. "Lawrence Westbrook sent me out here. He's already talked to Mr. Donahue."

"Lawrence, heh?" The man pulled off his cap and a surprisingly thick shock of steel-gray hair sprang free. He mopped the sweat from his brow with the sleeve of his shirt, light blue eyes peering at her from beneath bushy gray eyebrows. "So you know Lawrence, do you?"

"Yes. Very well. Look, Mr.—"

"Taggert. Graham Taggert. Tag suits me just fine."

"Tag." She smiled her very best smile. "Please, just call Mr. Donahue to verify this for me? I really need a place to live, and this is so perfect...."

"All right! I'll call him. But you stay put. No snoopin' 'round till I get back from the big house." Tag grudgingly gathered up his tools.

"Thank you," she said, adding hastily, "One more thing?" When he glanced at her impatiently, she shrugged. "I have a horse and dog that I don't want to leave behind."

He smiled, then. "You got guts, lady. I'll give you that. Yup, reckon I'll tell him."

Not only had Tag returned from the big house with good news, but Nicole had also noticed an expression of respectful curiosity in his eyes. And he was driving a pickup, pulling a tandem horse trailer. After a muttered, "Hell, these hedges can wait another day," he urged a surprised Nicole to climb into the truck. "We ain't got time to waste, girl. Boss says you're in no condition to be doin' any heavy liftin', what with your shoulder out of whack. Let's go."

She was moved in one trip: horse, dog and personal belongings. By nightfall, Nicole was sitting on the floor in the living room of the unfurnished cottage, her Doberman sleeping in front of the fire blazing on the hearth, her stereo blaring, towels tacked at the windows. In the barn at the main house, her Morgan mare was bedded down in a box stall, peacefully munching sweet hay.

If she was surprised by the swiftness of the move, she was more stunned by the amount of rent she was expected to pay for the cottage. It was a mere token, a fraction of what she'd expected. Plus, the estate picked up her utilities.

Even more puzzling was Theron Donahue's aloofness. On his rare visits to the estate, she'd seen him whiz by the cottage in what she supposed were rental cars, and not once had he so much as glanced in her direction, much less sought her out.

As one year passed, then another, Nicole began to wonder if she'd imagined his warm, strong hand on her forehead the night of her fall, or the dozen long-stemmed roses he'd sent during her hospital stay, or his note of condolence at the loss of her husband, with its simple statement:

If I can be of any help, Lawrence can reach me on your behalf. Speedy recovery.

Theron Donahue

It was hard to believe that two years had passed since she'd moved out here, and though she'd always be grateful to Lawrence for his part in making the move possible, it was the playwright himself who piqued her curiosity.

But would she ever have the chance to meet the elusive Mr. Donahue? Surely he couldn't reside on the estate and avoid her indefinitely, she reasoned as she parked beside the cottage, relishing the thought of removing her greasepaint and showering before returning the manuscript.

Thinking of *Images*, she groaned and glanced at her watch. It was barely one. Theron Donahue wasn't due in until late afternoon. There was plenty of time.

Still, she jumped nervously as a shadow fell over her. Looking up, she saw Tag standing beside the car, and a great sigh of relief rushed from her lungs.

"You're a bit skittish today, girl, heh?" The man who'd become as close as family grinned at her.

"You startled me."

"I can see that," he said. "Look, Nikki, if you want to shower, you'll have to use the facilities in the guest room at the main house. You got a busted water pipe here." He rubbed his chin. "I been workin' on it, but it's gonna be a couple more hours before it's fixed."

"That's just what I need today," she muttered quietly, and glanced over her shoulder. Everything she needed was in the backseat—jeans, a shirt, her Nikes. Carrying a change of clothes was more habit than anything else. Though she preferred being prepared, rarely did she climb out of her clown costume until she was in the privacy of her own home. Gunning the engine, she grinned up at Tag. "Well, if that's what I have to do, then I'd best get going, hadn't I? Thanks, Tag. See you later."

"Nikki, wait! A word of warnin', girl . . ." But his words were lost. The white Celica was already racing across the bridge and between the iron gates leading to the main house. He lowered his hand to scratch the ears of the Doberman sitting beside him. "Hell, Luke, looks like they're both in for a surprise." He chuckled. "Maybe what that man needs is a clown in his life. Sure won't hurt him none, heh? Now, let's get back to them pipes."

At the big house, Nicole scrambled out of the car, her arms laden with makeup case, clothing and the manuscript. Fumbling with the key to the front door, she let herself in. Though the house was empty, quiet, her spine tingled unaccountably, and a strange sense of urgency turned her hands clammy.

Before taking a shower, *before* changing her clothes, she had to return *Images* to its proper place in the study.

Nervously, she dropped her makeup case, grimacing as the metal cleats clattered against the Saltillo tile floor. The sound echoed through the house. Nicole anxiously glanced around, expecting... what? *He's not due in for hours,* she reminded herself, and taking a deep, calming breath, she pushed the case closer to the guest-room door, laid her clothes haphazardly over it and clutching the manuscript tightly to her breast, hurried out of the receiving hall and crossed the living room to the familiar paneled study.

Exhausted from the long hours spent in his car, Theron emptied his garment bag, hanging the few items of clothing that he'd brought with him in the walk-in closet in his bedroom, then prepared for a long-anticipated shower. He could almost feel the hot, pulsing water ease his tired, aching muscles and wash away the grime of the eight states through which he'd traveled during the past twenty-four hours.

He'd arrived much earlier than originally planned, but once on the road, once leaving his children and New York behind, there seemed little point in dawdling. He'd stopped for gas, for coffee. He'd napped in the car. Then he'd driven on again until the highway blurred and his hands seemed fused to the steering wheel.

Now he was in Florida—in a home that he should have moved his family to years ago but hadn't—*couldn't*—until now.

Pulling his sweater over his head, he tossed it on the king-size bed, frowning as he caught a glimpse of himself in the mirror on the dresser. A thick stubble of beard shadowed his face. His eyes were tired and bloodshot, his features drawn and haggard. A shower, a shave and a stiff shot of Scotch would do absolute wonders for him.

He sat on the bed, pulling off shoes and socks, and placed his watch on the nightstand, glancing at it briefly. If all went as planned, the movers would arrive soon. Once the trucks were unloaded, several hours of unpacking stretched before him. Hours, hell. *Days*. Thirteen rooms had to be organized. And of the thirteen, only three were even partially furnished now; his bedroom, with the bed, dresser and nightstand; the breakfast nook, with its old oak table and four chairs; his study, with its teak desk and chair and only a fraction of his vast library on the built-in bookshelves. He'd need every minute of the coming week to complete all that he planned to do before the children arrived for their first weekend in their new home.

Thinking of them, Theron frowned. As much as he disliked the idea of separation, Rusty, Julie and Jenny would be staying in New York with his sister-in-law until the end of the fall semester; until Theron could make arrangements for their transfers to schools in Florida. In the meantime, they'd fly in for the occasional weekend. He wasn't thrilled with the idea, yet there'd been no other choice.

No one, least of all Theron, had expected the Southampton house to sell within a few days of hitting the market. But it had, and with the sale had come the frantic plans for the relocation. He'd moved heaven and earth to make the necessary arrangements, to get things rolling quickly, and now everything the Donahues owned, with the exception of the children's clothing, was in transit.

The horses were here. The van had arrived shortly after Theron had climbed out of his Seville, and the animals, no worse for the wear, were now in their stalls. He'd helped unload them. He'd fed them and stayed with them until he was assured they were settled into their new environment.

While in the barn, he'd stopped to admire the dark bay dappled mare curiously eyeing her new stallmates. Stretching a hand out to stroke the animal's sleek neck, he'd thought of Nicole Ross for the first time since arriving, for the horse, he knew, was hers.

He lingered by the stall, thinking of the mare's owner. Though he vividly remembered Nicole's fall and the tears in her eyes, though he'd offered what help he could when she needed a place to live, he hadn't allowed himself to dwell on her. That fateful night in the Garden seemed a lifetime away in one instant, like yesterday the next.

Shaking his head, he abruptly brought himself back to the present and wearily strode to the bathroom, his mind still on Nicole. He hadn't been ready to meet her during his brief visits to the estate. He'd been too busy dealing with the ghosts rattling chains in his own mind to worry about Nicole, but all of that would soon change. No longer would he be able to avoid her. Not with her living on the estate.

Nor could he avoid the memories of Jessica, for they echoed through every room of the house. Yet, it was time to say goodbye. Time to move ahead with his life.

He reached for the water taps, stopping short as a sharp, clattering noise shattered the silence. Frowning, he listened. There it was again. Not as loud this time, it was more of a scraping sound coming from downstairs—a signal, a bold announcement of an intruder in his home.

Turning away from the luxury of the shower, he stalked out of the bedroom and down the open, railed upstairs hall, his frown changing to a scowl as he caught a glimpse of a woman dressed in ragged clothing dashing out of the receiving hall and disappearing into the living room.

A bag lady? A street urchin?

In his home?

Running down the stairs clad only in his trousers, he narrowed his eyes. His jaw tightened in anger as he surveyed the hall. There, on the floor, he saw the overnight case and clothing the woman had dropped. In long, determined strides he crossed the living room, coming to a stop at the open door of his study—a door he distinctly remembered closing not twenty minutes ago.

Outraged, he glared at the intruder. She stood behind his desk, her back to him. He stepped into the room, his body filling the doorway, blocking the only exit from the room.

Chapter Two

"Madam! Not only are you trespassing on private property, but you have gained illegal entry to my home!"

Nicole froze. Under the greasepaint, the color drained from her face, and for a moment, falling into a dead faint was a distinct possibility. Her mouth turned dry. Her heart pounded, and she clutched the manuscript so tightly that her fingers hurt. What she feared most was happening. She was caught in Theron Donahue's study with *Images* in her possession, and there was no doubt in her mind that the man delivering the reprimand was the master of the estate, in the flesh.

"Madam!"

She jumped at the harshness of the voice. It was bad enough that her guilt was so obvious, but to be caught red-handed while still in her clown costume bordered on the bizarre. Clowns didn't pry into people's personal belongings. Clowns were, supposedly, above reproach.

How, she wondered, could she explain that the play had held her so firmly, captured her so completely, tugged at her heartstrings so strongly that she'd been unable to put it down? Or that, while fully aware her action was an invasion of the author's privacy, she'd taken *Images* home in hope of finding a clue to how he intended to end the poignant tale? She'd pondered that subject for two weeks and still hadn't the slightest idea.

Quaking inside, she placed the box on the shelf behind his desk and glanced briefly at the framed photo sitting next to it. A publicity photograph, she guessed, in which he appeared studious in a three-piece suit and horn-rimmed glasses—rather bland, actually, except for his eyes. He seemed the intellectual type, she thought, and hoping that he was reasonable, as well, she took a deep breath, then turned to face the reality of Theron Donahue. Her prayer for mercy was silent but fervent, her guilt hidden behind the face of a clown.

Who was more surprised, Nicole would never be sure. She heard his muttered, "What the hell?" She saw his incredulous expression, and watched him blink twice in disbelief.

And there followed a heavy, astonished silence, while two pairs of eyes assessed, two mouths dropped open in amazement. Normally not at a loss for words, Nicole found herself utterly speechless. Theron was apparently dumbstruck, too.

Nicole stared at him. Studious? *Bland*? Not by a long shot! She blatantly studied the man standing in the doorway. He was tall. His very tan, very bare chest was sprinkled abundantly with golden hair. He was gorgeous and masculine and powerful in a lean, athletic sort of way. He was long of limb and sinewy. Broad of shoulder, narrow of waist. His feet were . . . bare? And tan?

Writers aren't supposed to look like this! she thought, raising her eyes to his beard-roughened face in time to catch the parade of expressions chasing across his features: waning anger, confusion, surprise, and underlying all, a reluctant suggestion of mirth. Framing his intriguingly lined face was a mussed, wavy shock of sun-bleached hair. Not quite blond, not quite brown.

He wasn't wearing glasses now, and for some reason that disturbed Nicole, made her wonder and hesitate. But finally she dared to look directly into his clear, blue-green eyes and would have laughed merrily at his utter shock if not for the seriousness of the situation.

She'd often wondered why the briefest of moments could stretch on interminably until it seemed as if hours had passed. Now she knew. Occasionally, time stood still, allowing people to thoroughly absorb what was going on around them, allowing a respite, a time to marshal thoughts, and while she wished the silence would end, she was frightened of what might happen when it did.

Ten fleeting seconds ago, ten abrupt movements of a hand on a clock, Theron had been ready to bodily throw a bag lady out of his house. Then she'd turned and, as ludicrous as it seemed, he found himself staring at . . . a clown? He opened his mouth to speak, to threaten her with the law, to do whatever was necessary to remove the vagrant from his home, then he closed it again, the angry lecture he was prepared to deliver dying on his lips. Instead, he stared at her with unmasked perplexity, wondering what the hell a man said to a woman sporting a pert putty nose, a ridiculous painted smile, blue freckles sprinkled on rosy cheeks and eyelashes that fanned out in dainty black paint streaks.

She moved toward him, her hand thrust into the pocket of her wild plaid skirt. Stopping an arm's length away, she withdrew it and held something out for him.

"Welcome home, Mr. Donahue," Nicole greeted, glad that she had Rossles's character to fall back on. When his lips twitched, she knew she had to play her role to the hilt, to appeal to the boy in him—if there was one. As he took the proffered bouquet of battered paper roses from her, her hopes for a reprieve soared. Their fingers brushed fleetingly. She felt the heat of his touch and his eyes, and she almost faltered. "I trust you had a good trip."

"Yes, I did. Thank you," he replied, gazing at the paper flowers in his hand, astounded that he'd accepted them. Looking back at the intruder, an incredible sense of déjà vu gripped him. "What is the proper response one gives, when receiving a peace offering such as this? Will a simple thank-you suffice?"

"It'll do very nicely." There was relief in her voice. "It's more than I expected."

"I can understand why." He turned the roses in his hand, studying the tattered bouquet, and for the first time since leaving New York, his mood lightened. *A clown*? Having never had occasion to go one-on-one with a woman who looked like a cross between Emmett Kelly and Carol Burnett, he contemplated the situation. Who the hell had put her up to this? Annabel? Lawrence, perhaps? he wondered, absently tapping the flowers against his hand.

"I wouldn't do that if I were you," the clown advised boldly. "Paper roses are fragile, but if you're careful with them, they'll last forever," she said, intentionally drawing out the moment. "Actually they're much easier to keep than the real McCoy if you follow the three basic rules of thumb in caring for them."

"Do those rules pertain to a thumb of the green or paper variety?" He'd play her game—for a while.

Nicole's eyes danced. The man had a sense of humor. That was good. "It depends entirely on what kind of roses you're dealing with. In this case, paper is definitely in order."

"Suppose you tell me what they are."

Stunned by the rich quality of his voice, Nicole fought to remain safely within her clown's character while the woman in her reacted in a totally disturbing manner. "It's really rather simple. They'll dissolve in water, burn if you put a match to them and shred if you keep hitting them against your hand."

"These appear to have been through several wars already, but I'll keep your advice in mind." He studied her, noticing for the first time that her eyes were green. A very deep, vivid shade of green. Like emeralds. "Is there any other information you'd care to impart?"

"Regarding the roses, no." She tensed, knowing the time of reckoning was close at hand.

"I see." His eyes darkened, the blue vying with the green for supremacy, and when he caught and held her gaze, it was with a fierce intensity that almost dared her to move. "In that case, why don't we get down to business. Before you *leave*, suppose you tell me who you are, who put you up to this, and who the hell gave you the right to go through my personal papers?"

Under her makeup, her cheeks flamed. "'Fess-up time?"

"I'd appreciate it."

Though he appeared outwardly composed and his voice was controlled, Nicole knew he was not a man to be easily fooled or put off. She returned his gaze with a directness of her own, and somehow managed to answer him in what she hoped was an equally controlled manner.

"I'm Nicole Ross."

"Nicole?" Off balance once again, he stared at her. God, what eyes! Bright, beautiful, well-remembered. Of course, it was she! He should have known the instant she moved out of the shadows of the room.

"Yes... I live in the gatehouse."

"I'm well aware of where you live."

"Of course you are." Self-consciously, she lowered her head, immediately wishing she hadn't. He stood mere inches from her, the muscles of his broad chest filling her vision, his musky scent teasing her senses with every breath she took. "I owe you an apology for taking *Images*."

"Taking it?" he snapped. "Taking it where?"

"Only to the gatehouse."

"My work does not leave this room. Is that understood, Ms. Ross?"

"Well . . . yes . . . but—"

"Is that understood?"

"If you'll give me a chance to explain—"

"How many times must I repeat the question?" He glared at her.

"I said I was sorry! It won't happen again, all right? But it's a darn good play, and I've spent the past two weeks trying to figure out why you didn't bother to finish it and how it would end if and when you ever do get back to work on it!" she blurted. "Now, will you *please* stop banging those flowers around before they fall to bits?"

Mortified by her outburst, Nicole waited for him to throw her out of the house, order her off the property. He did neither, and they stood like statues, glaring at each other, eyes meeting, challenging, neither backing down.

His hand stilled, and the roses nodded gently.

Her heart thumped.

His jaw tightened.

Her palms grew damp.

"So, you're a critic, as well as a clown?" he said finally, regarding her perpetually smiling face and angry eyes. The incongruity baffled him, and he found the entire situation bizarre. Grown men didn't fight with clowns.

"No, but I know what I like. *Images* is good. It's a shame that you've buried it instead of going the extra mile to finish it."

Her words pierced him like well-aimed arrows. He'd shelved the play three years ago when Jess died. It was a personal thing with him, one that he didn't care to discuss with anyone. Walking past her, he went to the windows overlooking the lush, tree-studded lawn that swept from the house down to the Intercoastal Waterway.

"I trust this won't happen again," he said quietly, ignoring her observation.

"You have my word on it," she promised, and sighed and wondered how the devil she would manage to live in such close proximity to this very attractive, very strong man and maintain her balance with any measure of grace. And, she wondered about the sadness that clouded his eyes when she'd upbraided him about *Images*. Then she remembered. He'd lost someone, too. "Look, Mr. Donahue—"

"It's Theron, please."

Surprised, her gaze shot to him, and she smiled hesitantly, then tried the name and found that it rolled almost sensually off her lips. "Okay...Theron. I am sorry. I had absolutely no right to read your work without your permission."

"No, you didn't," he agreed, his features set and stern. "I'm curious about something."

Nicole fidgeted nervously. "Oh?"

"Yes. You see it puzzles me. Your reason for being in the house in the first place," he clipped.

"Even an abandoned home needs airing and vacuuming occasionally, or neglect will take its toll," she replied frostily. "This house has been sorely in need of attention."

"That's Tag's job. Not yours."

Nicole bristled angrily. "Just in case you've forgotten the enormous size of this place, you might want to refresh your memory and take a good, long look around! Tag has his hands full with the gardening and yard work and keeping the fences up and the outbuildings in proper repair!" Her eyes flashed green sparks. "If helping out a friend is a crime, then by all means I'm guilty of that, as well. Now, if you'll please excuse me, I'd like to shower and get out of this makeup before I melt."

He lifted his eyebrows in surprise. She had spunk. He admired that. "If Tag hasn't finished the work on your plumbing, feel free to use the shower in the guest room. I trust you know where it is?"

"Yes, I do," she said and turned to leave.

Of course she knew, he reminded himself dryly. She'd aired the house, cleaned the empty rooms. She was intimately acquainted with his study. In all probability, she was more familiar with the house than he was at the moment. Why, he wondered, didn't that bother him? Why, instead, did it make him feel . . . good . . . knowing that she'd wandered the rooms in his absence, that perhaps her laughter had echoed through an otherwise empty house?

"Nicole!"

Her name, a single command, abruptly stopped her flight from the study. She stiffened, her shoulders held high and proud, one hand resting on the doorjamb, and for an instant before she turned to look at him, Theron remembered her in another way: as a young woman in a green-and-white spangled costume, smiling, whirling, flying, falling. Suddenly he wanted to see that woman again. The clown without the makeup and curly gold wig and custom-made tattered clothing.

"What?" she asked quietly, glancing over her shoulder, wondering if he ever smiled.

"Thank you for the bouquet."

"It was the least I could do."

The muscles of his jaw tightened, then he sighed heavily. "We didn't get off on the best footing."

"No, we didn't," she agreed warily.

"Suppose we try to remedy the situation," he suggested in a voice as warm as an August wind.

"What exactly did you have in mind?"

"I thought perhaps you might agree to join me for a drink after you've showered and changed?"

She pursed her lips thoughtfully. There were a hundred reasons to say no, not the least of which was the disturbing effect he had on her, the way he made her pulse race and her heart pound at the mere sight of him standing there, bare-chested and so very male.

"Yes, I'd like that," she said. A social drink with him would be strictly in the interest of establishing a peaceful coexistence, she hastily assured herself.

The corners of his mouth lifted slightly. "I have to shower, as well. Why don't we meet by the pool in half an hour? Will that give you enough time?"

"That will be fine."

Watching her hurry from the room, her step light and lively, Theron wished that he'd thought to pack his favorite pipe and tobacco in the car instead of shipping them. He didn't light up often these days. He hadn't, in fact, in several weeks. Now, he craved the rich taste of the tobacco and the feel of the pipe in his hand.

He stared at the empty doorway where the clown had stood, her eyes wary, her demeanor proud. Then he turned back to the window, realizing that his life would never be quite the same again. Certainly not with Nicole Ross living a stone's throw away.

It wasn't an unpleasant thought. Having her so near. Yet he pushed her from his mind, for there were things he had to put to rest once and for all, personal demons he had to deal with if he ever hoped to get on with his life.

His mouth compressed, his eyes narrowed, he gazed contemplatively at the sun-drenched beauty of the landscape and let his thoughts, his memories carry him one last time.

Everything he saw—the swimming pool, the stately trees, the gardens, the dock on the ICW—all of it was familiar and well loved, but he viewed it now with mixed emotions.

He looked at the magnolia trees close to the house, thinking of Jessica and how she'd loved them, and the shrubs that were neatly trimmed globes of green, and the gardens that bloomed in a riot of color.

He watched lazy shadows move on the grass as sunlight spilled through the boughs and fronds of the pines and palms peppering the grounds. A twinge of pain, of loss, cinched his heart. Oh, yes, Jess had loved this property. She'd wanted to move back to their Florida roots. So they'd built this house together.

How well he remembered the frantic pace at which she'd worked in designing the house, overseeing the construction, picking out tile and carpet and drapes. How well he remembered her excitement as the moving date loomed nearer and nearer. And oh, God, how well he remembered the night her life was taken by a drunk driver and the agonizing months that followed. Months of numb shock and anger and hatred.

He caught himself short. That was three years ago, and though Jess was a part of him forever, he knew he must try to accept her loss. Brooding about the senselessness of the accident wouldn't bring her back. He had his memories— memories that were soft and filled with love—and while he refused to lose them completely, he also refused to dwell on them. For Theron had his children, and in them he found an intense, satisfying joy. Each day of his life he looked to them as solid reminders of all that was and all that could be.

Still, he reflected, it had taken all this time to make the move down from New York, to face this house. Drawn to it, he'd flown in for a weekend now and again. He'd closed the gates behind him in hope of clearing his mind, in hope of working.

Work? He scoffed. Where had the ideas gone? The creative well that had carried him to the pinnacle of his profession, that had won him accolades and Tonys, was seemingly dry. The one play he'd written since Jessica's death had bombed miserably. And *Images*? Hell, he hadn't been able to look at the manuscript in three years.

Remembering the clown's words, he scowled fiercely. She'd read it and liked it and accosted him passionately on its behalf—for whatever that was worth.

Frustrated, knowing he was in a disastrous slump, Theron focused his thoughts and his gaze elsewhere.

From the study, he could see the gatehouse snuggled in the trees across the creek, and as he idly thought of the woman who lived there, he became conscious of a heavy loneliness deep in his heart. There were things he missed in his life: a woman's love and gentle touch, the sharing of laughter, a warm body curving against him in the darkness of the midnight hour, knowing that someone was there for him and the children, and the stability of a family life.

As he pondered these things, Nicole Ross inexplicably edged into his mind. She'd enchanted him from the moment he first laid eyes on her two years ago. After her accident, he despised himself for that enchantment. He had no right to feel anything other than compassion for her, yet no matter how hard he'd tried, he was never able to push her completely out of his mind. Now, thinking of her caused his blood to warm unaccountably, but the only image flashing in his mind's eye was that of a damned clown with big, green eyes and a putty nose.

Impatiently, he stalked out of the room. If he planned to shower before meeting her, it was time to get a move on, but as his bare feet hit the cool tile in the receiving hall he heard a truck lumber up the driveway and gears grind unmercifully. Theron cursed. It was the movers. He'd forgotten all about them.

Taking the stairs two at a time, he grabbed shirt and shoes from his bedroom and was waiting at the front door when the truck stopped.

His shower and the drink with Nicole would have to wait.

Her costume, wig and hat hanging on doorknobs in the empty room, Nicole wiped the last traces of greasepaint from her face and threw the oil-soaked tissues into the trash. Reaching up, she removed the pins holding her honey-blond hair in place and with a shake of her head sent the long tresses tumbling down her back.

Dear God, why were her hands shaking so? And her heart pounding? And her thoughts wandering?

She was a woman whose very survival for years had depended on total concentration, on absolute control of body and mind, and this idle woolgathering irritated her immensely. But she was powerless to block out Theron Donahue and the disturbing images hounding her as she readied herself for the shower.

Upstairs, he was likely doing much the same as she. Now stripping . . . now stepping under a hot, pulsating stream of water . . . now soaping his magnificent body . . . now toweling rivulets of water from his skin, his hands rough and gentle . . .

And what wonderful hands they were! A "hand" person, Nicole had noticed his immediately. Sprinkled with fine gold hair, they were well shaped and strong, with clever fingers that could fly over the keys of a typewriter. Experienced hands capable of fueling a woman's passion. Knowing hands that were, perhaps . . . demanding, seeking?

Annoyed, she tossed her towel aside and tried not to hurry as she dressed. She felt strangely restless, impatient, as she turned her blow-dryer on impossibly long, thick hair. When she looked in the mirror and saw the heightened color splashed across her cheeks, she chalked it up to the shower.

Skin always glowed after ten minutes exposure to hot water, didn't it? she reasoned as she swept her hair back and fastened it securely with a banana clip.

But she couldn't reason away the flutter of excitement curling through her nether region any more than she could account for its sudden presence. Her nerves were as taut as a tightrope, and her body fairly hummed with excitement. She felt...*alive*...for the first time in years, and on the heels of exhilaration came a sobering reality.

There was no room in her life for a relationship with any man. Not now. Most certainly not with someone like Theron. *Stay with your own kind, Nicole.* How many times had her father warned her about that over the years? And Gabriel Rossini was right. Especially in this instance. Theron represented everything stable and secure. He had a home to run and children to raise and plays to write. Nicole was a nomad who would soon be going back to the trapeze, back to the circus and life on the road.

Gathering her belongings together, she stacked them by the door. She'd have a drink with Theron. One. Then she'd beat a hasty retreat to the safety of the gatehouse. It was the only thing she could do, for he was far too tempting.

With that resolution firmly in mind, she opened the bedroom door and gaped in astonishment at the chaos greeting her. Packing boxes and crates were stacked everywhere. Men's voices drifted down from upstairs, and from the front landing came a volley of muttered oaths. Venturing a cautious glance at the perpetrator, she saw a heavyset, bull-necked man wrestle a loaded dolly into the house.

He spotted Nicole, and for all his hulk, he blushed. "Sorry, lady. No offense intended."

Accustomed to moving, and the frustrations that accompanied the chore, she smiled. "None taken. Where's Mr. Donahue?"

"In there." The man nodded toward the living room.

"Thank you."

Dodging man and dolly, she walked into a room, once empty, that was now cluttered with boxes and furniture. Across from her, Tag and Theron maneuvered a gleaming black lacquered baby grand into a corner that was flanked on one side by a solid off-white wall and on the other by paned picture windows. She eyed the placement with silent approval. It was perfect.

When Theron stepped back to view the piano, then went to work again, shifting the Steinway so it sat at an angle in the corner, Nicole's attention was diverted from the instrument to the man. She watched, fascinated, as the muscles of his arms and shoulders bunched and flexed from the strain of the task, and a shiver of awareness tingled through her.

"That's it, Tag. Tomorrow I'll make arrangements for someone to come out and tune the thing," Theron said, and turning suddenly, he caught Nicole watching him. Something flickered briefly in his eyes, then disappeared again, but there was no mistaking the catch in his voice. "So... you've finally finished."

"Yes." Her mouth went dry, her palms damp. She wanted to run from the intensity of his perusal, but her knees betrayed her by locking. "Is something wrong?"

"No... no, nothing at all," he assured her.

Tension filled the room. The air fairly crackled as eyes met in acknowledgement and spoke a language all their own, saying things Nicole couldn't begin to verbalize and only vaguely understood. Out of the corner of her eye, she was aware of Tag. She could have kissed the old man when he cleared his throat and broke the heady, nerve-racking moment.

"'Lo, Nikki. You're all set at the cottage. If you have any more trouble, let me know." He glanced from Nicole to Theron, then back again.

"Thanks, Tag." Oh, God, why did she sound so breath-less?

"Well, I'm gonna take a break. Drink a tall, cold brew with the movers, heh?" Tag announced. "Yup, that'll sure hit the spot right 'bout now."

"Go ahead, Tag. I may join you in a few minutes." Though Theron addressed the man, his eyes remained steady on the woman. Hell, he couldn't drag them away from her.

Tag ambled, whistling, from the room, leaving them alone in screaming silence.

"You're staring at me. Why?" Nicole asked finally, her heart slamming against her ribs.

"You look . . . oh, I don't know. Different."

"I certainly hope so." Her eyes grew merry, and the sound of laughter, the knowledge that it was erupting from her own lips, came as a complete surprise to Nicole. "Don't tell me you're one of those people who thinks a clown is a clown twenty-four hours a day?"

For the first time in years, Theron blushed. "No. I'm not quite that naive. I do recall, however, that the first time we met, you were in spangled spandex and theatrical makeup. And today you presented yourself as Freckles the Clown."

"Rossles," she corrected.

"Whatever." He almost smiled. "Somehow, I can't help but wonder if this is another of your many guises—or if it's the real you."

"It's the real me." She swallowed nervously. "I believe it's a case of what you see is what you get, so to speak."

His eyes wandered over her slender frame, rested briefly on firm breasts and curvy hips, then raised again to capture and hold her gaze. "I'm glad. I rather like what I see," he announced, adding a deliberate observation that made her pulse leap. "You're very beautiful nude."

The last word hung in the air, and Nicole almost choked. "I beg your pardon?"

"Without makeup."

"Oh."

He walked over to her. Crooking a finger under her chin, he tilted her head back fractionally and studied her features. "You're lovely, with or without the makeup."

"If you're comparing me to Rossles, then I'm not sure if I should take it as a compliment," she replied, shaken by his words.

He smiled, then, and laughed, and Nicole decided that he needed to do both more often, for his smile was dazzling, his laughter rich and mellow.

"I think you should take it as a compliment. Not all women can get by without the paint and putty, which isn't to say that Rossles doesn't have endearing qualities." He watched high color stain her cheeks. "The blue freckles." He touched her cheek and found her skin satiny. "The cute putty nose." He tapped the tip of hers before letting his hand fall to his side so that only his eyes rested on her full lips when he spoke again. "A very interesting mouth. Almost kissable." He punctuated the words with a pause, then added, "Of course, I'm speaking of Rossles."

"You're certifiably crazy," she stammered, her flesh burning where he'd touched her. "Any man who wants to kiss a clown is weird. The greasepaint's too messy."

"I may try it sometime." Though he was smiling, a subtle promise lingered in his words, and his voice had turned quiet, husky. From somewhere in the house—the kitchen, perhaps—boisterous laughter rang out, threatening but failing to shatter the mounting tension. Then much to her relief, he let her off the hook. "I'm afraid we're going to have to postpone our drink."

"I can see why." Grateful to be on safer ground, Nicole surveyed the room. "It looks as if you could use an extra pair of hands around here."

Surprised, he narrowed his eyes. "Are you volunteering?"

That was the last thing she'd intended to do, but the words had slipped off her tongue before she could stop them and it was too late to take them back. "I guess I am."

"Now, that's what I call enthusiasm."

"It's called being neighborly."

"I don't want to impose on you."

"It's not an imposition. If it were, I wouldn't have offered."

He looked at her thoughtfully, his eyes turning wary. "And are you as adept at critiquing home decor as you are my writing?"

She grinned impishly. "I'd rather think of it as constructive input. You know what they say about a woman's touch."

She groaned in dismay.

He smiled. "Oh, yes. I know about a woman's touch."

"Oh, God, you are impossible!" she muttered, wondering how the hell she'd gotten herself into this. "Do you want my help or not?"

"Offer accepted."

Chapter Three

It was late—well past nine—when Nicole slipped out of the house, unnoticed, and stood on the flagstone terrace, the cool night air refreshing her. Exhausted, she needed a break. They'd worked nonstop for five hours, accomplishing more than she'd thought possible, but with thirteen rooms of furniture, knickknacks, objets d'art, linen and dishes, and a multitude of other odds and ends, it would take several days to put the house in order.

Throughout the long hours, she'd learned much about Theron Donahue, and most of what she'd learned, she liked. Though stern, he was sensitive. Though stubborn, he was fair. Though quiet, he was a man of passion. She saw it in his eyes, heard it in his voice, sensed it in his very presence.

But the most important thing she'd learned while working at his side was the terrible emotional toll of the move. For a man who exuded self-confidence, a man who demanded attention simply by walking into a room, he was surprisingly vulnerable. He had turned to Nicole on several occasions to ask her advice on something. Sometimes he'd just looked at her with his marvelous blue-green eyes. Seeing pain in their depths, she'd smiled gently, and he'd smiled, and they'd gone back to work.

He seemed to need her, and more than once, he'd sought her out, staying with her, lending her a hand in whatever she was doing.

She'd been upstairs unpacking linen the last time he came looking for her. She'd ripped into one of the cartons and found, not the expected linen, but a box of mementos. Fascinated, she had kneeled on the floor to have a look. She pulled out a photograph of a strikingly beautiful, auburn-haired woman. Dressed in jeans, the woman sat under a magnolia tree, her expression one of sublime happiness. In the background was a house under construction—this house.

There was no doubt in Nicole's mind about the woman's identity. It was Theron's wife. Jessica Donahue.

Nicole found other things in the box. A book of poems that Theron had given his wife. There were other photographs of the Donahue family laughing, playing, celebrating.

Thoroughly engrossed in her discovery, Nicole wasn't aware of Theron's appearance next to her until his deep, quiet voice startled her. "You really do have a *thing* for going through my personal belongings, don't you?"

"I'm sorry. It was marked linen," she said and looked up at him. "Your wife was a very beautiful woman."

"Yes, she was," he replied as he picked up the box. "I'd better put these things up in the attic—get them out of our way."

There'd been something in his voice and eyes that made Nicole wonder if perhaps Annabel had been wrong. Perhaps Theron hadn't come to terms with his loss. Perhaps he never would.

Sighing, Nicole pushed the sobering thought from her mind and stood quietly on the terrace, drawing the cool night air deep into her lungs. With arms folded over her chest to ward off the chill of the night, she set off across the lawn. Walking slowly, she picked her way around trees, her feet cushioned by a thick pad of grass here, pine needles there, her destination the dock.

To the left, the lawn swept to a brick wall that held a dense jungle of underbrush at bay. To the right, the lights from the house shimmered on the smooth water in the pool. How strange those lights seemed after such a long stretch of darkness. And how wonderful the promise of soon hearing children's laughter echo through the house!

So why, oh *why*, did she suddenly feel empty and inexplicably lonely?

Shivering, she walked to the end of the dock, her sneakers soundless on the wood planks. She loved it here. This was where she dreamed. Often she'd sit with her legs dangling over the edge, watching, listening, thinking, while the water lapped soothingly against the pilings. During the winter months, she'd watch the parade of yachts migrating down the ICW toward Palm Beach, Fort Lauderdale and Miami. During the summer, it was here that she spread her towel and soaked up the hot rays of the sun.

But Theron was back, rightfully claiming his home and his privacy, and no matter how badly he needed her help now, she wondered how long it would be before he closed the gates, shutting her out.

She glanced around at all the things she loved. There was no moon tonight. The only lights were those flickering through the branches of the trees behind her, and across the waterway, close to the drawbridge, the lights from a fish camp twinkled brightly. Friendly shadows moved, and the barest whisper of a breeze rustled leaves and palm fronds.

Her gaze drifted up the canal. On the west side, a dense forest hugged the bank. On the east were homes with grassy, tree-studded lawns that rolled gently down to the water's edge, and docks that jutted into the canal. Rolling toward her, shrouding the waterway, was a thick blanket of fog.

Nicole sat down, and drawing up her knees, she clasped her arms around them, wondering how it was possible for one man to worm his way into her thoughts as quickly as Theron had. Just thinking of his name loosed a surge of confusing emotions. She couldn't remember ever meeting a man who affected her in such a profound manner, a man whose mere touch caused her blood to heat.

Adding to her confusion came a wave of guilt.

She tilted her head back. A light, cool sprinkling of mist dampened her skin as the bank of fog rolled across the dock and fanned inland, swirling around the trees, then moving on, swathing everything in its path in eerie white.

The guilt was new. But it was understandable, wasn't it? And normal, considering that this was the first time since Marc's death that she'd felt an attraction to another man? With reluctance, Nicole admitted to herself that it was a powerful attraction. It had hit her like a bomb the moment she'd met Theron.

Through her doubts, Marc's final plea played in her mind more clearly now than ever before, and tears welled in her eyes.

"You're no quitter, Nikki. Don't be afraid to go back to the trapeze because of this. It's your life!" His words were tortured, insistent. "After the baby's born, you've got to climb the web and wow 'em like you've always done, okay, babe? And promise me..." He'd gripped her hand tightly. Tears filled his eyes. "I want you to promise me that you'll find someone to share your life with. Someone who'll love you and the baby. Don't try to go it alone. Promise me that, Nikki!''

She didn't want to make the promise. Marc *was* her life. But for his peace of mind, she had.

Nicole wiped the tears of remembrance from her cheeks. Reaching up, she tugged at the clip holding her hair back and shook her head as if the motion could erase words uttered long ago on a dying breath. Both she and Marc knew and accepted the element of risk involved with aerial acts. Accidents happened. You trained hard, took meticulous care of the rigging, left nothing to chance, and most of the time...

Dear Lord, hadn't her family—and Marc's—performed for years with no major mishaps? Until that one damnable night!

The damp air chilling her to the bone, she stared pensively at the ever-moving water, the past tugging at her. There'd been no baby. She'd never know the pleasure, the completeness, of giving birth to and raising a child. The fall had ended that dream. And the shoulder injury she received had kept her away from the trapeze and rings.

But, oh, how she missed performing. Though the thought of climbing back up there sometimes terrified her, she had no other choice. It was in her blood and heart and soul, and she longed for the feel of the trapeze bar in her hands far more than she feared it.

That longing had driven her during the past two years. Through sheer grit and determination, she'd trained hard to prepare herself for the coming season with Circus Royale.

She was healthy and eager and scared silly and confused—for Theron Donahue's appearance presented a complication, a distraction she didn't want or need.

Worried because she'd been gone so long, Theron went looking for Nicole. He found her exactly where Tag said she'd be—on the dock. Stopping near her huddled form, he watched her a moment. Mist beaded on her hair, and her cheeks were wet. At first, he thought the wetness was caused by the moisture in the air, but when a board creaked under his weight and she tilted her head, he saw tears tracking down the lovely contours of her face. Quickly, she turned her head and dried her cheeks with long, tapered fingers.

The sight of her, small and fragile and alone, clawed at him with an unexpected, wrenching force. His mouth compressed, he pulled off his jacket and knelt beside her.

"Tag went to the beach to pick up hamburgers," he said, referring to Jacksonville Beach. "He'll be back soon." There was a tightness in his chest that he didn't understand. Draping the jacket over her shoulders, he wanted to do more—to touch, to hold, to comfort. "Are you all right?"

"Umm-hmm." Not trusting her voice, she nodded. Her cheek brushed against his jacket, and she breathed in his scent, letting it travel slowly through her. Warm, exciting, distinctly *his*. But she dared not look at him. Not yet. Not when tears still trembled on her lashes. "I'm fine, Theron. Really."

Unable to resist the powerful urge to reach out to her, he sat on the dock, settling his body mere inches from hers. It had to do with many things, he rationalized. Compassion, empathy, a need to help her through a difficult time, just as she'd helped him face the house with all its memories. And perhaps desire? So soon?

He didn't take time to analyze his actions. He had no choice but to lace his fingers through her hair and pull it out from under the jacket. Finding it thick and soft, he smoothed the silken strands before lowering his hand to cover her small shoulder.

Surprise, warmth, pleasure. Those were some of the things Theron felt when she pressed her cheek against the back of his hand. The silent, trusting gesture touched him deeply, and something soft tangled around his heart while something hot and fiery burned much lower.

They sat quietly, the mist swirling around them—two near strangers connected by an invisible bond during one of those rare moments when two people are perfectly attuned. Neither questioned the reasons for being together. Both accepted it as natural and right.

Behind them, the trees stood like tall, shadowy sentinels. Somewhere in the forest, a night bird cried out. In the bar at the fish camp, someone played the jukebox, the pulsing beat of the song carrying to them on the damp night air. On the waterway, a yacht moved ghostlike toward the drawbridge on its journey south. A loud blast from the boat's horn shattered the night, followed by the creaking of the bridge as it rose to allow passage.

"I love that sound," Nicole said softly. "It's one of the things I'll miss about this place."

Theron wondered at her choice of words, but he didn't press her. "It's special," he agreed. "This dock is older than I am. I remember when I was a kid and my granddad brought me here. We'd bait the crab traps and fishing lines and spend the whole day sitting right about where we are now," he told her, his heart thrumming heavily in his chest when she relaxed against him.

"Sounds like a scene from *Tom Sawyer*," she replied dreamily. "I love it out here. It's a good place to fine-tune feelings, evaluate priorities—"

"And solve the problems of the world," he interrupted on a chuckle.

"That, too," she said, wondering when he'd put his arm around her, when she'd rested her head on his shoulder, and why it felt as if *this* was exactly where she belonged. She thought about moving away, then discarded the idea. He felt good, strong. And it had been such a long time since she had been in a man's arms.

"So, which of the above were you doing?" he ventured, his warm breath ruffling her hair, the heat shooting straight through her from head to toes. "Or were you digging up bones?"

"What?" Lifting her head, she grinned.

"You heard me."

"Hearing that term coming from a sophisticated man from the Big Apple is a bit of a surprise."

Her smile warming him, Theron realized with startling clarity that he couldn't leave her alone any more than he could take wings and fly. His hand moved lazily on her arm. "I revert back to my roots occasionally."

"And that's here?"

"Ponte Vedra and Palm Valley."

Nicole sat quietly for a while, the heat of his touch searing her even through the layers of clothing she wore. Her stomach tightened, and her pulse quickened in a peculiar manner. "I was under the impression that this was more of a family vacation spot."

"You mean to say you've never heard of the dubious Donahues?"

She laughed. "I've heard of them, yes, but not in those exact words." She knew very little about his background and what she did know, she recited in four words. "Real estate. Grocery stores."

"And shipping. Don't forget shipping," he said, his brow beetling. "I thought you and Annabel were friends."

"We're good friends, but she doesn't talk much about your family."

"Smart girl, my cousin." An edge of bitterness crept into his voice.

Curious about the change, Nicole examined his shadowed profile. His features were harsh and set and lined.

Above his fine, aquiline nose, thick, dark eyebrows were drawn together. His mouth was compressed. Only the sun-streaked hair falling over his forehead softened his appearance. He looked fierce, imposing, and though she wanted to reach up and touch his cheek, to feel the texture of his skin, she resisted.

"Why did you leave?" she asked instead, her curiosity getting the best of her.

"As a protest, I guess. I was a rebel of sorts," he told her quietly. He didn't like talking about his past. He made it a point not to, yet with Nicole... in some way it was different. He felt comfortable with her, as if he'd known her a lifetime. So he continued, his eyes steady on the restless water. "Being an only child worked against me from Day One. My parents mapped out my entire life. They chose the college I'd attend and what courses I'd take. Who I'd date. Who I'd marry. How many children we'd have, and when, and what we'd name them. And of course they wanted to railroad me into the family business." He scoffed. "Writing had no place in their ultimate plans for me, so I moved to New York as soon as I graduated high school."

"That's where you met your wife?" she ventured cautiously.

"No, Jess came with me." Unconsciously, he drew Nicole nearer to him and rested his cheek on the top of her head. "Two kids out to change the world."

"And?" she prodded.

"And," he said after a long time, "that's enough about me."

"You still miss her terribly, don't you?"

"Jess was... Jess died three years ago, Nicole. It's time to get on with my life."

With her head resting in the crook of his neck, she mulled over all that he'd told her. That there'd be no more talk about Jessica, he'd made clear, so Nicole's thoughts drifted to his family. Remembering the bitterness in his voice when speaking of them, she couldn't help but think of the closeness binding hers together, no matter how great the distance that often separated them.

"And your parents? So much time has passed, Theron. They must be glad to have you back here, now." She turned troubled eyes on him.

"No, Nicole, even if they were still alive, they'd have preferred that I stay in New York," he replied brusquely, and before she could pursue the subject further, he rose, pulling her up with him. A mere wisp of a woman, she stood barely five-four and seemed tiny next to his six-foot frame. "We started with your bones. What do you want to do with them? Talk about them or bury them?"

She bit her lower lip thoughtfully. Things had gone too far already. He'd touched her heart in a way that she didn't understand, and to open up to him, to confide in him, would only serve to make matters worse.

"Bury them," she said. "They weren't important."

"Are you sure?" He didn't believe her for an instant, but when she looked up, her eyes jewellike and wide and utterly beautiful, his heart somersaulted. She quite simply took his breath away. She stood an arm's length away. The distance too great, Theron closed it and cupped her face with his hands. "If they weren't important, why were you crying?"

"Let's forget about it, Theron. They're not your bones." She shuddered. Lord, but his touch was potent! Good sense warned her to move away, to put some space between them. Miles of space. But the feminine, needing part of her made her long to lean against him and feel the warmth of his arms around her.

"Oh, I don't know about that." He let his eyes roam her features, touching high cheekbones, the straight, pert little nose, the stubborn jut of her chin. He grinned. "I rather like the idea of sharing your bones."

She laughed nervously and lowered her eyes. He had a knack for teasing. That was something else she'd learned about him in the few, short hours since they'd met. Then he tilted her head up, forcing her to look at him. Her heart stopped. His smile was gone. He gazed upon her with dark and hooded eyes, awakening needs, nudging desires she'd long ago relegated to the far reaches of her consciousness.

Their eyes met and held. Theron saw invitation in hers and wondered if she realized how it tempted him. Nicole became aware that her hands were resting on his chest and wondered how they'd come to be there, and why her fingers burned from the contact. The heat from his body seeped through her pores, warming her deliciously.

He was only a heartbeat away. So close...so very, very close. The sweet pungent smell of the forest and night air mingled with the clean scent of soap and after-shave. She wanted to reach up and touch his smooth, freshly shaved skin in the same way he was touching her.

She studied his mouth, thinking it a fine one, curious about its feel and taste. He studied hers, thinking the same things, wanting to find out for himself.

She closed her eyes when he traced the contour of her lips with the tip of his index finger, opened them again as he trailed the finger over her chin and down her throat.

The muscles of his jaw clenched, relaxed, then clenched again. She heard him inhale deeply, then let the air out in a long sigh. Looking into his eyes, the rest of the world seemed to spin away until Nicole felt as if she were floating in a white, swirling dreamland, the only reality being the sound of hearts beating, blood singing, soft, puffy breaths exploding from parted lips.

Just one taste, he thought, lowering his head to hers. Just one. And because it was what she needed, he was gentle. But, oh, dear Lord, he didn't expect the sweetness he found. Or the fire. Or his own response to her—those fiery needs that slammed through him when her bowed mouth parted under his.

Wanting to feel her closer, he wrapped his arms around her. She stiffened, sighed, then seemed to melt against him, her breasts pushing into his chest, her hips fitting perfectly to him.

Just as the kiss deepened and tongues touched and they desired more—much more—Theron groaned and held her away. Wordlessly he bent down to retrieve the jacket that had fallen, unnoticed, to the dock.

"You're shivering," he said as he draped it over her shoulders again.

"So are you."

Theron clamped his mouth shut and frowning, he regarded her for a long moment. She was so small, so trusting, so desirable, and for the first time in his life, he felt out of control and not at all sure that he liked the feeling. How was it, he wondered, that she could affect him so strongly in so short a time? One damned kiss! That was all it had taken to ignite a fierce desire to have more of her, to make love to her, yet that was a risk he simply wasn't willing to take, a responsibility he didn't want. Nicole Ross was *not* a one-night stand. She was a commitment.

It was a huge mistake. Kissing her like that. Starting something she wasn't ready for. Hell, neither was he. It was something he couldn't allow to happen again. And in the seconds that followed, Theron wanted to kick himself, for he realized that he'd put a voice to his thoughts.

She was staring up at him, her eyes filled with hurt and confusion. "A mistake, Theron?"

"Oh, God, no, Nicole. I didn't mean it the way it must have sounded."

"Oh, really?" Her cheeks burned with humiliation. What to her was a wonderful kiss, to him was a *mistake*? "At least you don't beat around the bush."

Cursing under his breath, he took her arm. Somehow he had to make amends, to take the hurt away. "Come on. Tag should be back with our dinner. After we've eaten, we'll talk."

"Look, it's late, and I'm really not very hungry," she said, trying to pull out of his grasp, but his fingers tightened on her.

"Nonsense. You're eating," he told her, pulling her along the dock. "No arguments."

Minutes later, Nicole sat at the oak table flanked on one side by Theron, on the other by Tag. She toyed with her food, finding it tasteless, while the men devoured hamburgers and fries. Silence prevailed through most of the meal, with Nicole keeping her eyes on her food, not wanting to look at either of them.

"Tag, if it'll make things easier on you, we can set up Rusty's bed." Theron finally broke the heavy silence. "You're welcome to spend the night here."

"Hell, I been sleepin' on lumps for so long my bones couldn't take a night on anything else." He glanced first at his young boss, then at Nicole. From the looks of them, all hunched over their food, Theron tense and brooding and little Nikki's face flushed and mad lookin'... well, mayhap some fireworks were in the making. Tag smiled.

"Thanks anyway, son, but I'll head on home. Reckon I'll see you two bright and early in the mornin', heh?" Tag said, and Nicole could have wrung his leathery, old neck when he added, "You gonna be here, ain't you, Nikki? Lot to do 'round here fore those young 'uns fly in."

"I'm...ah...not sure." She felt two pairs of eyes on her. *Damn you, Graham Taggert, you old busybody!*

"You don't have a bookin', do you?" Tag pushed.

"No." Nicole glared at him. He knew darn well she didn't.

"You goin' to work out, then?" he persisted.

"Probably," she groused and took a ferocious bite of her hamburger. It tasted terrible and she must have grimaced, for beside her, Theron chuckled—the clod.

"'Morrow's Saturday. You never go to winter quarters on Saturday," Tag stated matter-of-factly as he pushed away from the table. "Looks like we'll be seein' you. Get some sleep tonight, heh?"

"I'll do that," she muttered, furious with Tag for putting her on the spot.

"Well, then, now that that's settled, I'll be on my way." Walking behind Theron's chair, he clamped a broad, rough hand on the younger man's shoulder. "Good to have you home, son. Real good."

"It's good to be back." Amazingly, Theron found that he really meant those words. He looked from Tag to Nicole. "I should have made this move a long time ago."

"Yup, reckon you should've," Tag agreed and ambled out of the room.

The instant the door closed behind him, Nicole exploded in animated anger. "That crusty, nosy old—"

"He meant well," Theron interrupted, laughing.

Nicole glowered. "Talk about someone being railroaded! That old man is a master of manipulation! I may not have a party booking for tomorrow, and I may not be working out, but that doesn't mean that I want to spend the entire day unpacking boxes!" she fumed and wanted to bite her tongue.

"No, I don't suppose you do." The legs of Theron's chair scraped unpleasantly on the tile as he pushed away from the table and discarded the remains of his meal in the trash can.

"I'm sorry. I didn't mean it the way it sounded."

"Then it looks like we're even," he said pointedly, watching color touch her cheeks. Walking to the French doors, he stood with his back to her, one hand braced on the door frame. "Forget what Tag said. It was presumptuous of him."

"I don't mind *helping*, Theron. But I hate being backed into a corner."

"I understand." He stared unseeing into the foggy night. A scant thirty minutes ago, he'd wanted to apologize to her for his comment on the dock, to somehow try to explain the reasons behind it, but he couldn't do that now. Unwittingly, Tag had jerked in the reins, abruptly putting a halt to any relationship that he might have had with Nicole. Tag had said things that bothered Theron—angered him—and swinging around, he confronted Nicole point-blank, his features tight. "What exactly did Tag mean about you going to winter quarters?"

Alarmed, her eyes darted to his. "That's where my rigging is set up."

"Your rigging," he parroted her words.

"Yes. The trapeze and rings," she told him hesitantly. "I'm working with some friends of my father's until the show comes off the road."

"And then? What happens then, Nicole?"

Sensing something was dreadfully wrong, she swallowed. "Then...I rejoin the troupe. As a member of my family's act. The Flying Rossinis."

"I know the name of the act," he muttered, and all of the excitement and anticipation Nicole felt about working again withered instantly. Never had she seen features so angry or eyes so cold. His were cold enough to freeze hot water in hell.

Though she wondered about his reaction, and somehow feared it, she faced him dead-on and managed to keep her voice even. "I love flying. It's something I've done all my life—like you and your writing. I've worked hard for this, Theron! And it hasn't been easy, but I *will* be ready for the show's opening in New Orleans in March."

"Why?"

"Why?" She tilted her head slightly and thought a moment. "I guess for the same reason that people get back up on a horse after a fall. Or write play after play after play. You've got to keep going, moving ahead, doing what you love." She paused, then added softly, "I do love my work, and I'm grateful that I've been gifted with the talent to do it well."

"I see." A muscle in his jaw jumped. "Well...you certainly performed beautifully the night your husband was killed."

She blanched. "Damn you, Theron Donahue, you really are a bastard!" she hissed angrily, blinking hard to hold back the tears suddenly stinging her eyes. "That was a cruel thing to say!"

Normally a man sensitive to other people's feelings, Theron was horrified by his thoughtless comment. What the hell was the matter with him? Hurting her like that? But deep inside, he knew. It had to do with his youngest daughter.

Wearily rubbing his temples, he pursed his lips together, then sighed. "It was, Nicole, and I am very sorry. I had no right..." His eyes softened, and he shook his head slowly. "It's just that there's a hell of a lot at stake here. Things that I have to deal with that you couldn't possibly know about."

She didn't know what he meant—didn't care. Right now, the only thing she wanted was to go home, go to bed and forget she'd ever met Theron Donahue.

"Thanks for dinner," she said.

"Thank you for helping out today."

"Yes, well, see you around."

"It seems inevitable." He smiled an exhausted smile. "Do me a favor?"

Surprised, she met his gaze and found a warmth she didn't expect. "What?"

"Drive carefully. It's foggy out there tonight."

"The cottage is only a quarter of a mile from here. I can make the drive blindfolded."

"Just checking." A half smile touched his mouth. "The rent's due in a few days, and I'd hate to see something happen to you before then."

"I'll keep that in mind."

"Nicole." The quiet huskiness in his voice stopped her just as she was walking out of the kitchen to collect her belongings, and she turned to look at him. "I really am very sorry about that comment. It was totally out of line."

She let out a deep sigh. "Don't worry about it, Theron. It's late, and we're both tired. Good night."

Theron waited until he heard her car roar away from the house before turning off the lights and climbing the stairs to his bedroom. Hours after she'd gone, he lay in bed trying to make some sense of the day, of Nicole, of his life.

And into his thoughts crept Jenny and her dreams—dreams that were far too close to becoming reality. Dreams that he'd pushed out of his mind until news of Nicole going back to the trapeze brought them rushing into focus again. He couldn't help but wonder how much influence Nicole would have on his daughter—the little girl who had her sights set on a career on the trapeze.

Chapter Four

So? What'd ya think of my cousin?" Annabel set two glasses of iced tea on the white wrought-iron table between the lounge chairs.

Nicole grimaced. "You don't want to know."

"I wouldn't have asked if I didn't." Annabel grinned.

The morning was bright and cool, the October sky a hard blue without a trace of clouds. The sun climbed lazily, teasing them with the promise of heat later in the day. But now, at nine in the morning, it was so perfectly lovely that Nicole was content to lie back, sip the apple-cinnamon tea and let the warmth caress her while listening to the restless surf break on the beach fifty yards away from Annabel's swimming pool.

The last thing she wanted to do was talk about Theron Donahue, yet here she was in the company of one of her closest friends—who just happened to be the man's cousin. If it weren't for bad luck, she'd have no luck at all.

"Do you want a watered-down version, or the truth?" she asked dryly.

"Since when have you watered down anything?" Annabel lazed back on her chair, stretching luxuriously. "Give it to me straight."

"Okay, but remember, you asked. I didn't volunteer."

"Agreed."

"He's the epitome of arrogance. He has an ego the size of Manhattan. And he's probably the most insensitive man that I've ever met!"

"My Theron? Insensitive?" Annabel burst into laughter. "He's not a lapdog, granted, but he is one of the most sensitive, caring men in this vast, cold world!"

"Surely you jest," Nicole countered indignantly.

"No." Annabel wriggled, settling her long, lithe bikini-clad body into the chair, intent on making the most of the golden gift showered down upon them by the Florida sun. "You're leaving something out. What is it?"

"What are you? A masochist? We're talking about your cousin."

"I know." Finally comfortable, Annabel grinned. "Go on."

"All right." Nicole narrowed her eyes. "He's insufferable. A complete ass."

Laughter rippled through the clear morning. "That's good, Nikki. Very good. Now, we're getting somewhere." A therapist, Annabel was sounding more and more like her professional self.

Irritated, Nicole sat up abruptly. "You know, I'm beginning to see some very disturbing family traits here, Annabel. And, God knows, I had enough of your cousin's pushiness yesterday to last a lifetime! I don't need any more today." Taking a huge gulp of her tea, she scoffed. "If you're bent on analyzing, please do me a favor and pick on someone else. I'm not at all in the mood today."

Sitting up, Annabel swung long legs over the side of the lounge chair and pushed her sunglasses low on her nose, peering at Nicole over the top of the frames. "He really got to you, didn't he?"

"Truthfully?" Nicole directed big green eyes on her friend.

"What other way is there?"

"You never stop working, do you?" An unwilling smile curved full lips. She lowered her head and let out a long sigh. "He scares the hell out of me."

"If Theron did anything to hurt you, I'll wring his neck, and *that*, my friend, is a promise."

Feeling heat work up her neck, Nicole looked out over the sea, squinting against the shimmering silver glare. Oh, Theron had done things, all right. He'd drawn her in with a devastating kiss, then pulled away from her, cutting her to the quick with his words. But in the hours that had passed— the long sleepless night, her workout at the ballet bar and the long gallop she'd enjoyed on her horse at the crack of dawn—other aspects of his personality had crept into her mind. What haunted her more than anything wasn't so much *what* he'd said, but the look in his eyes, the infinite sadness, the needing that somehow tempered even his most withering expressions and harshest words.

She remembered his kiss, how at first it was gentle and then grew more insistent. She thought of his arms around her; strong, urging her close to his body. She remembered him stir with need. It was only then that he'd pulled away from her.

"No," she said firmly, knowing there was much about him that she didn't understand; knowing also that it would suit her to keep her distance. He was far too complicated a man. "He did nothing to hurt me."

"I'll buy that from a physical standpoint," Annabel remarked, watching Nicole intently. "But not from the emotional one."

Nicole turned on her angrily. "Will you stop it? Just let it go, Annabel! I'm not one of your clients. I didn't come over here for a hundred-dollar-an-hour mental puke session, and I don't appreciate being badgered like this, okay?" Rising, she paced the pool deck and cursed softly. "Damn. Between you, Theron and Tag, I can't get a moment's peace any more!"

"My, my, we are touchy today."

Nicole stopped in front of Annabel. "Is there anything else you'd like to know before I take a swim?"

"Yes, there is, Nicole." Annabel paused, then asked pointedly, "What happened between you two yesterday?"

"Nothing," she lied, her cheeks flaming. Some of the fight drained from her. "Look, he is a very sexy, handsome man, and I honestly think that if he tried hard, he might even be nice."

"Nice men don't scare the hell out of women, and you are scared right now." Puzzled by Nicole's strong reactions, Annabel frowned with concern. "Who are you really afraid of, Nicole? Theron? Or yourself?"

"I don't know. Maybe both," she confessed softly. "He's dangerous, Annabel."

"There! I thought so!" Annabel pronounced with the confidence of a woman who'd successfully tackled a sticky problem and solved it.

"There what?"

"Don't you see? It's a perfectly normal reaction when you meet someone you're attracted to! God knows, if a man with real force walked into my life, I'd be scared to death!" She grinned, her gray eyes dancing. "But definitely not frightened enough to run away. Life's too short not to take the occasional risk."

"I'm not running away."

"No?"

"I have other things to do today. Things that do *not* include Theron Donahue and his damned packing boxes."

"Do I detect a note of guilt in that dulcet tone?"

"It's not my place to help him. He's your cousin, for Pete's sake," Nicole countered. "But I don't see you breaking your neck to get over there."

"I have company," Annabel pointed out wryly. "It'd be rude to walk out on a friend in need. Look, why don't you do a few laps around the pool. After you cool off a bit, maybe you'll feel up to a round of golf. Mitch has the kids for the weekend, so I'm free as a bird," she suggested. "It might do us both some good. You know, get our minds off life's more pressing problems? If, that is, you can tear yourself away from all those *other* things you have planned for today?"

"They can wait." Nicole averted her eyes. "Why golf?"

"Believe me, where you're concerned, I'd prefer tennis." Annabel grimaced. "Unfortunately, I did a number on my knee last week. Chasing after your serves is out. Golf...eh..." She waggled her hands, palms down. "Maybe."

"Just remember, it was your idea."

"Does that mean yes?"

"Sure. Why not?" Nicole agreed. "But we'll have to swing by the cottage to let Luke out and pick up my clubs."

Theron downed his beer and swiped at his mouth with the back of his hand, then pitched the can toward the trash, smiling as it hit target dead center in the old Donahue drop shot. It brought to mind thoughts of his children. He'd have to get the basketball hoop and backboard set up before the kids flew in. It had been far too long since playing a rousing game with Rusty and Julie pitted against him and Jenny.

Jenny.

The thought of his youngest daughter both delighted and worried him. A bright, lovely child who was as sunny as a summer day, the little girl Theron thought was heading toward a brilliant career in ballet, had shocked him senseless by announcing two years ago that she wanted to become a trapeze artist—just like the beautiful Nicole who flew with the Rossinis.

Of course, he shouldn't be surprised. While all of his children adored Lawrence Westbrook and Circus Royale, it was Jenny who constantly begged Theron to allow her to spend time with Lawrence and the performers when the show was in New York. And he'd seen no reason to hold the child back. The *backyard* of the circus—in this case the train and the area behind the scenes in Madison Square Garden—was an exciting place, where Jenny was surrounded by friends.

Yet ballet had been a part of Jenny's life from age four, and Theron supposed now that he should have seen what was coming when the little girl insisted on enrolling in gymnastics, as well. But he hadn't. Nor had he been overly concerned about her growing interest in collecting circus memorabilia. Didn't all kids love circuses? He'd also failed to give her fascination with the aerial acts a second thought. The endless questions she fired at Lawrence stemmed from Jenny's insatiable but innocent curiosity. Nothing more. Nothing less.

The first real fear had coiled in Theron's stomach that autumn day two years ago when Jenny had watched Nicole perform, then had calmly announced that *that* was what she wanted to do. Jenny Donahue wanted to be just like Nicole Ross.

How well he remembered that day and Jenny's jarring announcement as they were driving home from the afternoon performance of the show. Once the children were safely home, Theron had wasted no time. Telling them he had a late business appointment, he headed back to the Garden to talk over Jenny's dream with Lawrence.

The two men grabbed a quick dinner together.

"I can cope with Rusty's passion for music, although I'd prefer that he stick to the guitar and leave the damn drums alone," Theron had told Lawrence over steaks. "And I can handle Julie's passion for horses."

"Is she still hoping to make the Olympic equestrian team one day?" Lawrence queried.

"She's determined to make it."

"That leaves Jenny."

"That leaves Jenny," Theron repeated, frowning. He sipped his coffee. "Has she said anything to you about training on the trapeze?"

"Not in so many words. She's fascinated by the aerial acts." Lawrence smiled broadly. "My God, I thought her eyes were going to pop out of her head when she saw Nicole perform this afternoon."

"But she's never expressed the desire to actually become a...leaper? I believe that's the term she used today."

"Not to me...wait a minute, Theron. Are you saying what I think you're saying?"

"She's plotting out a career on the trapeze."

Lawrence laughed. "That's a fantasy of children of all ages. 'Run away and join the circus.' It can be a very strong desire, especially in those magical hours immediately following a show like Circus Royale. People have spent two hours in another world. Laughing. Holding their breath. Escaping." Lawrence pulled out a cigarette and lit it. "I hear it all the time, but acting on that fantasy is quite another story." He leaned back in his chair, his black eyes intent upon Theron. "Running away to join the circus is about as obsolete as driving an Edsel. It just doesn't happen, Theron.

"Most of the performers come from generations of show people," he explained. "Take, for instance, the Rossinis. They're third-generation flyers. Nicole was born into flying and was groomed for it from the time she was old enough to walk. She's had extensive ballet and gymnastics that started when she was three, maybe four years old. Not to mention the years of grueling training while learning the intricacies of her profession. Even with her background, her training, she still had to prove herself and display the natural talent that goes hand in hand with leaping, and in her case, the rings."

Theron's mouth was set in a grim line. "Jenny's taking ballet and gymnastics. Has been for years."

"Well, the training certainly won't hurt her." Lawrence absently rubbed his chin. "But she's what...eight years old, now?...and she's never actually trained on a trapeze." He shook his head. "Personally, I think it's a phase. She'll outgrow it, in time."

"And if she doesn't?"

"Then, old friend, you could have a problem," he said, glancing at his watch. "I've got to get back. Why don't you come with me? Stay for the show? Afterward, I'll introduce you to Nicole. Tonight's her last performance. She's going into semiretirement, but I'm sure she'll be happy to give you some sound advice. She may even want to talk to Jenny. She's one of the best in the business, and she has a marvelous way with children." Lawrence paused. "Nicole may very well be the answer to your problem."

"How do you mean?"

"It's possible that by watching Jenny work out, Nicole can tell if she's made of the right stuff. Not putting Jenny down, but the chances are that she isn't." He shook his dark head. "Better to nip it in the bud early on, don't you think?"

Theron had watched Nicole perform and was quite simply awed by her beauty and grace. Then came the horrifying fall and the endless eternity of disbelief, when the only thing he was aware of were the soft swirling dust motes floating through the shafts of light illuminating a tragically empty, forlorn trapeze.

And, of course, he hadn't talked to Nicole.

Now, Theron stared at other dust motes. Those that were flitting through the rays of sunlight streaming into his kitchen.

Jenny's dream hadn't wavered one iota. If anything, she was even more determined. She'd experienced closing her small hands around a trapeze bar. She'd soared—not to great heights—but soared, nevertheless, and there was no denying the joy and excitement on her young face.

Theron frowned. Jenny would ask Nicole for help. Of that, he was sure. What he couldn't anticipate was Nicole's response. Whatever she decided, someone would get hurt. A no would devastate Jenny. A yes would throw Theron into worlds of worry. There would be no winners in this, and Theron wished, for the first time, that he hadn't been so quick to offer Nicole the gatehouse.

"You gonna sit there all day, son, or you gonna help me with that sideboard?" Tag's raspy voice cut through Theron's reverie.

"I'll be right there."

Tag studied Theron, seeing the lines of worry bracketing his mouth, the concern furrowing his brow. "Which one you broodin' over? Jenny or Nikki?" he asked, opening the door of the refrigerator and pulling out two cans of ice-cold beer.

"I don't need another." Theron waved it off.

"Drink it. It'll loosen the knots in your neck."

"You don't know when to back off, do you?" Theron grumbled. Having no choice, he took the beer thrust at him.

"So I've been told." Tag swung a chair around, straddled it and folded his hands over the high back. "Now, what's eatin' at you?"

"Nothing important."

Tag took a long swallow of his beer. "You might be able to pull the wool over the eyes of them highfalutin, fancy friends of yours, but you can't fool me. I was there when you came into this world buff naked, boy, heh? And I've known you better 'an anyone else, ever since."

Theron lifted his beer and downed three long swallows. "She's going back."

"Talk plain talk. Who's goin' back where?" Tag asked gruffly, but his voice was laced with unmistakable affection.

"Nikki...Nicole...to the trapeze."

"That comes as a surprise to you?"

"I guess it does."

"Why?"

"*Why*? Why the hell do you think?" Theron exploded, venting the anger that had been steadily, if irrationally, growing since last night; anger that burned even deeper this morning when, hoping to catch her at the barn, he'd hurried there only to find her Morgan mare already turned out to pasture and no sign of Nicole.

Slamming the can down on the table, he rose and cursed and muttered his feelings to a man who'd been closer than a father to him for thirty-five years. "Damn it, I was there when she was nearly killed! I saw her fall! Idiot woman has no business going back to the trapeze!"

"It's her life, boy! You've nothin' to say about it. You ain't her keeper."

Theron swung around, his features stormy. "No, I'm not, but that woman is going to exercise some influence over Jenny, and I don't like the prospect. I damn well don't want to see my ten-year-old daughter climb a web to fly thirty feet above a net that can be just as dangerous as the trapeze!"

"Since when is it your right to play God with other people's lives?" Tag's voice grew ominous.

"I have a *right* to protect my daughter!"

Tag's fist came down hard on the table, and when he spoke the windows rattled. "And Jenny's got a *right* to her dreams, Theron. As her father, you'd be well advised to give her the support she needs or, stubborn as she is, you're gonna lose her the same way your daddy lost you. Now, you young whippersnapper, you chaw on that for a spell. And while you're at it, why don't you do some thinkin' 'bout gettin' your own life back in order!" Tag's eyes glittered angrily. "You might not approve of what Nikki does with her life..." He shoved a massive, thorny finger under Theron's nose. "...but at least she's doin' somethin', which is more than I can say for you, flittin' as you been doin' from fancy woman to fancy woman and not paying attention to what you do best, which is, or *was*, writin'!"

They stood nose to nose, glaring at each other.

"Get back to work, old man," Theron muttered.

Tag ignored him. "And you'd best rein in that temper of yours. It ain't becomin', and it ain't 't'all like you. Kind of makes a man wonder if maybe you got feelin's for little Nikki, heh?"

"Are you finished?"

"Yup, reckon I am." Tag set his empty beer can on the table. "But as far as gettin' back to work? Don't think so. I don't know where you want things, and I don't think you know, either." A grin split his leathery face as he pulled another beer from the refrigerator. "I'm too old to be movin' furniture from room to room and wall to wall. When you decide what you want and where the Sam Hill you want it, son, call me. Meantime, I'll be down on the dock drinkin' this and mayhap settin' out the crab traps. I think we still got some chicken necks 'round here, heh?"

"You stubborn old coot, I ought to fire you."

Tag chuckled. "Yup, probably should at that, but you won't." Ambling to the French doors, he stopped. "By the by, that ladder you was lookin' for earlier is down at the gatehouse."

"What's it doing there?"

"I reckon I left it there."

Scowling, Theron watched Tag leave. The old fool ought to have been fired long ago, but Theron met the thought with the same resistance that his father and grandfather had before him. Tag was a valued constant in his life, and Theron loved him. They'd fought countless times before, and as surely as the sun rose each morning, they'd fight again.

The damnable, irrefutable fact of the matter had proven itself time after time over the years—Tag was usually right. Well, not this time, old man, Theron thought. Tag had no business sticking his nose into affairs dealing with Jenny, and no amount of shouting or verbal bulldozing would sway Theron's feelings one iota.

And you'd best rein in that temper of yours... Kind of makes a man wonder if maybe you got feelin's for little Nikki...

Tag's words played over annoyingly in Theron's mind. Grabbing his keys, he stalked out of the house, assuring himself that his anger had nothing to do with Nicole's decision to go back to the trapeze. As for the feelings Tag had suggested? Admittedly, Theron was drawn to Nicole. Physically. She was a beautiful woman, with deliciously soft curves that molded to him and a warm mouth that tasted like honey.

There wasn't a red-blooded man in the country who wouldn't respond to her, and Theron definitely fell into that category. But the lusty urges she fired in him didn't translate into serious feelings. Those took time to develop and nurture.

He had enough to worry about with Jenny. He didn't need to worry about Nicole, as well. If the woman hadn't the sense to know when she was well off, that was her business. If she wanted to leave the safety of the gatehouse, he had no right to stop her. If she chose to trade careers and leave Rossles behind in favor of the trapeze and the risk of another fall...

Unable to cope with that thought, he pushed it from his mind, started his car and squealed down the driveway toward the gatehouse.

Watching Theron's departure while comfortably seated on the dock, Tag smiled. "Yup," he muttered to himself. "Couple things that young fool don't know, but reckon he'll wake up soon enough, heh?" And he dropped the crab trap into the calm water.

Braking in front of the cottage, Theron climbed out of the Seville. There was no sign of Nicole, no sign of the ladder. Still seething with anger, he opened the wrought-iron gate and walked around the side of the house, realizing that this was the first time in two years he'd paid the slightest bit of attention to the gatehouse.

His anger lessening by degrees, he looked around. Flower beds abounded, and shrubs, and there were two recently planted magnolia trees, and a birdhouse and bath. He wondered to whom he should allow the credit. Tag or Nicole.

Rounding the back of the building, he caught sight of the screened-in porch. It ran the full length of the house and was almost as wide as the interior rooms. Feeling a curious pull, he stepped up to the screen and peered in. On the floor on one end were mats; tumbling mats, he guessed, although the room wasn't long enough to accommodate a zealous work-out. A wall of floor-to-ceiling mirrors was directly across from him, their continuity broken only by the door leading to the kitchen. Bracketed to the mirrors was a ballet bar. On a small table in the far corner sat a tape deck and hanging on a chair next to the table, he saw a pair of white satin ballet slippers.

For some reason, the small slippers caught and held his attention. He stared at them, the idea of the woman who lived here not only being a clown and aerial artist but a dancer, as well, entrancing him. How beautiful she must be when dancing, he thought, with her honey-blond hair flowing down her back.

"Damn it, anyway," he muttered irritably as he turned away from the vision. "Where'd the old man leave the ladder?"

He circled the house, finding nothing. In a last-ditch effort to locate the missing piece of equipment, he cupped his hands around his face and looked through the living-room window. There it was, leaning against a wall on the far side of the room. Behind closed doors. Inside of Nicole's home.

Dare he slip in to get it? It was his ladder, his property, his house, for Pete's sake, but it was her home. Private. Personal. On the walls were her paintings; on the tables, her treasures.

He groaned. Jenny would love the cottage, decorated as it was in early circus. The furniture was contemporary and comfortable-looking, and plants abounded, but he found himself fascinated with the paintings. Liberty horses and clowns. Elephants and tigers. Large framed photographs of her family flying high were placed here and there. Theron could almost hear the calliope, the drum rolls, the voice of the ringmaster, and an unwilling smile played on his lips.

Then, remembering why he was here, he wrestled with his decision for all of ten seconds. It would take him just about that long to grab the ladder and be out of the house again. What harm could it possibly do? He wouldn't linger. If the door was unlocked—which it probably wasn't—he'd get what he'd come for and be gone again.

Trying the doorknob, it turned smoothly, silently in his hand. A wave of guilt traveled through him, and he wondered if this was how a burglar felt when invading the private domain of his victims. Theron moved quickly across the room, his sneakered feet soundless as a cat. A sense of urgency made him hurry, made him wary, made him feel like hell for what he was doing. But it was too late, now. The ladder was in his hand. He was five seconds, five strides away from accomplishing his mission, but the door suddenly seemed miles and miles away and fraught with obstacles. . . .

For he heard a low, warning growl behind him.

He froze, the hair on the back of his neck standing up. The sound came from the deep shadows of the room. Eerie, ominous, it sent chills along his spine. He sensed movement, and too late, he remembered. Nicole had a dog; a very *big* dog, he judged, for the volley of barking that erupted sounded as if the gates of hell had opened wide.

Letting go of the ladder, he whirled around in time to see a huge, black animal streak toward him. Instinctively, his arm whipped up to shield his face. The animal leaped, teeth bared savagely, and ninety pounds of hurtling Doberman struck him in the chest. The floor came up to meet Theron's back with tooth-shattering force. The air whooshed from his lungs, and he lay there, gasping, sandwiched between the cold tile and the dog, waiting for the pain of teeth tearing into his arm.

It didn't come. Instead, there was a feeling of tremendous weight settling upon his stomach and the disconcerting sensation of a nubbin of a tail . . . Wagging? Absurd!

Silence fell in the room, broken only by the sound of the dog panting, the man gasping.

Cautiously, Theron moved his arm and slanted his eyes first to one side, then the other. Planted firmly on either side of his head were two large black-and-tan feet.

He peered up. The dog peered down. Ever so slowly, Theron let his arm rest on the floor above his head. The dog cocked his head watchfully, whined and curled his lip in what looked impossibly like a grin.

"Nice dog," Theron said, feeling confident and foolish at the same time. The animal's ears perked up, and a long, pink tongue suddenly lapped across Theron's face. He grimaced. "Good boy! Now that we're friends, why don't you let me up?"

But when he moved, the dog laid back his ears and growled menacingly, the curl of his lip becoming a definite snarl. Theron cursed softly.

"So this is how it's going to be," he muttered and letting out a sigh of resignation, he relaxed as best he could. Following suit, the dog settled his full weight upon the body of his prize, his tongue lolling from the side of his mouth, occasionally dropping to lick Theron's face.

"Someone is going to answer for this," he vowed softly. Listening, the dog cocked his head. "If I ever get out of here...."

The Doberman curled his lip again, then rested his great head on Theron's shoulder and panted close to his ear.

And they waited together. Man and dog. Neither moving.

"Were you expecting company today?"

"I wouldn't be golfing with you if that were the case." Nicole selected a Neil Diamond CD and adjusted the volume on Annabel's car stereo. "Why?"

"Someone's at the gatehouse. Do you recognize the car?"

Glancing up, Nicole frowned. "Nope. Do you?"

"Huh-uh. But I like it. Looks like the kind of car that Mr. Perfect would drive." Annabel grinned. "You know, the kind of guy who's eager to take on an easygoing woman and four rambunctious kids?"

"Remind me to introduce you to Lawrence when the show comes off the road," Nicole said with a laugh. She climbed out of the car, her laughter dying suddenly. "What does Theron drive?"

"I don't have the foggiest idea. The last time he was here, he rented a car." Annabel's gray eyes moved from Nicole to the car. "Why?"

"I don't know. Something feels...wrong." She shivered. "It's too quiet."

The two women walked through the gate and up the sidewalk toward the cottage, Nicole's unease growing with each step. The Seville was empty, and there was no sign of anyone in the yard.

"Oh, my God!" Nicole whispered, stopping abruptly.

"What?"

"Look. The front door is open, Annabel. Someone's in the house." She turned to Annabel. "Go on up to the main house and get Tag or Theron. Hurry!"

Annabel gaped at her friend. "You're not going in there? Are you *crazy*, Nicole? What if they've got a gun?"

"Luke's inside. I'll be fine."

"Great! A loaded gun against a Doberman!" she hissed. "Somehow I don't like those odds!"

"Oh, for God's sake, I dropped a ton of money into the training of that dog! He knows what to do! Now go!"

"Not on your life!" Annabel stubbornly stood her ground.

"This is no time to argue."

"Oh, Lord, are you sure you want to do this?"

"Yes," Nicole whispered, but she wasn't sure at all. She'd never been more unsure of anything in her life, yet when Annabel ran back to her Lincoln, Nicole drew up her shoulders and pushed open the front door, anger overcoming fear.

She moved cautiously, careful to dodge a coatrack, not quite sidestepping an umbrella stand. It toppled over, falling noisily to the floor.

Wide-eyed with fear, she froze, her heart in her throat, then a renewed surge of anger gripped her as from the depths of the house rang a disturbingly familiar male voice.

"If that's you, Nicole, you'd best get your butt in here and call off this black devil, then run like hell before I get my hands around your neck!" came the hoarse and winded bellow, followed by a low, warning growl. Theron Donahue's voice softened considerably. "Easy, boy. It's all right. I won't hurt her. Much. *Nicole!*"

"That rotten louse!" Nicole muttered. Clenching her hands into fists, Nicole marched into her living room breathing fire.

Chapter Five

Nicole stopped in the middle of her living room, placed her hands on her hips and glared down at Theron. He lay flat on his back, Luke's body stretched on top of him. Finding it a ludicrous sight, Nicole felt mirth undermining her anger.

"What's going on?" she demanded.

"If you'll call this hound off, I'll explain." Theron groaned as the dog shifted position.

"I will call the dog off after you tell me why you broke into my home, and not one minute before!"

"I did *not* break in. Your door was...humphf... unlocked..." Theron's words came out on great gushes of air. He glared up at her. "You...are skating...on...very thin ice...Nicole!"

"Hie, Luke," she commanded, struggling to suppress the laughter building inside of her. Obediently, the Doberman gave up his prize and walked over to sit at Nicole's side, his eyes still watchful. "Well? I'm waiting."

"That's the biggest damn Doberman I've ever seen. What the devil do you feed him?"

"Anything he wants."

"Somehow that doesn't surprise me," Theron grumbled as he struggled to a sitting position and gingerly tested his limbs.

Nicole watched him, concern edging out anger and mirth.

Though the dog was trained not to bite but to take down an intruder and hold him until help came, he'd never been put to the test. Granted, the dog hadn't bitten Theron, but Nicole knew the impact of an animal that size hitting a man, driving him to the hard floor, could cause injury.

Seeing that Theron was suffering a great deal of discomfort, she hurried to him and knelt down, instinctively running her hands over his shoulders and arms in the same manner one would check a child for injuries.

"Are you hurt?"

"I am bruised of body and ego," he announced tersely. "Nothing I won't recover from in time."

"I'm sorry," she said, withdrawing her hands.

"You've got nothing to be sorry about. If anything, I owe you an apology for coming in here when you weren't home."

"Why did you?"

"I needed the ladder. Tag said it was here. I naturally assumed he meant outside," he said, wincing.

"It was," she replied, color rising in her cheeks. "I brought it in last night to change a light bulb and forgot to put it back again." She looped his arm over her shoulder. "Come on. Let me help you up."

His eyes roamed over her small, delicate frame, trying not to notice the contrast of white shorts against the smooth, tan skin of her thighs or the enticing roundness of firm breasts pushing against the fabric of her green-and-white striped top. His blood warming, he looked away.

"Thanks, but I can manage on my own." But, oh God, was he stiff! As he slowly stood, it felt as if every muscle in his body was tied up in knots. He groaned. "I feel like I've gone one whole round with Mike Tyson."

"I am sorry about what happened."

"Why? The dog was just doing his job. He's well trained," he observed dryly. "I've got to give him that."

Nicole grinned. "At least now I know he won't bite."

"You mean I was his first hit? The guinea pig?"

"As a matter of fact, yes, you were." Laughter danced in her eyes. "I've often wondered what he'd really do if someone broke in."

"That's a comforting thought, Nikki."

Her nickname sounded like magic coming from him, and she looked up, everything inside of her going haywire. "Actually, he's a pussycat once you get to know him."

"Right. A pussycat." Theron turned skeptical eyes on the dog. "As long as he gets his way."

"That's the general idea."

"How is he with kids?"

"Terrific. He loves them. He spent his formative years on the circus train."

"That's one point in his favor." The faint hint of a smile played on his lips, but his eyes remained dark.

"He'll get used to you," Nicole said, suddenly feeling nervous. He was gazing at her so intently that she had to look away. "Why don't you make yourself comfortable while I fix some lemonade? It'll just take a minute."

He reached out and caught her shoulders before she could escape. "The lemonade can wait. I want to talk to you, Nicole."

"About what?" His hands, strong and insistent, sent her heart racing.

"About yesterday." His fingers moved lazily on the bare flesh of her arms, and a sense of male satisfaction coursed through him when he saw the effect his touch had on her. At the base of her throat, her pulse jumped. "I said some things that were way out of line last night. I'd like to apologize for them. For hurting you." His voice grew deep and husky. "There is a reason, and I'd like to explain."

Feeling herself melt under his warm caress, she swallowed. "Okay. Explain."

"Now?"

"Isn't that what you just said you wanted?" she challenged, wishing that he'd stop touching her, wishing that his eyes would turn cold and indifferent again instead of mirroring warmth and caring. These quicksilver changes threw her completely off balance.

"Yes, it's what I said, what I *want*, but I thought that we might talk over lunch."

She cocked her head. "And will that make the explanation more palatable?"

"You're not going to make this easy for me, are you?" he groused.

"I can't think of one good reason why I should, Theron."

He looked at her long and hard, then released her suddenly and stood frowning, his thumbs hooked into the waistband of his jeans.

"I deserved that," he said finally. "But isn't salvaging a friendship a good enough reason?"

"Is it friendship?" She doubted it. Too much tension flowed between them.

Theron doubted his words, as well. He wondered if the intensity of emotions provoked whenever he was near her didn't preclude all hope of a friendship ever developing between them, but he was determined to make a stab at it.

"I don't know what it is, Nicole. But I think that there is something worth saving, and being on neutral ground—in a restaurant surrounded by people—might keep the fireworks at a minimum." He grinned sheepishly. "Besides, I'm starving. My kitchen is so disorganized and understocked that all I had for breakfast was coffee and dry toast.''

An unwilling smile curved her mouth, and she lowered her head. ''What about unpacking?''

''Putting it on hold a couple of hours won't make a difference one way or another.''

''Annabel and I have plans.''

''This is *important*, Nicole,'' he told her urgently. When she glanced up at him, she saw it in his eyes—that vague, disturbing hint of apprehension, of vulnerability, that she'd seen last night. Then it was gone, and she wondered if it might have been her imagination. But when he spoke again, she almost staggered under the weight of his words. ''My youngest daughter has her sights set on becoming an aerial artist. You're her role model.''

The simple statement hung between them. Stunned, Nicole stared at him, fragments of their conversation the previous night hammering in her mind. He'd said there were things at stake that she didn't realize.

''Oh, God, I had no idea!''

''No, of course you didn't, and I'm sorry about dropping it on you like that, but I had to get your attention somehow.''

''You certainly succeeded.''

''Well?''

''Well what?'' She looked up blankly.

''Will you have lunch with me?''

''I'll have to talk to Annabel.''

''I'm sure she won't mind.''

Nicole couldn't help but smile at that understatement. Annabel had made the supreme sacrifice by suggesting that they golf. Although Nicole enjoyed the game immensely, she was notoriously bad—the ultimate duffer—and it drove Annabel crazy.

A sobering thought turned her smile into a frown, and her eyes grew anxious. "Theron, was Jenny there the night of the fall?"

"No, but she heard about it."

"It didn't change her mind?"

Theron smiled. "My children have the mind-set of mules. Jenny, in particular. If anything, it made her more determined."

"She sounds a lot like her father."

"Like I said earlier, you're skating on very thin ice, Nicole. Don't push me." Though his voice was gruff, there was an underlying teasing quality that he couldn't quite hide. "Now, then, are you going for some kind of a record in evasiveness, or are you going to give me a straight answer?"

"My car's still at Annabel's."

"For Pete's sake, we can swing by and pick it up after lunch." His patience was beginning to slip.

"Then I guess I'd better change clothes, hadn't I?"

"That means yes, I take it?"

"It means that I would very much like to spend time..." Her voice trailed off, and she felt blood rush to her face.

"Yes, Nicole?" He flashed a positively rakish smile her way.

Why the devil was it that he had the capacity to discombobulate her so? she wondered. And why did he seem to derive such great pleasure from her discomfiture? The least he could do was be a gentleman and let her off the hook. But he didn't, and in the end, it was she who gritted her teeth and with as much aplomb as possible, explained herself.

"What I'm trying to say, Theron, is yes. I would enjoy having lunch. That's all. Now, if you'll excuse me—"

"I wish you wouldn't change." He didn't have to lay a hand on her to stop her flight from the room. His words, the tone of his voice, the look in his eyes worked far more effectively. His eyes moved over her, inch by inch, touching her hair, her breasts, her hips, her legs, in a manner that heated her through and through. "You're perfectly beautiful just as you are."

The room became fraught with the timeless awareness between man and woman and the irrefutable knowledge that each held the piece of the puzzle necessary to make the other whole. Complete.

It was a heady moment.

Time stood still, rushed forward. Overlapped. Thoughts tumbled. His. Hers. Twenty-four hours ago, they hadn't met! And now? Here they were, their lives interwoven, bonded in an unfathomable manner that defied description, yet was, oh, so very basic! It was a far more dangerous scenario than anything even Theron's fertile mind could conjure up; the danger far different from that presented by Nicole's profession.

They'd shared a kiss. Too much, too compelling, too soon. Yet not enough.

A mistake, he'd said last night. Then, the words had hurt. Now, she understood what he meant and knew she should back away from him, break this mesmerizing spell before it was too late.

But it already was far, far too late, for his hand, rough and strong and warm, gently glided up her arm, barely skimming her soft flesh. Electricity crackled between them, and Nicole shivered.

Lost. Oh, God, she was so lost! she reflected on a sigh as he barely touched her shoulder, then cupped her cheek. She almost cried out as he tangled his fingers in her hair. She wanted him, just as she'd wanted more of him on the dock. He desired her with everything that pulsed inside of him, with every beat of his heart, he wanted full possession of this woman.

Eyes met, tangled, spoke volumes.

Nicole felt herself drowning in the calmest, yet wildest sea of blue-green imaginable.

Theron was drawn into the tempting depths of emerald fire burning hot and liquid, felt his blood fire and reason begin to slip away.

"We're going to make love, you and I," he murmured, his hand warm on her neck. God, how he wanted to take her in his arms now. To make good his promise, to feel her body molded to his, to know the pleasure of her embrace. Instead, he dropped a light kiss on her mouth: a promise, a prelude to what might happen. "One day, Nicole..."

"You sound awfully sure of yourself," she whispered.

"I am." He searched her eyes, looked into her soul and liking what he found, he gently reached up to brush a strand of hair away from her face. "And I think you know it, too."

Oh, yes, she knew. She was very close to throwing caution to the wind and locking her arms around him. She longed to feel his solid body pressed close to hers, to know more of him, then still more, in the most intimate way.

Feeling as if the very core of her existence had undergone a monumental change, she backed away, her legs rubbery. "We'd better talk to Annabel."

Almost before the words were out of her mouth, they heard voices outside, and Luke jumped up. Barking wildly, he trotted to the door.

Astounded, Theron watched the dog. "Why the hell didn't he do that for me? If I'd heard him bark, I wouldn't have come in."

"He only barks at people he knows."

"If there's logic there, I'm missing it."

"Think about it, Theron. If someone is determined to break into a house, a barking dog isn't going to stop him. Not if he has a gun. He was trained for sneak attacks," she tossed out blithely and opened the door for Annabel and Tag.

Standing quietly next to Tag, her arm looped through his, Nicole watched the warm reunion between cousins, liking what she saw. The easy familiarity, the affectionate hugs, the laughter. Intuitively she realized Theron Donahue was capable of great and abiding love, that he possessed a strong sense of family. The knowledge touched a chord in her, further disrupting her already fragile emotional state where he was concerned.

"...and so, if you have no objections, I'd like to steal her away for a couple of hours," Theron was saying, the heat of his gaze upon her jolting Nicole back to the here and now, bringing color to her cheeks.

"Objections?" Annabel laughed. "It's a reprieve! What I'd really like to do is go back to the house with Tag and dig in. Maybe run into town and buy you some groceries."

"Don't worry about that," Theron said, his voice somehow intimate, his eyes steady on Nicole. "We'll stop at the store after lunch and do the shopping."

Annabel smiled radiantly. "Well, then, it's settled. Tag, it looks like it's you and me and a houseful of boxes."

"Sure looks that way, heh?" Tag grinned and grabbed the ladder while Annabel ushered Nicole and Theron to the door.

"Out you go! I'll lock up for you, Nicole. Have fun, and try to relax a little." Though Annabel directed the comment to both of them, she'd meant it specifically for Nicole. Impulsively, Annabel hugged her friend. "Give him a chance," she whispered in Nicole's ear. "See you later."

In one way, Annabel's advice was easy to take. Nicole enjoyed Theron's company. Yet, their relationship had taken on a new dimension, and she became keenly aware of every facet of the man. Her heart skipped a beat each time he turned his eyes on her. Her pulse jumped when, at the restaurant on Jacksonville Beach, he placed his hand on the small of her back and guided her to their table on the weathered, ancient deck.

There were many things about him that she liked: his easy wit, his laughter, the low timbre of his voice. She noted the particular tilt of his head when he talked and the way the breeze tugged at his hair, making him look almost...boyish. There were the laugh lines that crinkled around his eyes and a smile that dazzled, and his quiet, inherent charm. She couldn't help but notice the way he moved with a calm authority and latent sexuality that turned the head of every woman they passed.

Seeing this, Nicole felt an inexplicable twinge of jealousy. It was the first time she'd given his personal life more than a passing thought, but now, seeing the admiration on their waitress's face as he ordered two seafood salads and tea, Nicole wondered if there was a special woman waiting for him in New York. Surely there must be. A handsome, sexy, compelling man, he was nothing to casually sneeze at. He was certainly not a man who lacked for female companionship. Of that she was sure, and the idea bothered her.

We're going to make love, you and I. The memory of his words heated her, and she wondered what it would be like wrapped in his arms, flesh against flesh, running her fingers through his thick mat of chest hair, feeling sinewy muscles under her hands, knowing him...completely.

As the waitress left, Theron looked at Nicole, caught her staring, and smiled. "Is something wrong?"

"No. I was just thinking..." She lowered her eyes. "...about how beautiful it is today."

"It's almost like midsummer," he agreed. Having seen the light in her eyes, pleasure welled in him. Ah, yes, he was glad he'd made the move, glad to be in this woman's company, glad that he'd chosen this restaurant. Small and casual, it was located on the beach. The deck on which they were seated was perched near the rocks forming the break-water. He took a swallow of tea, then leaned back in his chair and studied the woman sitting opposite him. "So...tell me all about Nicole Ross."

"I thought we came here to talk about your daughter."

"We did, and we will. But I'd like to talk about you right now. Writers are curious animals. We like to learn as much as possible about people." He paused. "Especially those people who impact on us so strongly that we know we'll never be able to forget them."

Nicole laughed. "My but we're turning formal."

"Not at all." Theron chuckled. "It's ice-breaking."

They talked for two hours, each logging away bits and pieces of information to draw out and ponder later.

They talked of seemingly inconsequential, yet somehow monumental things. Likes and dislikes. Theron preferred classical music, especially when he worked. Nicole, having a background in ballet, enjoyed it, as well, but her love was light rock, and she often turned her stereo to the highest decibel. He grimaced at that. She laughed. Nicole thrived on bright, happy colors; Theron, muted ones, although he admitted reluctantly, he found the chaotic decor of the gatehouse fascinating. They talked of the sea and how it soothed, and the beauty of the gardens on the estate and how the fragrance of the flowers filled the soft night air, and how they both enjoyed cantering their horses through the misty hours of an early morn.

They talked of many things, left out many more.

After the waitress brought them their third glass of tea, Theron fell silent. He gazed over the calm, metallic sea and in that instant, Nicole sensed the turmoil within him, sensed it went far beyond his daughter. The expression on his features mirrored raw, naked sadness, and she fiercely ached for him. The feeling wound around her heart, formed a lump in her throat.

Wanting to ease his pain, she reached across the table and hesitantly rested her hand on his. Meant only as a small gesture of comfort, it turned into much more.

Still gazing at the water and the rolling, eddying of the surf upon the sandy beach, he laced his fingers through hers and talked about Jenny, telling her the same things he'd confided to Lawrence two years ago and had fought with Tag over just a few hours ago. While he talked, he absently massaged the soft flesh of her wrist.

"With winter quarters nearby, and you living in the gatehouse . . . well . . . Jenny's talked about nothing else," he finished, and sighed. "She's going to ask you to help her, and I have to know what your answer will be."

The small hand intertwined with his, stiffened, then pulled away. Curious, he studied her. She'd grown very still, her eyes distant, haunted.

"Why me? I haven't performed in two years," she said on a soft rush of air, feeling as if a great weight had dropped on her. Pain clutched her heart.

Puzzled by her reaction, he frowned, intuition telling him to tread carefully. "Because you're one of the best. Because Jenny is drawing from your past, Nicole." He paused again, and when she turned frightened, questioning eyes on him but didn't comment, he continued. "Apparently your debut was postponed because of an injury—"

"That's not at all the same thing! I was only fourteen, then! I fell off a horse and hurt my ankle!" she interrupted, desperation heavy in her voice.

Taking a chance, hoping to ease the tension, he grinned. "Certainly not the same horse you have now."

It worked. She sat back and smiled.

"Lord, no! She's only five. The horse that dumped me is long gone to that pasture in the sky. But the point is, Theron, it was a different incident."

"True. And my daughter understands that. But, she's still an impressionable child who possesses an unwavering belief that because you once overcame obstacles, you'll do it again," he said, adding meaningfully, "Apparently, she's right."

Much to Nicole's relief, their waitress sidled up to the table, interrupting the flow of conversation. "Excuse me, will there be anything else, sir?"

"Nicole?" Theron looked across at her pinched features, saw her shake her head, and gave the waitress a credit card. Moments later, the receipt tucked into his wallet, he rose and pulled Nicole up with him. "Come on, let's go for a walk on the beach."

Mutely, she let him guide her out of the restaurant and down the driveway to where it intersected with the beach access road. Sitting on one of the granite rocks of the breakwater, they removed shoes and sandals. Hand in hand, they strolled silently toward the water's edge.

The unseasonable heat of the day brought the sun worshippers out in droves. Bodies slick with oil lay on beach towels and lounge chairs. A man played Frisbee with his dog. There were joggers and waders and beachcombers and swimmers. Cars cruised the hard-packed, wet sand. Radios blasted. Gulls soared and squawked. The sea rushed over bare feet, then receded again with a soft sucking sound and a power that tugged at the sand upon which they stood.

Spying a small, round stone that was out of place on the beach, Theron picked it up and flung it toward the water.

"I don't want the responsibility," Nicole said the moment he released it. He stood very still, waiting, the sun beating down on his head. Standing behind him, Nicole watched as he looked toward the heavens. "Jenny will have to talk to my father. I can't help or advise anyone right now."

"Why?" He turned and gently rested his hands upon her shoulders. She sounded defeated. Gone was the spirited bravado of the previous night. In its place he saw fear, and again, he was puzzled. "Tell me why, Nicole."

She shrugged noncommittally. "I just can't do it now, Theron." Her composure began to slip, and she felt close to tears. "I just can't . . ."

The need to comfort her strong, he pulled her into his arms and smoothed back her hair. "It's all right. I'll talk to Jenny. Don't worry about it. It'll be okay."

But as they stood under the hot sun, both wondered if what he'd said was true.

Theron didn't broach the subject again. Not during the time they laughed their way through the grocery store, filling two baskets. Nor did he mention it while they unloaded the car and stocked the cupboards and refrigerator to capacity.

And he kept silent the following day, Sunday, while working with Annabel, Tag and Nicole. The four of them put the finishing touches on the ground-floor rooms.

Monday morning Theron, having learned from Tag that Nicole religiously went to the winter quarters at nine, made it a point to be there well before she arrived. Obtaining a day pass at the security gate, he drove to the aerialists' center. Minutes later, his car parked out of sight, he entered the door of the cavernous building, and when Nicole arrived Theron was leaning against a wall opposite her rigging, a baseball cap covering his hair, tinted glasses hiding his eyes.

Excitement charged the air when she appeared, this small, leggy woman wearing a black leotard, her hair pulled back in a neat bun, her wrists taped. She was met by two men dressed in sweat suits. A short conference ensued before Nicole climbed the long rope to the Roman rings and began a series of body-bending gymnastic exercises that sent sympathy pangs through Theron's muscles.

"Is that what you meant, Ralph?" she called down to the older of the two men, her smile vibrant.

"Almost. I'd like to see a little more extension on the shoulder lifts, but that'll come as you build up your strength. Let's put it all together. Take it from the top, and we'll see how it looks. All but the opening arabesque," Ralph told her, then turned to the younger man. "Gus, get that rope out of her way."

For the next nine minutes, all eyes were riveted to the dynamic woman performing thirty feet above them. If possible, she went through her routine with even more vitality now than when Theron had first seen her. She was beauty and grace and perfection, and when she slid down the rope, there was a moment of total silence, then came cheers, whistles and applause, and Nicole was caught up in a series of backslapping bear hugs.

But later, after a long break, as she moved to the trapeze, Theron saw a different woman. Gone was the radiance, the excitement. She stood near the net and gazed up apprehensively. A tension so heavy that it was almost palpable tainted the air as she walked around, pulling on guy wires, testing the net, all the while staring at the platform above.

Ralph and Gus, now shed of their sweats and clad in tights, climbed the web—Ralph to the catcher's trapeze, Gus to the fly bar.

Nicole followed slowly, and Theron caught the expression on her features. It was the same one she'd worn on the beach. It was pure terror. He had to force himself from calling out to her to come back down. Yet, another part of him wanted to shout out encouragement.

Nicole strapped the safety mechanic around her waist. Across from her, Ralph took his position, while Gus loosened Nicole's fly bar from its moorings and swung out easily. Nicole stood on the pedestal, her features closed as she watched them warm up. Then Gus was standing beside her again, holding out the fly bar for her to take.

Theron's heart seemed lodged in his throat as she whipped off the pedestal, her body fluid. She swung once, then again...higher. When Ralph cued her, it resounded through the vast room. There wasn't a person watching whose heart didn't stop beating at that crucial moment.

"For God's sake, Nicole!" Theron muttered under his breath when she hesitated, stiffened. Then her body went limp. Closing her eyes, she lowered her head and swung long legs up and over the bar. Sitting up, Nicole clung to the now gently swaying trapeze like a frightened child.

On the ground, anxious eyes watched and heads shook.

"I'm sorry, Ralph," she said, her voice wavering.

"It's all right, babe. You've got everything that it takes to come back strong. As soon as you get past this hurdle, you'll do fine," Ralph assured her. "Take a minute. Catch your breath, then we'll try it again."

But Theron couldn't stay for the next time. Slipping out of the side door, he hurried to his car and drove home, his heart aching for Nicole.

Late that night when sleep refused to come, he wandered down to his study. Absently taking a pipe from the rack, he filled the bowl and lit it. He felt lousy for having gone to the winter quarters, felt as if he'd intruded on a very personal part of her life, yet in the same breath, he was glad. For he'd learned something about Nicole today.

He'd learned a lesson in courage, and that was something he'd not soon forget; it was something for which he greatly respected her.

Courage.

The word relentlessly stalked the corners of his mind. He had no doubts whatsoever that she would persevere until she overcame her fear of letting go, until she flew again. She was facing a painful part of her past with bravado, and he understood the emotional toll exacted because of it.

Setting down his pipe, he turned toward his bookshelves and stared at the box containing *Images*. Maybe it was time that he, too, came face-to-face with a past that he couldn't seem to shake.

Hesitantly, he picked up the box and took out the manuscript, reading it for the first time in three years.

Chapter Six

Theron ran downstairs dressed in jeans, a pullover, boots and a lightweight suede jacket shortly before six the next morning. Cutting through the large family room, he went directly to the kitchen where he found Tag already at the table, the inevitable morning paper and plate of rubberized eggs and burned bacon in front of him. A strong aroma of chicory coffee permeated the air.

Some things never change, he reflected gratefully, suddenly anxious for his children to arrive so they, too, would come to know Tag in the same way Theron had while growing up.

"'Morning, Tag," Theron said, slapping the old man on the back as he passed him.

"Yup, that it is. Coffee's fresh if you want some." Tag laid the paper down and slurped his brew. "What the devil you doin' up so early? I saw the light on in the study when I drove in at five."

"I worked last night and fell asleep on the couch," Theron told him, filling a mug with coffee. Turning around, he leaned against the counter.

Tag gave him a long look of appraisal. "I gotta admit to bein' a bit surprised. Glad, but surprised."

"Not half as surprised as I am," Theron admitted, frowning.

"How'd it go?"

"It was tough," he replied candidly. Truth was, he'd almost put *Images* back on the shelf several times, and would have—if not for the nagging memory of Nicole's determination and courage. "Damn tough."

"Nothin' worthwhile's easy, son. Don't lose sight of that." Tag's eyes mirrored approval, then concern. "You know, an honest day's work can't hurt anyone, I reckon, but a man can get old before his time if he don't take care of himself. Get the proper rest he needs to keep goin'. In a proper bed."

Theron laughed. "Hell, old man, your coffee will kill me long before I ever get close to old age. What are you going to do when I hire a housekeeper?"

"Train her proper, I 'spect," Tag grumbled and went back to reading the paper.

Theron took a long swallow of the hot liquid, savoring the rich chicory taste, then set the empty mug on the counter. "Keep the pot hot. I may force down another cup when I get back from the barn."

"You goin' ridin'?"

"The thought crossed my mind." He'd thought of nothing else since waking up, for he knew that Nicole rode every morning at the crack of dawn.

"It's gonna be a mighty pretty sunrise, heh?" Tag said without looking up. He cleared his throat. "Yup, reckon little Nikki's gettin' that Morgan mare of hers ready for a ride right 'bout now."

Theron smiled. "You trying to play matchmaker, Tag?"

"Confound it anyway, there just don't seem to be no sense in two people who're goin' ridin' to ride off in separate directions, now does there?" Tag groused. "God didn't mean for a man to live alone."

"You have."

"Only because there's not a woman in the world who'd put up with me for more than five minutes, and I ain't 'bout to change." He glanced out the window. "Hadn't you best get a move on it before you waste the whole mornin'?"

Needing no further prodding, Theron walked outside. It was cool and still in the predawn hour. The dampness of the night hung heavily in the air. Above, stars began to fade in an ever lightening sky. Below, his boots thudded dully on the asphalt as he strolled toward the stucco-and-wood six-stall barn not thirty yards away from the house.

It was odd, he thought, that he didn't feel exhausted. Though he'd struggled with the past, and doubts had plagued him the previous night while reading *Images*, though he hadn't fallen asleep until after two in the morning and then had slept restlessly for three short hours on the leather couch in his study, he felt unaccountably good. A feeling of expectation, of anticipation, of urgency had gripped him the moment he'd opened his eyes, and he knew he simply *had* to see Nicole.

When he did, his breath caught in his lungs and he paused a moment, unwilling to let a single detail of the scene before him escape his attention.

Dressed in faded jeans and a denim jacket, she was standing in the middle aisle of the barn grooming her horse. Her hair was pulled back from her face, held in place by a headband, but it cascaded down her back in a luxuriant river of honey blond that picked up a touch of gold from the light above her. She worked diligently, her lithe body moving and swaying as she brushed the gleaming coat of the dozing horse. While she moved around the animal, she spoke softly, soothingly.

Smiling, Theron knew he would be content just to stand outside watching her, but her Doberman suddenly appeared in the aisle and barked. The horse, spotting Theron, pricked her ears and whinnied. Nicole swung around.

"Hi! You're up and about awfully early," she said as he walked into the barn. Her eyes sparkling, she smiled softly.

"Hi, yourself," he replied, somewhat taken aback by her sunny disposition. After what he'd seen yesterday at winter quarters, it caught him off guard, and he couldn't help but wonder if it was a facade. Approaching her, he saw that her eyes were sparkling and her smile was genuine. What inner well of strength did she survive on? he wondered, a new respect building inside him. "This is the best time of the day."

"Somehow I didn't take you for a man who rose before daylight," she replied, quickly turning back to her horse. Oh, God, it was happening again—the fluttering in her stomach, the wild thumping of her heart, the boneless feeling in her knees.

"Have you forgotten our discussion over lunch so quickly?" he asked, walking up to stand directly behind her.

"No." She remembered every detail of that day. "I just don't know you well enough to know if I should take you seriously on everything you say."

"You'd be making a grave mistake not to, Nicole. I don't say things that I don't mean," he warned.

"I'll remember that." Shaky, her voice was so *shaky*! Desperately, she wished that he'd move away from her, that he'd give her some space, but he didn't. He stood solidly behind her, sandwiching her between the warmth of her horse and his masculinity.

Not having seen him yesterday, she'd been able to put their encounters into the proper perspective. A fact that was especially important after the fiasco on the trapeze. She simply had to work through her problems, in order to let go and fly again, and harboring a preoccupation with Theron Donahue wouldn't help. He was far too distracting.

Yet here he was, his presence filling the barn. Her perspective vanished, and a tremor shot through her that she was sure would register a full eight on the Richter scale.

"If you don't stop brushing that horse's rump, she's going to go bald," Theron commented, his breath ruffling her hair, a smile lifting the corners of his mouth. So she felt the chemistry between them, as well, he thought, the knowledge warming him, reinforcing his already strong feelings for Nicole. "What's her name?"

Embarrassed, Nicole stopped brushing the horse. "Pockets. M T U Pockets," she said a little too breathlessly for her own liking. "Say it fast, and you'll know what I had to do to buy her."

Laughter rumbled through his chest, and when he reached out to stroke the mare, Nicole felt the heat of awareness surge through her as their bodies came in contact. His laughter subsided, and in its place she heard him draw in a quick, sharp breath. Had she turned around as she was tempted to do, would she have seen desire in his eyes and felt his mouth warm upon hers? Was she right in sensing that's what he wanted to do at that moment: hold her—kiss her?

Silence screamed through the barn for several long moments, both of them piercingly aware of each other and the strong currents flowing between them.

"The name suits her," Theron said finally and stepped back to appraise the mare. "She's a good representative of the breed. Nice crested neck...fine head...lots of mane and tail. Good disposition." He narrowed his eyes. "She is a beautiful animal, Nicole."

"Thank you," she murmured, wondering what she was really thanking him for—the compliment, or for moving away and allowing her some much needed space.

"Are you riding this morning?" he asked.

"Yes."

"Do you mind if I join you? I think Thor is ready to get out and stretch his legs a bit."

"No. I don't mind, at all," she told him, smiling. *Thor*? That figured—the lord of the manor riding a mount named for the Norse god of thunder. Curious, she glanced up to see which stall he went to. So the big black gelding was his, and from the looks of it, man and horse suited each other very well. Draping her arms over the back of her horse, Nicole watched quietly for a moment. When Theron looked up suddenly and caught her staring, she flushed and grinned and shrugged. "Sorry. I was just curious as to how a mere mortal handles a god."

"With a great deal of caution," he told her. "If you don't get busy and saddle up, we're going to miss the best part of the morning."

Minutes later, they led their mounts outside and swung easily into the saddles.

"Where do you want to go?" Nicole asked, noting with approval how natural he looked astride his mount.

"That depends on you and how much time you have before going to the winter quarters."

"My coach has a doctor's appointment this morning. I don't have to be there until ten."

He studied her intently, a muscle in his jaw jumping, then ventured, "How're the training sessions going?"

"Just fine," she replied a little too hastily and turned her attention to her horse, hoping that Theron wouldn't pursue the subject. The trapeze and rings were the last things she wanted to talk about this morning, so she quickly changed the subject. "How would you like to see what's been done on the backside of your property? Maybe go to the creek?"

"You are offering *me* a tour of *my* property?" His eyebrows lifted slightly.

"Why not? Somebody's got to do it," she said, thankful that the conversation was on safer ground. She grinned at him. "You haven't seen it for so long, you'd probably get lost if you went alone."

"I'm beginning to wonder who's the tenant and who's the landlord," he groused, but he was smiling.

They rode away from the barn, Luke bounding ahead of them. Riding in silence, they followed the fence line, both of them lost in the beauty of the morning, both enjoying quiet reveries, yet each of them keenly aware of the other's presence. During the quiet moments, a feeling of intimacy bound them, for they were sharing something they loved.

Theron's eyes moved to rest on the woman riding beside him. She sat straight in the saddle, her features relaxed, her expression almost dreamy. Gone was the panic he'd seen first on the beach, then at the winter quarters, and again a few minutes ago when he'd asked about her training. Gone, too, was the guilt he'd been harboring since his visit to the winter quarters, for it had provided him with the insight necessary to better understand her. It was odd, he thought, this sudden need to have her trust him, yet he knew he couldn't push her.

Still, as they rode silently through the pale light of early morn, the horses' hooves thudding softly on the dewy grass, the leather of the saddles squeaking comfortably, he felt helpless. He wanted to do something for Nicole...but what? Hell, how could he help her when he was having trouble getting his own life in order? Frustration gnawed at him, deepening the lines of his face.

The trail took them deep into the three-hundred-acre piece of property, and when Theron saw the enormous amount of work that had been done, his frustration ebbed, and he looked around with interest. What had once been impassable because of dense underbrush was now almost parklike. The brush had been cleared away and the lower branches of pine trees lopped off. Now and again, they passed groups of palmettos which looked as if they'd been landscaped into the property. The grass grew lush and green over much of the acreage. And everywhere he looked he saw scrub oaks and holly bushes and towering pines interspersed with palm trees.

"Like it?" Nicole asked, smiling.

"It looks a hell of a lot different from the way I remember it," Theron admitted, his voice husky. "Yes, I like it very much. It's a perfect place for the kids to ride." He paused. "Tag's been busy."

A strange sense of relief surged through Nicole at Theron's almost reverent approval of what was, after all, his property. But surge, it did, and she felt warmth flood her. Reining in her horse, she glanced around.

"Yes, he has," she agreed softly. "He picked two or three places like this to clear out, but the rest of the property is in its natural state. There are some really beautiful trails farther back, Theron." She turned in the saddle and pointed toward the house. "Later on, I'll show you the area he cleared out for Julie's arena, but first there's something else that you need to see. Come on."

Following a two-rut trail that wound through the trees, they kicked their horses into a canter, now and then scaring up a bird or surprising an armadillo. As they rounded a curve in the trail, Nicole pulled up her horse.

They'd stopped not five yards from the bank of a stream that flowed across the property and emptied into the ICW. Nostalgia gripped Theron when he saw the two ancient timber tracks bridging the stream—timbers that had been there for as long as he could remember. While the trail continued through a thick stand of trees on the opposite bank, this side had been cleared and was utterly beautiful with its large shade trees and thick carpet of grass.

"There's a good oyster bed down by the ICW. Tag cleared a path so it's accessible by land or boat," she told him as the sun rose over the tops of the trees, warming her. "This is another one of my favorite places."

Wordlessly, Theron dismounted and walked around to lend her a hand. After tying their horses to low-hanging branches of a nearby tree, he turned to look at her.

"How much did you have to do with this?" he asked, his voice low and sandpapery.

Alarmed, afraid that he was angry, her eyes shot to his. "I helped Tag a little, when I had time." There was a tremor in her voice. Clearing this spot had been her idea. "It's so beautiful back here, I thought there'd be no harm in cleaning it up so you and the kids can enjoy it."

"Somehow I've never visualized it looking this way," he said simply and walked out to stand on the timber tracks, Luke trailing along at his side. He stood there for several long quiet moments, staring at the water, absently scratching the dog's ears while Nicole watched apprehensively from the bank.

Her mouth went dry, and her heart beat crazily. If only she knew him well enough to read his moods . . . but she wondered if anyone could ever do that, for there were times when his expression was so closed and distant that reading him was virtually impossible. This was one of those times, she decided. He stood tall and proud, his jawline hard, his mouth compressed, deep lines furrowing his brow. He had the appearance of an angry man, and it wasn't until he returned to the bank that Nicole saw the infinite sadness reflected in his eyes. It tore through her, made her want to go to him, but she held back.

"It's been a long time since you've been back here, hasn't it?" she observed hesitantly, her eyes steady on him.

"I was just thinking three years, but it's probably been closer to five or six. Possibly even longer. I don't know. All sense of time seems to have gotten away from me." His voice was thick with emotion. "This place brings so many things into focus."

"Memories?"

"More than I can count." He shook his head and smiled. "Memories of being fifteen years old and almost killing myself by racing across those timbers in a dilapidated old Jeep. Of hunting with Lawrence and Granddad." His eyes sought hers. "Memories of the oyster bed you were talking about."

A long silence fell over them.

"And of Jess?" The question slipped out before Nicole realized it was even on her mind, and she saw Theron's jaw clench.

"Yes," he replied, frowning.

Fidgeting nervously, she wished there was a graceful way of climbing back on her horse and riding away so he could spend some time alone—if that's what he wanted.

She swallowed against the tears in her throat. "Are you angry with me for this, Theron?"

"Good God, no, Nicole!" Going to her, he scooped her into his arms and held her tightly. "Not on your life, sweetheart. It's beautiful, and I'm glad that it's done." He dropped a kiss on the top of her head, the sweet fragrance of her hair rushing through him. "I guess I just wasn't expecting the place to affect me as strongly as it did."

"If you'd like, I'll go back to the house," she told him quietly.

"You'll do no such thing." Tilting her head back, he gazed into the green eyes he was coming to adore so much. "I want you with me," he said, and lowering his mouth to hers, he showed her how much he meant those words. Slowly, he savored the softness of her lips, the sweetness of her, the feel of her body pressed close to his. Breaking the kiss, he sighed. "God, but you taste good. So...good." He grinned and nodded toward the horses and dog curiously watching them. "If we didn't have an audience, you could find yourself in big trouble."

"They're a snoopy lot, aren't they?" she managed shakily, her lips still tingling from his kiss, her breasts from their contact with his hard chest. When he sat down and held out his hand for her, she sank gratefully onto the grass beside him and after a moment, she turned large, curious eyes on him. "What happened with you and the Jeep when you were fifteen?"

"You don't want to hear."

"Yes, I do." She wanted to know everything there was to know about this man. "Was it bad?"

"Bad enough so I almost didn't survive the crime or the punishment." He laughed. "Lawrence and I were hotrodding in Granddad's Jeep. We came tearing around that curve doing about forty or so. I slowed down some before we hit the timbers, but I also miscalculated the distance between them. Needless to say, the Jeep slid halfway across on its frame. Somehow it managed to balance on one of the timbers, but both Lawrence and I were thrown into the creek. Thank God, there was no top on it, or we'd have both been killed." He shook his head in remembrance. "Once Granddad got a hold of us, our luck ran out. That old man was hell with a belt when he wanted to be."

They laughed together, then Theron told her about other things in his life: how his parents had disinherited him when he left Florida, and how they were killed when their private jet went down a few years ago; about his grandfather leaving him this piece of property and another large parcel of land right across the highway from here, with its old hunting lodge that he one day wanted to rebuild. He told her about the family empire going to Annabel's father and brother, and how it caused a rift between Annabel and her

parents. He confided that Tag was the only real father figure he'd ever known.

And as the day came alive around them and birds flitted
about in the trees and a big sun warmed them, he told her
how he and Jess had planned and built the house.

"She had to have her hands in every phase of the construction," he said, a faraway look in his eyes, then he fell
silent.

"What happened to her, Theron?" Nicole asked gently,
wondering if he'd ever be able to put his memories to rest.

The question whispered on the breeze, and she thought
that he hadn't heard her. Then she saw his jaw clench, and
he rose. Walking to the bank of the creek, he stood with his
back to her, his broad shoulders sagging, his head lowered.
After what seemed an eternity, he turned back to face her.

"If I seem clumsy about this, it's only because I've never
been very good at talking about it." There were things involved with Jessica's death that he had trouble accepting,
for he blamed himself.

"I know it's hard, Theron. It was almost impossible for
me to talk about Marc for a long time." The tension growing inside of her was almost as unbearable as the pain she
felt for him. "If you don't want to, I'll understand. I'm not
trying to pry."

"You're not prying, Nicole," he said quietly, his eyes
haunted, the intensity of his inner struggle mirrored on his
features. "Jess and a good friend of ours were killed in an
automobile accident. The driver of the other vehicle was
drunk."

"Oh, Theron, I am so sorry!"

He let out a heavy sigh and wondered why it was so easy
to talk to this woman; why he suddenly felt as if he wanted
to tell her what happened, when he'd steadfastly refused to
discuss the loss of his wife with anyone else over the years.

"The irony of it is that Jess did a lot of volunteer work at a drug- and alcohol-abuse center. It was because of her work that *Images* was born, and it was largely because of that damned play that she was killed."

"I don't understand the connection," she said, but she completely understood why he'd shelved *Images*, for it dealt with a woman's fight against and rise above chemical addiction. Though it was a provocative, sensitive piece, it had to have torn Theron to pieces after his wife's death.

"Jess and I were supposed to attend a fund-raising dinner for the center at our country club one evening, but I got tied up with the play. It was rolling so well that Jess suggested I stay home." He frowned. "She was a damned slave driver when it came to *Images*. She passionately wanted the play finished and in production. So, I stayed home and worked." Pausing, a muscle in his jaw twitched. "A friend of ours picked Jess up. Two hours later, the police showed up on our doorstep. They said the pickup truck was doing sixty when it ran a stop sign and plowed into Jerry's Porsche. Jerry and Jess were killed instantly. The three kids in the truck survived."

Tears misting Nicole's eyes, she watched him closely and knew exactly what he was doing. She stood and went to him and wrapped her arms around him. "Don't do this to yourself, Theron. Oh, God, please, *please* don't blame yourself."

"How can I not, Nicole?" he demanded. "If I hadn't been so damned single-minded about the play...I can't help but think that if I'd gone, if I'd been driving, it never would have happened."

"And what if you'd both been killed?" she asked insistently, the mere thought of it making her sick. "What, then? Who would the children have, Theron?" When he looked at her doubtfully, she continued. "Sometimes things happen that we have absolutely no control over! It took me a long time to accept the fact that Marc, a man who'd been performing since the age of nine, a man with an uncanny sense of timing, could make a mistake. I was so bent on blaming myself that months passed before Dad finally convinced me to watch the video Mom had made of the performance.''

"Sweet Jesus, Nicole, that must have been rough.''

"It was horrible! But there it was. Big as life! Someone let go of one of those silly balloons, and it distracted Marc long enough to miss his cue—and we collided. He just couldn't get himself in control before hitting the net, and that's what killed him. He broke his neck.'' Her eyes were soft and wet and sad. "I had one hell of a good cry after watching that tape, Theron. Then I decided that if I didn't get on with my life, they might as well bury me next to him, and I sure wasn't ready for that. So I called Lawrence.''

"And...here you are.'' Pulling her into his arms, he felt closer to her at that moment than he did to any other person on the face of the earth. It was a good feeling, he decided. "You and Rossles—the perfect little clown.''

"Rossles saved my sanity. She put laughter back in my life,'' she told him. "You've got to try to do the same thing. Blaming yourself will make you crazy. I know. I've been there.''

"I'm working on it,'' he said quietly. "Now, then, if we don't get you back, you're going to be late.''

They rode back to the barn in companionable silence, both lost in private thoughts. So much had happened during the past two hours, so many confidences had been shared, that the entire scope of the relationship had shifted. What was needed now was, very simply, time to assess thoughts and feelings.

After grooming and turning out their horses, Theron walked Nicole to her car, smiling as Luke leaped across the console and settled into the passenger seat in a proud and princely fashion.

"I read *Images* last night," he said, as Nicole slipped behind the wheel.

Surprised, her eyes shot to his. Having learned the story behind the play, she'd vowed never to mention it again. "You did?"

"Yes, I did."

"And?"

"And... I don't know. I read it, that's all." He paused. "Would you mind some company again tomorrow morning?"

"No. Not at all," she told him, pushing aside the warning that stalked her mind. Things had subtly changed during their ride. She felt connected to him somehow, and closer. Much closer than she wanted to feel toward any man, but as she drove away, a sense of anticipation worked through her.

They rode almost every morning that week.

The knock on her door came shortly after two o'clock Saturday afternoon. Curious, Nicole closed the book she'd been trying to read, wondering who it could possibly be. Everyone she knew had plans for the weekend. Theron's children had flown in the previous night, which meant Nicole probably wouldn't see him or Tag until Sunday. Annabel was busy with preparations for a family cookout scheduled for that evening. Everybody else Nicole knew was out of town.

Smoothing back her hair, she went to the door, her eyes widening with surprise and pleasure as she opened it and saw Theron looking impossibly handsome, his hair tousled, his smile broad.

"Hi! I wasn't expecting to see you today." Was her voice really as whispery as it seemed?

"I can't imagine why not." He laughed. "I need all the support I can get this weekend."

She smiled. "Where are the children? Surely not at Annabel's already."

"Nope. As a matter of fact, I'm here as official spokesman for the family." When she cocked her head quizzically, he explained. "We took a vote, and the decision was unanimous."

"What decision?"

"That you go riding with us."

"Oh, Theron, I don't think . . ." Her voice trailed off as he stepped aside. Behind him, on the other side of the front gate, she saw the Donahue children. Mounted on their horses, they waited patiently.

"You don't really have a choice in the matter, Nicole." He touched her cheek gently. "Go put your boots on."

Moments later, she walked down the sidewalk with Theron, her eyes moving from one child to the next as they approached the gate. There was Rusty, the spitting image of his father, sitting astride Spooky, his light bay gelding. In his hands, he held Thor's reins. Next to him was Julie with light brown hair, astride Cantata, her huge gray show jumper. Last of all was Jenny, with long, flowing auburn hair—a perfect likeness of her mother—mounted on Mickie, a delicate little bay mare. The beaming child held the reins of Nicole's horse.

Sitting in front of his newfound friends was Luke, panting happily.

Sensing Nicole's nervousness, Theron placed a reassuring hand on her shoulder as he made the introductions. Just as he'd known they would, Rusty and Jenny responded enthusiastically to Nicole, but a frown furrowed his brow as Julie, in her cool, reserved manner, acknowledged Nicole with nothing more than a slight nod of her head.

Nicole walked to her horse, apprehension heavy in her heart as she took the reins from Jenny, the little girl who wanted to fly, the child who'd chosen Nicole as her role model. Oh, God, what would she ever do if Jenny began plying her with questions about the trapeze, Nicole wondered anxiously.

"Dad says that you're a clown now," Jenny enthused as Nicole mounted, and her tension began to ebb by degrees.

"I sure am, Jenny," Nicole confirmed.

"Hey, squirt, that's right up your alley," Rusty piped up, laughing. "You don't even need makeup!"

"Russell, mind your manners, and stop teasing your sister," Theron admonished as he swung into his saddle. But, of course, the teasing didn't stop, or the laughter. As they rode back across the bridge and through the iron gates of the estate, the banter and noise escalated. Theron grinned at Nicole. "See what I mean about needing support?"

"You love every minute of it, Donahue," she tossed back lightly and nodded toward Rusty and Jenny. "Are we going to let them think we're fuddy-duddies, or are we going to catch up with them?"

As they cantered through the sunny afternoon, Julie fell in line with Nicole and Theron, closely flanking her father.

Late that night, Nicole lay in bed mulling over the day's events. Once back from riding, it had been impossible to turn down Theron's invitation to join them at Annabel's.

How wonderful and natural it had felt to sit between Theron and Annabel watching the Donahue children and Annabel's four play in the pool, turning the calm water into a frothing playground. The rapport with Jenny and Rusty had been instant. Only Julie had seemed standoffish and watchful of her father and Nicole. But something puzzled her. Not once had Jenny mentioned the trapeze. Perhaps, Nicole thought, Theron had talked to the little girl. Or perhaps the questions didn't come because of the general lack of privacy and the excitement that pervaded the night.

Nicole sighed, knowing that those questions would be forthcoming. If not on this visit, then on the next. Most assuredly she'd be forced to face the reality of Jenny's dreams once the children moved permanently to Florida.

Burrowing under the covers, Nicole thought warmly of the drive back from Annabel's. It had seemed the most normal thing in the world to her when, shortly before midnight, they'd corralled three tired children and set off for home with Julie and Rusty in the backseat and Jenny fast asleep on the front, her head cradled on Nicole's lap.

As the car moved smoothly through the darkness, Theron had looked first at his sleeping daughter, then had raised his eyes to Nicole's, the silent communication so filled with contentment and meaning that Nicole's eyes had misted. It had been years since she'd felt such a strong sense of family, of rightness, with a man.

What terrified her was that she hadn't wanted to leave him. She had imagined the ease of going home with him, of sending the children up to bed, then climbing the stairs with Theron and spending the night curled against him. But of course no matter how pleasant the thought, it was a fantasy. When he'd stopped the car at the gatehouse, she'd insisted on seeing herself inside and shifted Jenny so that she lay on the seat. Nicole said goodnight to Rusty, Julie and Theron, and walked to the cottage alone.

Oh, dear God, how was she ever going to cope with the multitude of feelings swiftly growing within her regarding Theron and his children? Yet somehow she had to, for he was a man who needed a full-time wife rather than a nomad who lived in a stateroom on a train nine months out of the year.

She drifted to sleep, glad that she had a party booking the following afternoon, glad that Theron's busy social schedule and her work commitments would allow almost a full week of breathing space. She'd need every bit of that time to marshal her feelings and get her thoughts back on track again.

If that was possible.

Chapter Seven

Nicole's stomach tightened uncomfortably when she saw the picture in the newspaper the following Saturday morning.

Dressed in leotards and leg warmers, she was sitting at her small glass-and-rattan kitchen table, a sheen of perspiration from a vigorous workout still on her forehead. In one hand, she held a glass of orange juice. In the other, the newspaper. Drawing it closer, she frowned. There, right in front of her in black-and-white, was Theron Donahue, his dazzling smile frozen for eternity.

Seeing the photograph didn't surprise or bother her. To the contrary, she'd become accustomed to it. That the Jacksonville area adored its homegrown celebrity and was welcoming him back in royal fashion had been made abundantly clear during the past week. Photos of Theron had popped up almost daily on the society or entertainment pages, or sometimes both.

What did bother Nicole more than she cared to admit was the woman at his side, a woman around whose shoulder Theron's arm was protectively draped. A woman whom Nicole recognized instantly as the very beautiful, very talented actress, Shelly Ballinger—the toast of Broadway.

"Looks like you were worrying needlessly about an involvement with the man, Nikki, girl," she muttered to the empty room and pushed the paper aside. But as she finished her juice, another thought skittered annoyingly through her mind. *So that's why he canceled lunch on Wednesday.*

The message he'd left on her answering machine came back clearly. "Nicole, Theron here. I've got a break in my schedule today. If you're free, maybe we can have lunch together. Call me when you get back from the winter quarters." Then came the second message. "Sorry, funny face..." She'd smiled at that. "...something came up that I can't get out of. I'll talk to you later."

Of course something had come up, Nicole reflected irritably. Shelly Ballinger. Glancing once more at the photograph, she scoffed and went to take a shower. Not that it would have made any difference. Lunch with Theron would have been virtually impossible. Finding five minutes to herself had been a challenge during the past week.

A creature of habit, Nicole had rolled out of bed at four every morning. She'd gone directly to her ballet bar, limbering her body with a series of *demi-pliés*, *grand battements*, *dégagés*, and a variety of other exercises she deemed crucial in order to maintain her style and grace. From the bar, she moved to the mat, executing handstands and splits and back bends that would snap a normal person's spine.

After the workout, her day got really crazy. There was a quick shower, a hurried trip to the barn to feed her horse, then she was off to the winter quarters for a two-hour training session. By eleven she was home, gulping down a sandwich before applying the greasepaint that transformed her into Rossles. Then she was racing away from the gatehouse again, in order to fulfill her work obligations.

Nicole stripped and sighed and stepped into a hot shower. It seemed as if every children's ward in every hospital within a fifty-mile radius and every children's home in the area had booked Halloween parties during the past few days. As much as Nicole enjoyed clowning, she could only do so many pratfalls before suffering an acute case of fanny fatigue. Especially when most of those falls brought her in contact with hard tile floors.

Turning in the shower, she lowered her head and let the water soothe the aches from her shoulders and back, frowning as she thought about her disastrous workout at winter quarters the previous day. Tired, frazzled and frustrated, she'd done poorly enough to evoke a tongue-lashing from her normally calm coach and, for a while, she'd been afraid that Ralph would quit.

"Damn it, that's enough, Nicole! Come on down before you kill yourself!" he'd bellowed, and when she slipped her legs out from the rings and slid down the long rope, he railed at her for a full fifteen minutes. "If Lawrence had seen that little display, he'd have you shoveling camel dung instead of headlining you!" His next words knifed through her. "Oh, hell, maybe you should find someone else to work with, Nicole."

She fought back tears. "Why, Ralph? Because I'm thirty, you think I'm too old to go back up there? Is that it?"

"No, it isn't, and you know it," he grumbled, then hugged her. "Why don't you get out of here? Take a few days off. Get some rest. When you come back, we'll see how it goes."

Once the ego-battering trauma, with its tears of frustration, had subsided, Nicole began to look forward to time off, to the possibility of seeing Theron again.

Until this morning, that is. Until picking up the newspaper and seeing him with Shelly Ballinger.

She soaped her limbs, wondering why a man who was obviously enjoying the company of the gorgeous Ms. Ballinger would have bothered to call last night. The message he left on her machine was simple: "Nicole, call me as soon as you get home."

But he'd already left the house when she got home from a booking at nine. The only information Nicole had gotten was that the strange female voice answering the phone was Theron's new housekeeper, Mrs. Pierce and, no, Mr. Donahue hadn't left a message for Nicole.

"Probably wants to make sure he gets his rent check today," Nicole muttered caustically as she poured shampoo into her palm and vigorously lathered her hair. "One day late, and he's worried, the cretin."

Theron finished the last of his eggs and pushed the plate away.

Finally it was over. That grueling week of obligatory receptions and parties was at an end, thank God. During the course of the hectic days, he'd been presented with honorary keys to the cities of Jacksonville and Jacksonville Beach. He'd attended receptions at three of the major country clubs in the area and luncheons given by various community and university groups, and he'd lectured at a local university as well as a writers' group meeting.

But it was last night that stood out in his memory, he reflected, sipping his coffee. It was sitting in a high-school auditorium watching the students give an enthusiastic performance of his award-winning play, *Glory Bound*, and the warm reception that followed, that gave his work meaning.

The only damper on the evening was that Nicole hadn't been free to join him and his sister-in-law for the performance. Perhaps, he rationalized, he'd wanted Nicole with him for primarily selfish reasons, as *Glory Bound* was one of his best plays, and admittedly he wanted to share it with her. Yet there was more than ego involved. He'd wanted her by his side simply because he missed her, and that admission was difficult for him. He hadn't missed the company of a specific woman since Jess.

The situation could be remedied easily enough. Upstairs, Shelly was packing, and as soon as her car arrived to take her to the airport for her return flight to New York, all that stood between him and Nicole was a hot shower and dressing. And if Theron had anything to say about it, and Nicole's schedule permitted, they'd have the rest of the weekend to laze around, take in a movie, have dinner or ride.

Gulping the last of his coffee, he pushed away from the table and picked up the dirty dishes, stopping in the middle of the room when the knock came at the door.

"It's open. Come on in!" he called, smiling as Nicole pushed through the door. "Good morning."

"'Morning. I brought your rent ch—" she began, her throat constricting when she saw him standing there, clad only in a dark green velour robe. He looked deliciously tempting with his tousled hair, hooded and sleepy eyes, and his wonderful expression of...contentment. Like a satisfied cat, she mused, her heart caroming against her ribs, then skipping a beat as the full implication of the scene hit her. A wave of unutterable embarrassment washed through her for having burst in on him, for in his hands he held not one, but two plates. He wasn't alone, and as images of Shelly Ballinger lying in his arms flashed through Nicole's mind, she edged backward toward the French doors. "I'm sorry, I shouldn't have...I didn't mean to interrupt you." Her face grew hot. "I'll come back later."

"There's no reason for you to leave, darling," a sultry, well-modulated voice assured her, and Nicole's heart sank as a tall, leggy woman impeccably dressed in a navy blue silk shantung suit made an elegant entrance into the room. She walked to Nicole with a slender, bejeweled hand outstretched. "You must be Nicole."

"Yes, I am," Nicole replied with a stammer.

"I'm Shelly Ballinger," said the woman, shaking Nicole's hand firmly. "I've heard a lot about you and had hoped that we might have a chance to get together for a little chat. Unfortunately, our schedules just didn't permit it." Shelly Ballinger smiled expansively. "Maybe next time?"

"That sounds...delightful." Nicole almost choked on the words, but somehow she managed a reciprocal smile.

"Well, then, until next time?" The Titian-haired, blue-eyed beauty turned away from Nicole and went to Theron. Wrapping her arms around him, she kissed him on the cheeks. "I've got to run, love. My car's here. It was wonderful, as usual." Swinging around, Shelly waved and winked at Nicole. "He's all yours. Take good care of him, darling. He's a very special man. Ciao." And Shelly Ballinger swept out of the room.

"My, but she's generous," Nicole muttered through clenched teeth.

"What did you say?" Theron asked.

"I *said*, aren't you going to be a gentleman and walk her to her car?" she bristled, fighting back the unfamiliar emotion threatening to overwhelm her. It was ridiculous. She had no right, no *reason* to feel as she did. Theron didn't belong to her. They'd made no commitment to each other, and the likelihood that they ever would was zilch.

"Shelly knows the way," Theron replied, amused and pleased by her reaction. "Would you like some breakfast?"

"No, thank you. I don't like leftovers." She stood near the doors, her cheeks flushed, her eyes flashing. "But I will take some coffee." Heading toward the cupboards, she helped herself to a mug, filled it and grimaced as she tasted the steaming liquid. "My God, this stuff is terrible!"

Theron leaned against the counter watching her, loving the glow of her skin, the dark gold halo of hair framing her face, the fire dancing in her eyes. "Any particular reason why you're in such a good mood this morning?"

"No." She glanced at the clutter on the table. "Any reason why you were doing your own housework? I thought you hired a housekeeper?"

"I did. Gladys Pierce." He grinned. "It seems Tag has taken quite a shine to her. He drove her to town this morning to help with the grocery shopping."

"Stands to reason," Nicole grumbled. "It must be mating season around here."

Laughter rumbled from Theron. "You might have something there. At least where Tag and the widow Gladys are concerned."

"Whatever, it's none of my business," she replied, surprised by the strength of the resentment she felt. Could it be that Theron regarded relationships so casually? But this wasn't a relationship, she countered silently. Suddenly anxious to get away from him and sort through her muddled emotions, she pulled a folded check from the back pocket of her jeans and handed it to him. "Here. I'm sorry I'm late."

"Ah...the rent. I was worried about this, you know," he said, regarding her thoughtfully. Was he reading her right? Was there really a hint of the old green-eyed monster in her eyes? In her behavior? Or was it wishful thinking on his part? Watching her every reaction, he shook his head solemnly. "You know how this goes, don't you?" When she eyed him warily and said nothing, he continued. "A day late this month, two days next, and before you know it ... eviction."

She lifted her chin stubbornly. Here she stood, inexplicably crushed, and he was teasing her? "I'll be sure to be on time next month. That way you won't have to call and ask for it."

It was his turn for surprise, and he narrowed his eyes. "Is that why you think I called you last night?"

"Considering your busy social life, yes."

"I called because I was hoping that you'd be home in time to join Shelly and me for dinner, a play and a reception."

"Right. And I've got a bridge in Brooklyn," she countered and turned to leave. "I've got to go, Theron."

"Nicole!" He caught her in two strides and swung her around to face him. "Please, if you're upset about Shelly—"

"Your personal life is none of my business!" she interrupted, not wanting to meet his gaze, but he forced her to look at him, forced her to bare the hurt in her eyes.

"Shelly is my sister-in-law, Nicole. She's Jess's sister. The kids are staying with Shel and her husband until the holidays," he said so quietly that she wasn't sure she'd heard him correctly.

"She's your what?" Nicole met his gaze, relief and embarrassment and anger washing through her simultaneously. Shelly Ballinger was the Aunt Shel the kids had raved about? Oh, God!

"My sister-in-law," he confirmed.

She stood in shocked silence for a moment before exploding. "Damn you, Theron Donahue! Why didn't you tell me that in the first place instead of letting me make a complete fool of myself?"

"I thought you knew. The kids talked about her enough while they were here."

"Somehow, matching Aunt Shel to Shelly Ballinger is out of my realm of comprehension! The woman isn't *aunt* material!"

"Granted, she's not your typical cookie-baking type, but she's great with the kids," he said, grinning. His eyes, devilish and sparkling, sought hers. "You know, you're kind of cute when you're mad."

It was the wrong thing to say.

"I am *not* mad, and I am definitely not cute! I have never been cute, and I will never be cute!" She scowled. "I *hate* cute! The only thing I hate more is being teased!"

"I'll be sure to keep that in mind," he assured her, laughing.

"Please do," came the haughty retort, but her anger ebbed and was replaced by an electrifying jolt of awareness when he reached out and cupped her shoulders with hands that were strong and warm and sure.

Her eyes shot to his, questioningly, and the desire and need she found in them took her breath away. Unable to break the gaze, she felt helpless against the barrage of unbidden thoughts and visions washing through her mind.

It was a heady moment, fraught with tension, laced with excitement.

While she wanted to push the robe from his shoulders in order to feel the long, lean length of him next to her, he wanted to remove her shirt, to hold the weight of her full, straining breasts in his hands. While she desired the feel of his lips upon hers, he longed to trail his mouth over her flesh from head to toe, to taste the sweetness of her, to learn the secrets of her luscious body.

"You're right," he murmured thickly, moving his hands exquisitely over her shoulders and up to cup her face with hands that were shaking slightly.

"About what?" she whispered, mesmerized.

"You're not cute." He lowered his head, brushing his lips across hers in a kiss that was as light as the touch of a butterfly's wings, but more potent than dynamite. "You are a very beautiful, very desirable woman."

"Oh, God, what are you doing to me?" she breathed softly, her words lost in his mouth as he claimed hers in a deep, sensual kiss that left her weak and clinging to him.

If the urgency of the kiss frightened her, it was only for a moment, for fear had no place in his arms. If logic told her it was wrong, she paid no attention, for his caress brushed logic aside, and in its place came hot, fiery desire.

"I've missed you, Nicole," he whispered touching her cheeks, eyelids, forehead and chin with his lips before bringing his mouth back to hers.

"I've missed you, too," she admitted, moaning softly as she felt the heat of his hands gently brushing the underside of breasts that were full and longing for more of his touch.

When he lifted his head, it was Nicole who wound her arms around him, plunged her fingers into his thick hair, and pulled him back to her. How good he felt, his body taut and hard against hers! How wonderful the sensation of firm male lips moving on hers, now gentle, now demanding, his tongue seeking, finding, tangling with hers. His early morning beard brushed her cheeks. She inhaled the musky scent of him, reveled in the erratic beat of his heart.

A heightened sense of femininity surged through her, overpowering the last vestiges of reason. Heat warmed her loins, followed by an ache of desire so strong that she thought she might die. In his arms she could find fulfillment, and that knowledge came to her with breathtaking swiftness.

Isn't this what it was all about? Man and woman, firing needs and desires, then quenching them in the most spiritual union of all? Oh, dear God, how long had it been since knowing the pleasure of making love? And oh, how easy and natural and beautiful it would be with Theron!

"I want you, Nicole," he said raggedly against her mouth. Cupping her bottom in his hands, he pulled her tightly against his thighs, giving her undeniable proof of the strength of his desire. "I want to make love with you until we can't breathe." Hungrily, he kissed her. "And then I want to love you some more."

Feeling the full impact of his arousal pressing against her, Nicole felt a tremor shoot through her. Oh, yes, she wanted him, too. She couldn't live another moment without knowing him completely, and she was just about to tell him so when the sound of car doors slamming outside, followed by laughter, edged through the fog of desire gripping her and she sagged against him.

"Damn," Theron muttered, holding her gently now. "I didn't expect them back so soon."

"Tag and Mrs. Pierce?" she mumbled, grateful for the support of his arms around her. Her legs felt so rubbery she was sure she'd crumple to the floor in a heap the instant he let her go. Against her cheek, his chest was warm, his heartbeat strong and fast.

"Yeah…Tag and Mrs. Pierce." Letting out a deep, shaky breath, Theron dropped a kiss on the top of her head, then looked at her, concerned. She was trembling. "Are you all right?"

"I'm fine," she replied shakily, wondering if she'd ever be all right again. What the devil had gotten into her, anyway? She'd been too close—far too close—to losing herself to this man, and while the thought was intriguing, it was also frightening.

"Well, I'm not," he said on a long sigh. "Why don't I run up and take a long, cold shower and dress, then you and I can make a run down to St. Augustine? Make a day of it?"

Before she could answer, Tag and Gladys bustled through the door, arms laden with groceries.

"'Lo, Nikki. 'Bout time you remembered us long enough to stop in, heh?" Tag greeted her, his voice somehow different, somehow…lighter. "You haven't met Gladys, yet."

He turned to the kind-looking, gray-haired woman standing next to him. "Gladys, this here's little Nikki."

"It's nice to finally meet you." Gladys Pierce offered her hand to Nicole and smiled warmly. "But, I'm still not sure if you're little Nikki, like Tag says, or Nicole."

"Either one is fine, Gladys. It's a pleasure meeting you," Nicole told her, instantly sensing the goodness and energy in the woman. She smiled. "You know, these two are going to give you more trouble than the children ever will."

"Don't you worry your pretty head one bit about that," Gladys assured, her hazel eyes turning steely. "I know exactly how to handle both of them," she added, and Nicole didn't doubt her for an instant.

Tag shifted uncomfortably and turned his attention to Theron. "What the devil you doin' in your robe at this hour of the day? A man ain't supposed to be walkin' 'round lookin' like he just climbed out of bed in the middle of the mornin'."

"I would have been dressed an hour ago if Nicole hadn't distracted me," Theron replied, smiling lazily. "Actually, I've been trying to convince her to take a day off and go to St. Augustine with me."

"Yup, reckon it's a mighty pretty day to be out and about." Tag turned to help Gladys unbag the groceries, and Nicole knew instantly that Theron was right: the crusty old man was enamored with Gladys Pierce. It was in his eyes and in his voice. "Well, then, hadn't you two best get a move on 'fore you waste the whole day?"

"He's right, you know," Theron said quietly to Nicole.

Warning bells clanged and gonged in her mind, but she paid them no heed. After all that had transpired during the hectic week, after the stress of the past twenty-four hours and the doubts she harbored about her future, an afternoon of total relaxation might be exactly what she needed.

"Yes, I'd like that very much," she said.

"Good." His eyes were warm on her. "If I pick you up at the gatehouse in an hour, will that give you enough time?"

"I'll be ready." She smiled and watched him leave the room, her heart light, almost singing.

A volley of barking greeted Theron when he knocked on the door of the gatehouse an hour later. "Looks like the old boy has finally accepted me," he said when Nicole stepped outside and into the sunlight. Theron dropped his hand to scratch the dog's ears. "What'll he do if I kiss you?"

She looked into blue-green eyes and smiled. "You've kissed me before, and he hasn't done anything."

"Yes, but we were on my turf, then. This is yours, and I have vivid memories of the lengths he'll go to in order to protect his mistress," Theron reminded her, then muttered, "Oh, hell, it's worth the risk." Pulling her into his arms, he kissed her soundly, a muffled groan rumbling through his chest when her lips parted under his. "I wonder if you have any idea of what you do to me, Nicole. Any idea, at all."

She had a very good idea, and while it spelled danger, it was also enticing. She soared to heights she'd never been to before, every time she was near him, every time she considered that she could arouse such a powerful, compelling man as Theron.

But, then, he had the same effect on her. Even now his hands warmed her flesh and the taste of him lingered on lips that were still tingling.

"Maybe we'd better go." She took a step backward, out of the warm circle of his arms.

"Yeah . . . you might be right," he agreed.

"Stay, Luke," Nicole commanded the dog, then turned and fell in line with Theron, marveling at how natural it felt when he draped his arm around her shoulder. "I wonder if St. Augustine is ready for us."

"That sounds ominous. What are you planning on doing when we get there?" He glanced at her appreciatively. She looked lovely in the cranberry slacks and the long-sleeved, cream-colored shirt she was wearing.

"Eating. I'm famished." She slid into the plush seat of the Seville, grinning as he climbed behind the wheel and started the engine. "Hot, fresh-baked bread from a little Spanish bakery, cinnamon cookies and blueberry fudge."

"That's obscene! What kind of training program are you on that allows gluttony?" he teased and unwittingly hit a nerve. He sensed it in her sudden stillness and, curious, he glanced at her. She was staring pensively out of the side window. "Nicole? What's wrong?"

"Nothing. Everyone is entitled to a change of pace occasionally," she replied so quietly that her voice was almost inaudible.

Theron's jaw tightened. There it went, again. That damnable wall she erected every time they touched on the subject of her work. He'd encountered it every morning that they'd ridden together, and it bothered the hell out of him.

"Something has happened. What is it?" he prodded gently.

Nicole twined her fingers together and closed her eyes as she thought of a future on the rings and trapeze that was questionable at best. Ralph's tongue-lashing pounded through her mind. *Maybe you should find someone else to work with... When you come back, we'll see how it goes.* They were ominous words that she hadn't thought about since going to the main house to see Theron, words that she didn't want to consider. Certainly not now. So she drew in a deep breath, forced a smile, and looking at Theron, she lied, each word sending a stab of guilt through her.

"Nothing's happened. The training couldn't be going better," she said, her voice sounding strained even to her own ears. Quickly, she looked away again. "Look, I'll make you a deal. Being as this is a day off, I won't bring up your work if you don't bring up mine, okay?''

His mouth set in a grim line, his jaw clenched, he followed the lane to the highway and turned east, anger stirring in him as they swept over the drawbridge. Perhaps if he hadn't seen for himself the trouble she was having on the trapeze, perhaps if he didn't care for her, he could brush off her comment. But he *had* seen her and he *did* care, and the idea that she could so blithely shut him out of an important part of her life hurt. Worse still was the fact that she'd lied. That infuriated him, and this time he wasn't about to let it go. Too much was at stake.

''No deal,'' he snapped and without warning, he pulled off the road just beyond the bridge and braked.

Surprised, Nicole's eyes shot to his. ''What on earth are you doing?''

''I'm going to find out, here and now, if this relationship has a future, Nicole.'' He regarded her with eyes that were dark and ominous. ''I can understand if you don't trust me enough yet to share certain parts of your life with me. It might hurt a little more than I like, because I care a great deal for you. But trust takes time.'' When he paused, she ventured a glance at him and shivered at the intensity of his gaze. ''But the one thing that makes me madder than hell is being lied to! And it's damn disappointing coming from you.''

''I don't know what you're talking about,'' she whispered tremulously. The idea that she had the ability to hurt him had never crossed her mind. Her heart lurched miserably.

''Don't you?'' Desperately he wanted to reach her, but she seemed bent on tuning him out. ''Look at me, Nicole!''

She lowered her head, unsure and afraid. She hadn't confided her doubts and fears to anyone—except Annabel, and then unwillingly. Talking about her failure was too humiliating. "Can't we please leave it alone, Theron?"

Frustrated, he stared unseeing out the windshield, squinting against the sun, his heart heavy. "I wish you wouldn't do this to us," he said, letting out a deep breath. Cursing, he struck the steering wheel with the palm of his hand. "Damn it, I'm not asking you to bare your soul to me! All I want is a little honesty, but apparently I've misjudged you." Why the hell was she being so stubborn? he wondered as he shifted into drive and looked over his shoulder to check for traffic. "I think we'd better call this afternoon off."

"No!" Her hand shot to his arm. Tears trembled on her lashes as she realized how close she was to losing the only man she'd cared about in years. She swallowed. "How did you know?"

"Because you're a lousy liar." Relief surged through him in giant waves. Turning to her, he cupped her cheek with his hand and braced himself for her reaction to his next words. "And because I saw one of your workouts," he said. When she blanched and tried to twist away from him, he quickly added, "I *had* to, Nicole! I was concerned about you!"

"Why haven't you said anything about it before now?" she challenged.

"God knows I wanted to, and I tried, but a wall ten-feet-thick materialized around you every time the subject came up," he told her, a teasing smile playing on his mouth. "And all this time, I've thought myself to be a rather trustworthy kind of guy. Someone easy to talk to." He wiped a tear from her cheek, his heart growing lighter when she smiled back. "Until you came along, that is."

She closed her eyes and took a deep, steadying breath. "It's pretty awful on the trapeze, Theron," she admitted, and felt oddly relieved that he did know, that she could talk to him.

"I didn't see it as awful, Nicole. I saw a very courageous woman climb that web and try to overcome what must be one hell of an obstacle, considering what happened to you and Marc. If you think that makes you a failure, you're dead wrong." Leaning across the seat to her, he kissed her lightly. "If I hadn't gone to the winter quarters that day, I might never have read *Images*."

Surprised, she raised her eyes to his. "Because of me?"

"Because of you, funny face." Releasing her, he pulled back on the road, heading east, toward the beach highway, A1A, that would take them to St. Augustine.

"Theron?"

"What?"

"I didn't mean to hurt you."

"It wouldn't have been just me, Nicole." His voice was husky. "It would have hurt us. There's something special between you and me. Call us kindred spirits or soul mates. Or maybe it's the beginning of love." He glanced across at her and saw her eyes widen. "It doesn't make any difference what label you put on it. It's special, and I think you feel it as well as I."

Stunned, she stared at the man who was becoming so dear to her. But was it *love*? Love didn't happen so fast, did it? It grew and blossomed over a long period of time. Still it had to begin sometime, somewhere, with that one special person, and God knew, Theron was that. She'd known it the instant she met him.

"Something did happen yesterday," she told him softly as they skirted the silvery water of the Atlantic, and the words tumbled out in a torrent, as she confided her fears, her triumphs, her hopes and her dreams to him.

Throughout the wonderful afternoon, she felt the bond between them strengthen even more, a bond she at once desired and feared. What would become of them when the show pulled out in March? Why did leaving him suddenly promise to be difficult, if not impossible? she wondered as they parked the car and walked through the City Gate in the partially reconstructed wall of the Castillo de San Marcos. Then he took her hand in his. Feeling his warm strength, all thoughts of the future slipped away, and she seized the moment.

It was a perfect day. Big, puffy clouds floated across a hard blue sky. The sun shone down brightly upon them. A light breeze tugged playfully at their hair, ruffling Theron's over his forehead, Nicole's across her face.

Strolling along St. George Street, they ate cinnamon cookies that were still warm from the oven and listened to the Spanish music filter down from the wrought-iron balconies of authentically restored buildings in this, the oldest city in the country.

Laughing, they ducked into the shops of artisans lining the streets—here, a glassblower; next door, a silversmith. Theron pulled her into a tobacco shop where the air was pungent with the rich smell of fresh leaves, and they watched while the shopkeeper hand-rolled cigars for a friend of Theron's. Nicole dragged him into a confectionary, where he watched in astonishment as she ordered and promptly devoured a huge slab of blueberry fudge.

"Oh, no! We're not going to have time to go through the fort!" Nicole commented as they walked out of the old Spanish Treasury building and into the dusk of evening. The Castillo de San Marcos, a symmetrical structure built of coquina with its four bastions and ten-foot-thick walls was one of her favorite places in St. Augustine, and she often spent hours prowling around the fort and grounds.

"We'll hit it next time," Theron promised. "Right now, I'm ready for dinner. Real food. Not the junk you've been stuffing in your face all day."

They lingered a long time in a small, quaint restaurant where the waiters were dressed as monks, savoring a delicious meal of salads and red snapper, sipping their wine, enjoying the easy flow of conversation.

All too soon it was over, and they were back in the car heading for home.

"Would you like to come in for a drink?" Nicole invited when he walked her to the door of the gatehouse. A full moon cast a magical spell around them, and as she looked up at his strong, shadowed features, she wondered if she'd ever feel as close to another human being as she did to him right now.

"Not tonight, Nicole." He ran a finger along the line of her jaw, thinking her the most beautiful woman he'd ever laid eyes on. Irresistibly drawn to her, he scooped her into his arms and closed his mouth over hers in a long, deep kiss that left them both breathless. Letting go of her again was the hardest thing he'd done in a long time, but he had no choice. Though she was soft and willing in his arms, though her mouth was eager under his, he sensed her vulnerability and feared the repercussions that might arise if he stayed and did what he so desperately wanted to do—make love to her until the light of dawn.

"I had a wonderful time today," she said softly.

"So did I," he replied, realizing with surprise that this was the first time since Jess died that her memory hadn't haunted him. His heart and mind were totally occupied by the woman he now held in his arms. There were so many feelings to sort through, he reflected as he dropped a kiss on Nicole's forehead. "I'll meet you at the barn in the morning."

"I'll be there."

Out of his arms, she felt chilled and oddly empty. As she stood in the doorway watching him walk away, a sudden shiver shot through her. God help her, she was falling in love with Theron. He'd said she had courage. She wondered about that. If it came down to choosing between him and performing, would she have the courage to walk away from either one?

One thing was certain. She couldn't have both.

Chapter Eight

There was no other place in the world where Nicole felt as free as she did while performing on the rings. Up here she was in command, and safe, and secure. No one could hurt her. Up here she was happy, and that happiness, that joy radiated from her, touching everyone watching her go through her routine.

Working to the slow, romantic beat of the music she'd chosen, she finished the aerial ballet and as the song built to a crescendo, she began the high swing; the swing that launched her toward the rafters. When she let go of the ropes and fell forward, her hair flying loose, a huge smile curving her mouth, excitement rippled through the aerialists' hall.

Nicole Ross was back in form. The rings, at least, belonged to her, and as she slid down the long rope, Ralph met her with a bear hug that took her breath away.

"If you perform like that in New Orleans, Nicole, you're going to bring them right out of their seats!" He whomped her on the back. "That was one of the finest nine minutes I've seen in a long time!"

"It felt good, Ralph. It really *felt* good!" she replied breathlessly. "Did I have enough extension on the circle swings?"

"You were as long and sleek and smooth as a bullet." He grinned. "You know, I've been wondering who lit the fire under you and put the sparkle back in your eyes. I don't suppose the young gentleman waiting to see you has anything to do with it, does he?"

Nicole glanced in the direction Ralph had indicated and seeing Theron, she smiled. "Maybe."

"I thought so. He's a townie, isn't he?" Ralph used the slang term for all non-circus people.

"Yes, but he's a good friend of Lawrence's." She slipped into sweatpants. "He's a playwright."

"Be careful, Nicole. I'd hate to see you get hurt again," he warned, then smiled. "Go ahead and take a break. Hell, who knows, maybe he can give you some inspiration for the trapeze."

Nicole walked toward Theron, her eyes soft and shining. She couldn't remember a time in her life when she'd been happier. Since their trip to St. Augustine, she and Theron had spent every minute of their free time together—riding, enjoying long lunches, going out for dinner when she didn't have a party booking. They'd taken walks on the beach, and sometimes they just sat on the dock and talked for hours.

If she thought it strange that he hadn't pressured her for anything more, she was also grateful. She already harbored deep feelings for the man. Making love with him would push her over the edge, and that was something she couldn't handle right now, no matter how badly she wanted him.

But, dear Lord, it hadn't been easy for either of them, and she knew there would soon come a time when Theron's patience would wear thin. And it certainly wouldn't take much for her own resolve to break down. Not when the man turned her to jelly every time she was near him.

"Hi." She kissed him lightly.

"Mmm. That was nice, but there wasn't enough of it." Bringing her back to him, he kissed her more fully, then smiled. "Hi."

It would never be easy for them, she decided as she ran her fingers along the lapels of his black suit coat, thinking how sexy he was. "You're looking mighty dapper all decked out in your power suit."

"I sure as hell don't feel powerful right now," he admitted, his voice husky. "I don't think I'll ever get used to seeing you let go of those damn ropes. It's bad enough when you've got the net set up. It's going to be pure torture when you work without it." He brushed her hair away from her face. "But you were magnificent, sweetheart."

"You say the nicest things!" She beamed with pleasure.

"I meant it."

"Now, if I could do the same on the trapeze…" Her voice trailed off, and she glanced apprehensively at her rigging.

"You're worrying about it too much, Nicole. It'll happen."

"I hope so." She sighed, then dragged her eyes away from the rigging and back to him. "Are you staying for the workout?"

"I can't. I have to be at the university by eleven to lecture a group of theater arts students." He grinned. "It seems they think I have something to say."

"I can't think of anyone who knows the ropes better than you. And … you're writing again. Maybe a little sporadically, but writing, nevertheless," she pointed out, pride welling in her.

She was right about that, he agreed silently, wondering when he'd fully be back in stride. "I hate to leave, but if I don't, I'm going to be late." He kissed her once more, lingering over the taste of her, then turned to go. Remembering the piece of paper in his breast pocket, he stopped, pulled it out and handed it to her. "I've got the information your father wanted about Jenny's coach in New York. It's a woman by the name of Gina Marin. They've been working together about six months, now."

Frowning, Nicole glanced at the paper in her hand, looking for confirmation. There it was—in Theron's bold script—*Gina Marin*. Astonished, her eyes shot to his. "Are you sure about this?"

"Yes." His eyes narrowed fractionally. "Why?"

"Gina's one of the best in the business, Theron. She doesn't take on just anyone." Nicole's mouth went dry.

His jaw tightened. Apprehension worked through him. Though he wanted all of his children to set goals and succeed in life, he hadn't allowed himself to consider that Jenny's passion for the trapeze would come to fruition. He'd almost convinced himself that the phase would pass, and if not, that his daughter wouldn't quite make the cut when the time came. But there was something in Nicole's expression that alarmed him.

"Maybe it's a case of money talking," he suggested and immediately felt guilty for denigrating his daughter.

"Maybe," she said quietly, knowing that it wasn't. Gina Marin was temperamental, demanding and tough. More than that, she was selective. Nicole knew the woman well enough to understand that money took a backseat to talent where Gina was concerned. How would Theron cope with Jenny having a real talent? Talent that might pull the family apart? With great effort, she forced a smile. "No problem. I'll tell Dad when I talk to him."

Theron glanced at his watch. "I've got to run. Break a leg, okay?"

"Oh, God, I hope not!"

He smiled. "You know what I mean. I love you."

And he walked away, leaving Nicole alone, gaping, wondering if she'd merely imagined the magical words. *I love you*? Her heart soared, then trembled. But there'd be no time to consider the implications of his words, for Ralph was calling to her.

"Are you going to stand there all day, Nicole, or can we start this torture session?" he teased good-naturedly.

"Smart ass," she muttered, smiling. It had been a long time since any of them—Ralph, Gus or Nicole—had so much as cracked a smile during training, and the effect of Ralph's easy manner soothed Nicole, made her relax.

Maybe today, she mused as she stripped off her sweats and checked her equipment. Fifteen minutes later, the safety mechanic strapped around her waist, she wrapped her hands around the fly bar and left the pedestal, her swing fluid and graceful. She was soaring. Body, mind and soul. *This* was going to be her breakthrough! She could feel it as she swung once, then again, building momentum. Ralph cued, and Nicole let go of the bar... but her body stiffened, her arms refused to extend, and she fell, coming to a tooth-jarring, bouncing stop at the end of the safety line.

"Are you all right, Nikki?" Ralph called to her.

Dazed and breathless, tears stung her eyes. "Do I look all right?"

"At least you let go," he observed encouragingly.

"Fat lot of good it did," she groaned, and minutes later she was back on the platform, trapeze in hand, but her eyes were clouded, and nausea rolled through her stomach.

"You're late," Annabel announced as Nicole sank into a chair opposite her. "I've already had two glasses of wine."

"Then you're early." Nicole glanced around the crowded dining room of the Ocean Club. Outside the solid wall of windows, the Atlantic rolled gently on the sandy beach. It was the perfect setting in which to relax body and spirit after the abuse she'd suffered during her training session. "It's not even one, yet."

"Our reservation was for twelve," Annabel reminded her.

"Oops, I must have misunderstood." Nicole grinned and ordered a glass of Burgundy from the waiter while Annabel looked on in astonishment. Nicole never drank anything harder than lemonade during the day, and she rarely drank at night.

"You must have had a horrendously bad morning," Annabel quipped, sipping her Chablis.

"I did more bouncing than a paddleball, today," Nicole said, frowning. "Sometimes I wonder if it's worth it. Maybe I should forget about performing again. It'd be a lot less painful if I concentrated on developing Rossles a little more, and settled down here for good." She paused while the waiter set her wine on the table. "That's what I wanted before I lost Marc and the baby. You know—the cottage with the picket fence?"

Annabel eyed her friend closely. "You might be able to do that someday, but I honestly don't think you could live with yourself if you don't see this trapeze thing through. You've got to overcome your fears, Nicole."

"If I'm afraid, then why isn't it affecting my performance on the rings?" she demanded.

"Because, damn it, Marc wasn't killed on the rings! You didn't lose your baby because of a fall from the rings!" Annabel pointed out quietly, emphatically. "Sweetie, when you're on those rings, *you're* in control. When you're on the trapeze, you're depending on another fallible human being to catch you. You don't *have* total control! Subconsciously your warning system kicks in, and you freeze instead of letting go," she said, adding, "One day, though, something is going to click inside your head and you'll fly again."

"I wish it would click before I end up in a body cast."

"It'll happen, Nicole, and you probably won't even realize you've let go until it's over and the applause begins," Annabel assured her and smiled. "I hope it happens soon, because I'm losing a fortune on you with these free counseling sessions. Let's eat. I'm starving."

They ordered spinach salads and shrimp quiche and talked their way through lunch, Nicole feeling a stab of envy as Annabel chattered about her children.

"Joshua is madly in love with this little girl! Of course, Steffie, Amanda and Lindy have been teasing the poor kid mercilessly for days!" Annabel laughed, and shook her head wistfully. "Puppy love. Poor Josh is walking around in a daze from morning to night with this dreamy look in his eyes. Kind of like the one in yours right now."

Nicole almost choked on her quiche. "I may have a tired look but certainly not a dreamy one."

"Tired from too many late nights with my cousin?"

"You're incorrigible."

"Wrong. I'm curious. I haven't seen either of you since the kids were down," Annabel observed as she stuffed a forkful of quiche in her mouth. "So? Are the rumors true?"

"What rumors?" It was Nicole's turn for curiosity.

"That you and Theron are a hot item. That the two of you are either seen together or not seen at all." She glanced around the room, her silky brown hair swinging lightly around her face. "Half the single women in this community are green with envy. The other half are ready to scratch your eyes out for taking him out of circulation before they had a fighting chance with him." She sighed. "Must be nice to be that much in demand."

"You would be, too, if you'd give up on Mitch," Nicole told her candidly, noting the sadness in her friend's eyes.

"I've given up on him, Nicole," Annabel said quietly. "Funny, I always thought he'd come to his senses and come home to me and the kids."

"But?"

"But, he's remarrying next week."

"I'm sorry, Annabel. I had no idea..."

"Of course you didn't, and really, it's all right." But her eyes had misted. "Oh, hell, how'd we get on this subject, anyway?"

"You were trying to make me admit that Theron and I are a hot item, and it backfired," Nicole reminded her.

"And now you're going to keep me hanging?"

"I should, but I won't. Yes. We're dating."

"You two are good for each other. And you are good for those kids. I saw that the night of the cookout."

"I don't know if I am or not," Nicole admitted, and told Annabel about Jenny's situation. "I talked to Dad before coming over here, and when he learned that Jenny's training with Gina, he immediately agreed to coach her. What worries me is how Theron will handle it if Jenny shows enough potential to train seriously." She sipped the last of her wine. "He loves those kids so much that being separated from one of them will tear him apart."

"Theron is a strong man, Nicole. He'll handle it. If Jenny is committed and has the talent, he won't stand in her way." Annabel leveled big gray eyes on Nicole. "You're in love with him, aren't you?"

Nicole sighed. "I don't know. I don't want to be. What kind of a relationship could we possibly have after I leave in March?"

"It would be hard but not impossible, Nicole," she replied. "Love is too precious and too hard to find to toss it aside. Maybe you should talk to your folks about it when you fly to D.C. for Thanksgiving next week. Your father's a wise man." When Nicole didn't answer, Annabel frowned. "You are still going, aren't you?"

"I'd like to. I haven't seen any of my family since last summer, but three weeks is so long!"

"Then don't *stay* three weeks. Cut the trip short. Fly back from Washington right after Thanksgiving instead of traveling to Atlanta with the show."

"I don't know, Annabel. We'll see." *I love you.* Theron's words curled around her heart. Letting out a deep, shaky breath, Nicole glanced at her watch, noting with surprise that it was nearly three. "I've got to run, or I'll never make my booking on time."

"Bye. Let me know what you decide on Thanksgiving."

"I will. Thanks for lunch. Next time's on me," she said, and fairly flew out of the restaurant.

An hour later, her skin tingling from a shower, her hair pinned on top of her head, Nicole sat at her dressing table. She'd just begun tapping on the white, grease-based pancake makeup that would transform her into Rossles when the knock came on her door.

"Damn!" she muttered impatiently as she grabbed a shirt and ran through the house. Opening the door, she found herself staring at a shocked, incredulous Theron. As he threw back his head and roared with laughter, Nicole wriggled her toes and wanted to sink through the floor. Here she stood in her hot pink pantaloons, bright red socks, clutching the front of an old shirt, her hair a mess, and her face caught between clown and woman. "I have a party booking tonight, in case you've forgotten."

"I'm glad. I'd certainly hate to think you were getting ready for a date," he choked, his shoulders shaking with laughter. "Do you mind if I come in?"

"Why? So you can torment me?" Moving aside, she allowed him entrance.

"God knows, the opportunity is ripe."

She ignored the comment, wishing it were as easy to ignore the man, but that was impossible. His presence made the cottage seem smaller, more intimate. Closing the door, she started through the living room. "If you want to talk to me, it'll have to be while I finish my makeup. I'm running late."

He followed her to the bedroom, watching the rows of ruffles on the backside of her pantaloons sway as she moved. "Ruffles?" he commented on a low chuckle. "Interesting place for them."

"I'm warning you, Donahue, any smart remarks and you're in big trouble." She grabbed a tube of greasepaint from her dressing table, whirled around and pointed it at him. "I hold the weapons around here. I control the dog—"

"He's outside," Theron interrupted, loving the sparkle in her eyes.

"That's right. He is, isn't he?" She grinned. "Well, I still have this, and I can turn you into instant clown."

"Then I'll just have to disarm you." Reaching out, he took the tube from her, set it aside and captured her shoulders in strong, warm hands, studying her intently for a long moment. There were three large patches of white on her face—one over and around each of her eyes, one around her mouth. He smiled. "If I could figure out where to kiss you, I would."

"Chicken," she taunted, feeling breathless, boneless.

Rising to the challenge, he lowered his head and nuzzled her neck, felt her shiver, then whispered softly against her ear, "We'll take up that issue later, funny face, but right now, you'd best get busy or we'll be late."

"We?" she asked, moaning softly as he nibbled the sensitive flesh of her earlobe.

Lifting his head, he gazed down at her, his hands moving lazily on her arms. "Would you mind terribly if I drove you to your booking? I'd like to see Rossles in action. I've kind of missed the old girl.''

"Yes...I mean, no. I don't mind, at all. If you're sure you want to put yourself through the ordeal." Was there no end to the surprises in this man? "There's going to be about fifty kids there."

"Then you might need some help blowing up balloons or whatever it is that clowns do." He moved toward the bedroom door. "Do you have anything to drink?"

"Umm-hmm. Apricot nectar and lemonade. Help yourself." She sank down on the bench in front of her dressing table and began tapping flesh-colored greasepaint around the patches of white on her face. With trembling fingers, she covered forehead, cheeks and neck. Was it possible that she hadn't been mistaken this morning? But it was too fast! And there were too many reasons why love couldn't work with them!

When he walked back into the room carrying two glasses of lemonade, she smiled shakily, a tinge of regret working through her. How could a man be so right for her, yet so wrong?

"Thanks," she mumbled, taking the proffered drink. "How'd the lecture go?"

"Great." He sat on the edge of her bed, watching her blend red greasepaint over her cheekbones. "They're a good group of kids."

Sipping his drink, he told her about his day at the university, confiding his feelings as easily as if it were the normal routine for them, all the while his eyes remaining intent upon her as she finished her makeup. Sprinkling baby powder on a puff, she applied it liberally over the greasepaint to set it, then dusted the excess off her face and drew in lashes, freckles, brows and mouth.

"Did you talk to your father today?" he asked.

"Yes. He's agreed to work with Jenny."

A heavy silence fell about them.

"I'll tell Jenny over Thanksgiving," he said quietly. "How'd training go? Any progress?"

Watching his reflection in her mirror, she told him about almost letting go.

"I have faith in you, funny face. You'll beat this thing," he offered in encouragement, but she thought she saw a hint of sadness in his eyes. "Are you almost ready?"

"Yeah." She slipped into Rossles's blouse and skirt, plopped on her wig and hat, and grabbed her tattered coat and oversize bag. "That's it."

"Not quite," he said, and when she eyed him quizzically, he laughed. "You forgot your nose."

"Oh, Lord, I did, didn't I?" She rummaged through her makeup case. "Where the devil is it?"

"Right here." He was tossing it around in his hand. "First time I've ever held a woman's nose." He grinned. "It's a damned odd feeling. How do you keep it on?"

"It's self-adhesive." Taking the small blue putty nose from him, she pressed it in place and smiled at him. "Ready?"

"Ready," he replied. "I'm almost afraid to ask this, but where exactly are we going?"

"Downtown Jacksonville."

"Do you always drive to and from jobs with that makeup on?"

"Umm-hmm."

"With no accidents or traffic jams?"

"None so far." His hand on her arm was warm.

"Amazing."

And Theron Donahue, the handsome, sought-after playwright dressed in an exquisitely tailored black suit, drove Rossles the Clown downtown and escorted her a full block to the building where she was to entertain fifty underprivileged children.

As they walked, Nicole's size-thirteen shoes clomping on the sidewalk, Theron smiled, knowing that this was perhaps the strangest date he'd ever been on; knowing, too, that it would be one of the most memorable.

Leaning against a wall in the back of the large room, he watched her go to work, drawing the children to her almost as if by magic, making them howl with laughter, making Theron wince each time she executed a pratfall on the hard tile floor.

This morning he'd told her he loved her. The words had slipped from him of their own volition, and he'd wondered about his feelings all day long. Now, standing in this room, seeing her with the children, seeing her exchange those ridiculous shoes for a pair of tattered ballet slippers, seeing her dance with a grace and fluidity that was remarkable, he no longer wondered. He knew.

Not only was she a dazzling performer and a perfect clown, but she was also the perfect woman for him. Tenderness filled him, and two hours later when they left, he drew her close to his side and they walked wordlessly to the car.

"Tired?" he asked as they pulled away from the curb.

"Exhausted and famished."

"How about if we pick up a pizza on the way home?"

"That sounds heavenly," she enthused.

Nicole stripped off her makeup the minute she walked into the cottage, leaving Theron to build a fire and pour the wine he'd bought.

Pulling on a robe, she hesitated a moment before joining him. For some reason, she was nervous. He'd changed during the course of the evening. Granted, it was a subtle change, but it unnerved her. She'd sensed it the moment he'd come to the front of the hall to help her blow up balloons for the children. Their eyes had met, and she'd plainly seen the depth of emotion reflected in his, then he'd looked away again. He had shed his suit coat, loosened his tie and joined in the fun, treating the children with a deference that warmed her through and through.

Everything about him had been different. He'd touched her with more tenderness than before. He'd drawn her protectively to his side while they walked to the car. In response, she'd curled her arm about his waist with an easy familiarity that felt, oh, so good. And when he'd reached across the seat to take her hand in his, hadn't she laced her fingers through his and held on tightly, luxuriating in the strength she found?

Maybe they'd both changed tonight. Maybe the entire relationship was moving beyond her control. Maybe it was time to take matters into her hands once again. Three weeks away might be the perfect answer for both of them.

"Sorry I took so long," she said quietly as she joined him in the living room, and her heart began to race. He'd cleared off the coffee table, replacing the magazines and ashtray with pizza and glasses and wine. He sat on the floor, his shirt sleeves rolled up, the top buttons unfastened. His hair was rumpled, his eyes smoky and intent, as he looked up at her. Golden firelight played on his features, for the only light in the room came from the flames dancing on the hearth.

"Come on, before it gets cold," he invited, patting his hand on the braided rug on which he was sitting. In front of the hearth, Luke raised his head to watch his mistress, then lowered it again, his eyes on the pizza. Theron grinned. "He's been eyeing our dinner ever since I took it out of the box."

Intuition screamed that tonight would be the night that Theron would ask more of her than she could give. Her throat went dry and her palms grew damp, for she knew that one of his deep, seductive kisses would be all that was necessary and she'd melt like butter in his arms.

"Would you like some wine?" he asked as she sat down next to him.

"Please," she replied, her heart flipping.

He poured the wine and handed her a piece of the sausage-and-mushroom pizza. They ate in silence, listening to the hiss and pop of the logs burning. Now and again one of them threw a small piece of pizza to the Doberman lazing comfortably a few feet away.

"That's it for me. I am stuffed." Theron finally broke the long, intimate silence. Leaning back against the couch, he smiled contentedly as he watched her polish off her fourth piece. "Your appetite amazes me." He felt her shiver when he ran his fingers through her silky hair, now touched with gold from the firelight. Desire stirred in his loins. "But, then, you're an amazing woman."

"No, I'm not, Theron," she said softly, wishing that he wouldn't tempt her so with his gentle words and touch.

"You're beautiful—inside and out—and talented and warm and funny." He paused. "And sometimes, whether you like it or not, you're cute."

She sat cross-legged on the floor, staring into the fire, his words weaving a magical web around her. Turning to look at him, she felt a surge of love so powerful that it almost overwhelmed her. His eyes mirrored naked desire and power and passion, and, yes, love.

"I'll let you get away with that this one time," she replied, an unwilling smile playing on her lips.

"I should think so, considering I've seen you in your pantaloons...ruffle butt." He chuckled. Lazily moving his hand along her shoulder to her neck, his eyes grew serious. "You are the kind of woman a man could easily fall in love with and marry, Nicole."

"No, Theron..." She averted her eyes quickly, lest he see them mist.

"You're wonderful with children. I watched you with my three, and then again tonight…" He was stroking her cheek gently, loving her softness, wanting more of her. "You'd be a natural mother. The kind of woman who could surround herself with a passel of kids and love every minute of it."

She lowered her head. "That's something I'll never know about."

"Why not, Nicole? You're young and healthy. There's no reason why you shouldn't have a houseful of kids." He studied her profile, frowning. "Unless you don't want children."

"It's not that I don't *want* them." She hesitated, as if some great decision was weighing on her mind. When she raised her eyes to meet his, they were haunted with sadness. "I can't have children," she began, wondering if he would think her less of a woman. "I was leaving the show because I was pregnant. It seemed as if one minute Marc and I had the world by the tail. So much to look forward to, then all of a sudden…poof!…a whole lifetime of dreams ended." She felt Theron's hand warm upon her arm. "I blamed the fall for losing the baby, but the doctors said that I wouldn't have carried to full-term even if they'd restricted me to bed. There were other problems. And being as another pregnancy would have been life-threatening, they performed a tubal ligation before releasing me from the hospital." She fell silent a moment. "I guess it was better, in the long run, to lose the baby early on rather than later…after feeling life. That would have been unbearable."

"Oh, sweetheart, I am sorry. So very sorry." The words, though heartfelt, seemed inadequate, so he pulled her into his arms, pulled her down so her head was resting on his chest. "It doesn't have to be the end of your dreams, Nicole. There is such a thing as adoption."

"I know. But a lot of men balk at that," she observed quietly. She hadn't wanted this closeness. Yet, here she was half sitting, half lying in his arms, the beat of his heart steady and reassuring against her cheek.

"And a lot of men don't." He crooked a finger under her chin, tilting her head back. "Some of us even have ready-made families who are waiting for a woman like you to come along and fill the void." He lowered his head, his mouth hovering a whisper above hers. "You never know...you might open your door one day and find us on your doorstep."

He closed his mouth over hers, wondering about her tension, her hesitation, then he wondered no more, for she melted against him, allowing him access to the moist treasures of her mouth.

Because his long-denied need of her was great, the kiss quickly turned intense. Hungrily, he claimed her with a deep, mind-shattering kiss that sent Nicole's senses spinning out of control. Shifting her in his arms, he lowered her gently to the floor, his heart pounding heavily as she wrapped her arms around him, clung to him, arched her body against his.

His hands found the ties of her robe and loosened them. As he felt her cool skin under his palms and cupped the soft fullness of her breasts, he groaned. "God, but I want you, Nicole. I didn't think a man could ever want a woman this much," he murmured thickly. Pushing the robe aside, he gazed reverently upon her, then, ever so slowly, he brought his mouth to her flesh, nuzzling, nipping, tasting, teasing her breasts. "So sweet...so beautiful..."

His words, his touch, the feel of his mouth on her, threatened to consume Nicole. Wild with desire, she eagerly accepted his weight, loving the feel of his long, hard body pressing against her, offering proof of the force of his need. Oh, the glory of being in his arms! How badly she desired him, how badly she wanted to give herself freely to this sensual man who was chasing reason away. And perhaps she would have, had he not uttered the beautiful words that terrified her the most—the words that represented a commitment she couldn't give.

"I love you, you know," he murmured against her mouth, and she froze, reality crashing down on her.

"No, Theron...please..." She turned her head away from him and grew very still.

Stunned, caught in a rush of desire, he stared at her. "What did you say?"

"Please... we can't do this," she whispered.

Forcing her to look at him, he searched her eyes. Seeing that she was serious, frustration knotted his stomach. "Suppose you tell me why we can't? We both want. We both need," he demanded, and when she tried to twist out from under him, he cursed softly and let her go. Rolling onto his back, he stared at the shadows dancing on the ceiling as he fought to control the desire pounding through him. "What are you afraid of, Nicole? Of me? Of falling in love again?" When she didn't answer, but instead sat up and pulled her robe over her exposed breasts, he reached out and grabbed her arm, anger replacing desire. "Answer me, damn it!"

"I can't handle it right now, Theron."

Rising, he stood with his back to her, his shoulders broad and strong. He took a deep, shuddering breath, then rounded on her, his face tight with rage. "And I'm not doing such a good job of handling these turn-ons and turn-offs! I don't know what you think I'm made of, but I'll tell you something right now. I'm getting damned tired of you playing referee with this relationship!" He pinned her with hard eyes. "What in the hell do you want from me?"

Tears welled in her eyes. "I... I don't know."

"That's bloody terrific, Nicole," he muttered, running a hand through his hair. "How long do you suppose it's going to be before you *do* know?"

"I need time to think!" Unable to face the anger and hurt in his eyes, she lowered hers. "I'm flying to D.C. to meet the show. To spend Thanksgiving with my folks."

He clenched his jaw. "Right. The going gets a little tough, so you run home to mom and dad."

"It's not like that at all!" she countered hotly. "Life doesn't revolve around you and your lusty libido! I've got a life of my own, and right now it's pretty damned mixed up!"

The pain twisting through him was as great as if she had knifed him. A few minutes ago he'd been holding a warm, loving woman in his arms. Now they were shouting at each other, shredding the very essence of the emotions that had drawn them together in the first place. Was it possible that she regarded his love so lightly?

"You want to play games, lady, you'd best do it with someone else, not me," he warned, his voice ominously quiet. When he reached down to grab her arms, she was powerless to fight. He dragged her to her feet and shook her once, the fury in his eyes searing her. "I will *not* put up with it." He ground out the words, then set her free so abruptly that she almost lost her balance. Grabbing his coat and tie, he sighed. "While you're gone, Nicole, you'd best do some hard thinking about us. A relationship can't stay in limbo. It has to either move forward . . . or end. And you'd damn well better have some answers for me when you get back."

Nicole jumped as he walked out the door, slamming it so hard the windows rattled. Devastated, she crumpled up on the couch, her eyes blurred with tears. What had she done to him? To them? She hadn't wanted to provoke a fight. She hadn't wanted to hurt him, yet she'd cut him to the quick, and in doing so she'd seriously wounded her own heart. She sat staring into the fire, wondering if anything in her life would ever be right again.

At home, Theron stormed through the house, passed Tag and Gladys without saying a word. Going directly to the bar in the family room, he poured a double Scotch. When it didn't ease the pain, he poured another, and for the first time since his college days, Theron Donahue got very drunk.

Chapter Nine

Nicole sat in a window seat of the wide-body jet, listening as the engines changed pitch, signaling that their descent into Jacksonville had begun.

Taking a deep breath, she stared out the window, wondering what she'd find upon returning to the gatehouse, wondering whether Theron would see her, and if he did, whether he'd be willing to listen to her. She couldn't blame him if he refused, for the pain she'd inflicted was great and, oh, so needless.

Trying not to speculate on what lay ahead, she closed her eyes and let her thoughts drift over the past few weeks. They had been miserable. That was the only word she could find to adequately describe her life since the horrible fight with Theron. Absolutely miserable!

The tension on the estate had grown unbearable during the week between the argument and her departure for Washington, D.C. Even Tag and Gladys seemed to tiptoe around, talking in hushed tones, their faces pinched with concern.

As for Theron? Nicole had seen him once. She'd been at the main house having coffee with Tag while they discussed the feeding schedule of her animals, when Theron, looking impossibly handsome in dark brown trousers and a tan shirt, ambled into the kitchen.

"Don't you have work to do, old man?" he'd groused as he passed them, glancing at Nicole with cold, dispassionate eyes. "I'd like to have those hedges trimmed today, if you can tear yourself away from the house long enough to do them."

"I reckon they'll get done, son," Tag replied quietly.

"You might want to tell Gladys that I won't be home for lunch today. I'm meeting someone," he'd clipped the words—words that had ripped straight through Nicole's heart—and moments later he was gone, his car roaring away from the house.

Tag shook his head. "Boy's not himself these days, Nikki. Yup, reckon somethin' must have happened. When he's not locked in his study, he's off to the Ocean Club. Been spendin' too much time there the last few days." Tag looked at Nicole. "But…guess it ain't none of my business, heh? So, girl, when you leavin'?"

"Tomorrow morning," Nicole had managed to push the words past the tightness in her throat.

"Sure hope you know what you're doin', Nikki. It'd be a shame to see somethin' good wasted," he said, then in a gesture that surprised Nicole, he hugged her close and patted her roughly on the back. "You have a good time with your folks, and don't you go worryin' none 'bout Luke and that Morgan. Reckon you got enough to sort through as it is."

Numb, feeling as if she were walking through a nightmare, she'd boarded the plane the next morning, hoping desperately that being with her family and friends, being in an environment that she'd known since early childhood, would lessen the pain and emptiness threatening to tear her apart.

But it hadn't. None of it had helped, and for the first time in her life, Nicole felt herself a stranger in the midst of everything she'd once held so dear. Something was missing. Something that the excitement, the warm animal smells, the laughter and the blaring music couldn't give her. She'd laughed and talked with friends and family, but the loneliness seemed to grow rather than ebb. More and more often, she stayed behind when her family left the train for work in the mornings and spent her days cleaning the Pullman car that was the Rossinis' home for nine months of the year.

The circus seemed lackluster. It had lost its power to overwhelm her. It had lost the mystique that once enticed her, and she'd thought little about the Roman rings or the trapeze.

What she had thought about was Theron. His words echoed in her mind, haunting her day and night until she thought she was going crazy. *You're the kind of woman a man could fall in love with and marry.... I love you.* Wonderful words, heartfelt and so full of promise, yet she'd refused to listen to him and instead had cut him to the quick by twisting those words, reducing them to strictly sexual come-ons. Fool! She'd hurt the one man she cared for, a special man who was capable of loving so deeply.

And for what reason? Because she was afraid? Because she loved him and couldn't bear the thought of allowing that love to grow, only to lose it again if and when she rejoined the show? She scoffed when that thought arose. *If* seemed more probable than when, for she was in no condition to perform. She'd been nervous and shaky since leaving Jacksonville, and now she stood a good chance of losing both Theron and the career she'd been trying so hard to re-build.

Sometimes it seemed as if she couldn't have one without the other. Yet that was impossible, wasn't it?

Round and round the questions rolled in a circle without end.

Her father had finally cornered her the night the train pulled out of Washington en route to Atlanta. He'd walked into the kitchen of the car close to one in the morning and found her sitting at the table, sipping old coffee, staring out at the passing darkness.

"There's only one thing that can make a person more miserable than being in love," he'd said, without preamble, as he started a fresh pot of coffee.

"What's that, Dad?"

"Being in love with a townie."

Nicole smiled genuinely for the first time in weeks. "How'd you know?"

"Ralph. I talked to him. He said there was a young man who'd put a kind of sparkle in your eyes that made you glow all over." Gabriel Rossini, a tall, well-muscled man with salt-and-pepper hair and dark eyes, sat down across from his daughter and took her hand. "But I certainly haven't seen any evidence of that sparkle. Neither has your mother or David or Cherie or Adam or Margo. Even Lawrence is worried about you." When she turned to gaze out of the window again, Gabe squeezed her hand. "You're a grown woman, and you have to handle your problems on your own, but I think you're ready to self-destruct on this one. If you need help, we're all here for you. Your mom. Me. Your brothers and sisters."

"I know, Dad, and I appreciate that."

"Do you love this man?"

"Yes."

Gabe regarded his daughter for several long moments. "Knowing a bit about the situation, and knowing you like I do, I'd guess you haven't told him, and you're probably fighting it every step of the way."

"I didn't want to fall in love with him. Not now. Not when I'm trying to get my professional life back together. Especially not before going back on the road in March."

"If you don't get your head straight, you won't be going anywhere in March, Nick." Gabe had called her Nick since the day when, at age seven, she'd whacked off her hair. By the time Simone—her mother—had evened it out, it was shorter than her brothers' hair. "What are you afraid of? That he's a townie? That you might lose someone else you love, like you lost Marc?"

"I guess it's a combination of everything," she admitted, accepting the fresh coffee he poured for her, and as the train rumbled comfortably through the night, its steady motion soothing Nicole, she talked openly and honestly with her father. By the time she finished, it was well past four a.m. "It might not be so bad if he weren't a family man. But he is, and what he wants and needs is a full-time wife and a mother for his kids. He doesn't need a woman who's off chasing rainbows most of the year."

"So you've asked him what he needs?"

"No, of course not!" she blurted in surprise.

"I didn't think so." Gabe smiled gently. "Somehow I have a feeling that a man such as the one you've just described is better qualified to know what his needs are than you, don't you think?"

She bristled. "Let's just say that your advice to stay with my own kind stuck, all right? He's not one of us!"

"My advice to you—and to your brothers and sisters— was given when you were young, impressionable teenagers traveling from city to city. It was given in order to protect you from falling head-over-heels in love with some local boy who'd break your heart when the show left town, Nick," he told her. "You're old enough now to make your own decisions on who is right for you and who isn't. And, if you don't stop hiding behind that wall of yours, you just might burn a bridge with this man for good, and something tells me that would be a grave mistake." Gabe's comment prompted Nicole's curious look. Her father grinned. "You sparkled like a diamond while you were talking about him."

"He is a wonderful man, Dad. You and Mom would like him."

"We may never have the chance to meet him if you don't get off your high horse and fly back home. Mend a few fences before it's too late. I'd hate like hell to see you live a life of what-if's. Take it one step at a time. It might be worth the risk, honey. If you really love each other, you'll find a way to work around the problems." He glanced at the clock on the stove. "It's five. I've got to get some sleep before we pull into Atlanta. You should, too." He kissed her cheek. "Think about what I said?"

"I will, Dad. Thanks."

He stopped at the door of his bedroom. "This is Jenny's father? The little girl Gina's working with?"

"Umm-hmm."

"Jenny's got to be good, or Gina wouldn't have taken her on. That must mean that she's committed to the trapeze, and if that's the case, that child will be spending a lot of time on the road," Gabe observed, and Nicole wondered what he was leading up to. "I can't imagine any woman better suited to that family than you. Good night, Nick."

The conversation with her father had taken place only a few short hours ago. It hadn't taken Nicole long to make her decision. She'd booked a flight back to Jacksonville the minute they'd arrived in Atlanta and had called Annabel to make arrangements for a lift home from the airport.

Now here she sat, anxious to get home, terrified that she might already be too late. Below her, the wheels of the plane met the runway, bounced once, then settled down smoothly and they rolled toward the terminal.

Deplaning, she scanned the faces of the people at the arrival gate, looking for Annabel. But the familiar face that she found wasn't Annabel's. Nicole froze. Not twenty feet away from her, Theron stood watching her. A lump formed in her throat. Her heart hammered heavily behind her breast.

Oh, dear Lord, he was the most beautiful man she'd ever laid eyes on, and she prayed fervently that somehow they could make this work, that somehow she could undo the damage she'd done.

Apprehension grew in her as they wended their way through the milling crowd toward each other—for she could see the guarded, wary expression in his eyes. The lines on his face seemed deeper now than before, his mouth more compressed, and his jaw clenched a little more tightly. Though he stood tall and proud, though his presence was still commanding, Nicole detected a weariness that tore at her.

"Hi," she said, stopping close enough in front of him so she could feel his body heat radiate out to her. Yet, he was still much too far away. She wanted to throw herself headlong into his arms, to feel the power of his embrace.

"Hi, yourself," he said, a deep huskiness in his voice.

"I wasn't expecting to see you here. Where's Annabel?"

"She couldn't get away from the office," he told her, reaching down to take her carryon luggage from her. Their hands brushed, sending a jolt through both of them. Theron's eyes shot to hers, and a muscle in his jaw jumped. "I offered to come in her place."

"I could have taken a cab," she said, her mouth bone-dry.

He looked at her a moment. "Would you have preferred that?"

"No!" she assured hastily. "I just hate to be an imposition on you."

"You're not an imposition." Far from that. Had Annabel not been tied up this morning, he would have still insisted that he pick up Nicole. The past weeks had dragged by interminably, each day a little more intolerable than the last. Looking at Nicole now, he wanted to hold her, to kiss away the sadness in her eyes, to show her somehow how much he did care for her. Instead, he said, "You look tired."

"I am. Dad and I sat up talking until five this morning."

"Well, then . . ." he began, but someone jostled into Nicole, pushing her against Theron. The contact was potent, and a shudder worked through him. She trembled and their eyes met. Both wanted the same thing: to make amends, to hold, to touch. Yet, both shared the same fears, the same apprehensions, so they backed away from each other. Theron cleared his throat. "Why don't we get the rest of your luggage and go, so you can get some rest?"

They walked side by side, careful not to touch each other, and when Nicole's luggage was loaded into the trunk of the waiting Seville, they set out on what was the longest hour's drive of her life. Tension, thick and heavy, stilted their conversation, made breathing almost impossible, made her wonder if they could ever get back on track.

"How was your trip?" he asked, not looking at her.

"Fine. How was Thanksgiving?"

"Good." He checked the rearview mirror before changing lanes.

"Did you tell Jenny that Dad's going to evaluate her?"

"Yes."

"And?"

"She's excited."

Nicole swallowed nervously. "How are Rusty and Julie?"

"Fine."

They drove in silence, Nicole painfully aware of every nuance of the man next to her: the way he sat leaning against the door, one hand draped over the steering wheel, the way he squinted against the sun, the inevitable tension in his jaw, the sound of his breathing, the wonderful scent of his after-shave. She smiled. He was the only man she knew who rubbed the scent into his forearms which made for a de-lightfully sensual experience when he draped his arm around her shoulder.

"When you said you were going to spend Thanksgiving with your folks, you didn't tell me you planned on staying three weeks," he commented after a long time.

"You didn't give me a chance to," she reminded him.

"I guess my lusty libido got in the way of a lot of things that night."

"Theron, please . . . I'm sorry. I didn't mean that."

"Don't apologize. Once I got used to the term, it gave my ego a boost. It's been a hell of a long time since a woman has thought me lusty," he remarked easily. Glancing at her, he saw her cheeks dapple with color. "You cut your trip short by a week. Why?"

"Because I missed you," she said simply, honestly.

The silence in the car was deafening. Two hearts pounded. His. Hers. His hands tightened on the steering wheel. She laced her fingers together to stop them from trembling. His mouth went dry. She wetted her lips with the tip of her tongue. Both of them stared out at the road ahead of them, wishing the miles would drop behind them more quickly, wishing they were out of the car so they could talk and, perhaps, touch.

"I missed you, too, Nicole. More than you'll ever know," he said huskily as he turned off the highway onto the road that wound through Palm Valley. They were almost home. Letting out a heavy sigh, Theron frowned. "Maybe we can talk after you've had a chance to rest."

"I don't think I'll be able to rest until we've talked."

They were quiet for the remainder of the drive that took them over the drawbridge and down the long, tree-lined lane to the gatehouse. Silently they unloaded the car and carried her luggage inside, setting it down in the living room.

It was so good to be home, she thought, tossing her purse on the couch. So good to be back in familiar surroundings with the soft, sweet scent of flowers everywhere. *Flowers?* The room was alive with the scent of...roses! Looking around, her eyes misted, for on both of the end tables and the coffee table sat bunches of long-stemmed roses in crystal vases. On the coffee table beside the roses was an ice bucket with one glass and a bottle of champagne.

She gazed at Theron—the man whom she loved—and wondered how she could have been foolish enough to push him away. "They're beautiful, Theron, but you didn't have to do this."

"I wanted to, Nicole." What he wanted to do was take her in his arms, but he'd made a promise that he intended to keep, no matter how difficult it was; he simply wouldn't push her anymore. "It was the only way I could think of to put emphasis on the apology I owe you for trying to force something on you that you weren't ready for." His features tense, he nodded toward the champagne. "That you can crack later when you're ready to sit back and relax."

"Theron?"

"What?"

She felt suddenly giddy and terribly unsure of herself. Drawing in a deep, sustaining breath, she met his gaze directly. "Do..." she began, but her voice cracked. She cleared her throat. "Do you still want to make love with me?"

She heard his sharp intake of breath and saw him close his eyes a moment. "No games, Nicole," he said huskily. "I'm on a very ragged edge right now." He pinned her with a blue-green gaze. "Yes. I want you. But until you stop play-ing referee, the answer is no."

"What if I throw away my whistle? What, then?"

"If you were serious, if you meant it, then I'd ask you to come to me, to hold me, to love me." His eyes darkened. "The ball's in your court."

"I really hurt you badly, didn't I?" she whispered. He was wary, and she couldn't blame him.

"We hurt each other," he told her, desire building in his loins. "Look, Nicole, maybe I should go. We can talk about this later."

"No, please, Theron, don't."

He smiled wearily. "There's a bit of irony in those words, don't you think?"

"You're not making this very easy."

"No, I don't suppose I am. But then, you haven't ex-actly made things easy for me, have you?" he reminded her. "I just want to make damn sure that you know what you're doing, Nicole. Because the next time something flares up between us, I have no intention of stopping. You need to know that up-front. You're a very desirable woman, and I'm sure as hell not made of steel." He studied her for a long time. "The last thing I want is for you to feel obligated or pushed."

She smiled shakily. "So instead, you're going to make me throw myself at you?"

"Only if you want to." He wanted nothing more than to possess her, to love her fears away.

"I can't stand it another minute," she confessed softly. Going to him, she wound her arms around his neck. "Please, please, hold me."

A great shudder worked through him as he felt her soft curves pliant against his body, but he held her gently for several long, quiet moments, drinking in the sweet fragrance of her perfume, of her hair. When she nuzzled his neck, he held her away to search her deep green eyes.

"Are you very, very sure about this, Nicole?" he asked, feeling desire build swiftly, powerfully inside of him. "I want more than anything to make love with you, but it has to be right for both of us."

"I'm sure, Theron," she whispered, cupping his face with her hands. "I've missed touching you ..." She pressed her lips against his cheek. "I've missed this ..." Dipping her hands into his hair, she brought his mouth down to hers, kissing him fully. "And this ..." She unbuttoned his shirt, luxuriating in the feel of his hard chest, tantalizing him with mouth and hands before raising soft, luminous eyes to his. "I've missed you. Every single, solid inch of you. Now I want to know what I've been missing."

"Good God, woman, I had no idea you could be such a seductress. I don't think you could stop this now if you tried," he said thickly.

"I don't want to stop anything," she said, kissing his throat.

He lowered his mouth to hers and the kiss seemed to go on and on, sensual and delicious, slow and languid, both of them savoring every intoxicating sensation and taste and heartbeat.

Nicole sensed the great restraint he was exercising and wanted to set it free, but he insisted on drawing out the moment, holding her gently, when her whole being strained to feel him pressed hard against her.

"Slowly, Nicole," he murmured against her mouth. "We've got to take it slowly."

But the urgency of his kiss belied his words, and the urgency of her response only served to heighten a need that was already strong.

Scooping her into his arms, he strode to the bedroom and set her down next to the bed. With trembling hands, he unbuttoned her blouse, pushing it off her shoulders, then reached around to unfasten the lacy white bra she wore.

Gently, reverently, he leaned down to nuzzle her neck. Nicole felt her legs turn rubbery as he touched her with a flutter of warm kisses that left a moist trail down her throat, along her shoulder, down to breasts that were full and throbbing.

With maddening deliberation, he dropped a light kiss on her mouth, raised his head, and unfastened the clip holding her hair back. Tangling his fingers in the long, silken mass of gold, he fanned it over her shoulders, watching it curl temptingly around hardened nipples.

"I want to touch you, Theron," she breathed softly, and he shuddered as she reached out to pull his shirt free, then dipped her fingers through the crisp mat of hair covering his hard, broad chest. Her eyes steady on his, she trailed her fingers down through the curly light hair to where it disappeared below his belt.

Groaning from the exquisite pleasure of her touch, he drew her close and claimed her lips thoroughly. Mouths clinging, he pushed her back to the bed, lowering her until she lay on the cool sheets. He stretched out beside her, his tongue surging into her mouth, and she felt the wonder of his hard body pressed close to hers.

They undressed each other, and then they lay together, flesh to flesh, touching, stroking, drinking their fill each of the other.

To Theron, she was impossibly soft to touch, yet her body was firm and supple, her breasts ripe and begging for his attention. To Nicole, his flesh was hot, the sinewy muscles of his arms and shoulders tingling her hands as she explored, touched, and touched again. She burrowed her fingers into his hair when he lowered his head to her aching breasts, suckling each in turn, loving her, and when he brought his mouth back to hers, she moaned and arched against him, needing to feel the full length of him close to her... closer.

"Oh, God, Nicole, I've wanted you for so long," he said raggedly, moving to cover her. "For too long..."

Warmth flooded her, and a great, aching need throbbed at the very core of her. She wasn't sure where she was—only that she was soaring. He was her guide, his experienced hands knowing just where to touch, to stroke, to tantalize. Then she took over, marveling at the strength and fierceness of his growing passion, gasping when she felt the force of his need pressing against her thigh, then dipping into her, filling her completely.

Wrapping her arms and legs around him, she moved with him, the ache inside of her growing. Mouths clung, hands moved, bodies surged, then suddenly he stopped.

"Don't move," he warned thickly, kissing her damp cheeks. Her body shifted under him. "Nicole...I said...don't *move*...."

But she had to for she needed him as badly as he needed her. Tightening her legs around him, she brought him full into her again, and it sent him over the edge. Moaning, he moved powerfully against her, into her, his arms encircling her so tightly she thought they would meld for life, and with a great shuddering moan, he found release, leaving her one step away from paradise. Gulping in deep, ragged breaths, he collapsed on her and buried his forehead in the pillow next to her head.

Thoroughly awed by his great hunger for her, by the power of his release, Nicole held him tightly, her body still aching. They lay quietly for several minutes, Theron wondering if his heart would ever stop hammering, Nicole loving the feel of his body on hers.

"I was afraid that was going to happen," he said finally, kissing her shoulder. "The next time I tell you not to move, Nicole, *don't*."

She pressed her mouth to his neck, drinking in the salty taste of him. "It's all right, Theron."

"No, it isn't. You're as much a part of this as I am." Raising his head, he looked into her eyes, then lowered his head to taste the sweetness of her mouth. "I've just wanted you too much and for too damned long." He grinned. "You have no idea of how sick I was getting of taking cold showers."

She was only beginning to understand what went on inside of this man, to understand the depths of his feelings. The more she learned, the more she wanted him. It hurt her to think of the pain she'd put him through. Pulling him to her, she remembered all those times when they'd been so close to making love, yet she'd pushed him away.

"I'm sorry," she whispered, kissing his mouth, his cheek, his shoulder.

"You have nothing to be sorry about, sweetheart," he assured her, groaning as she traced his lips with the tip of her tongue. "Mmm, that's very nice." Closing his mouth over hers, he kissed her languorously, deeply, and a surge of renewed desire hardened his body. This time he made love to her slowly, taking time to explore the secrets of every curve, every contour of her luscious body. Learning what she liked, he tantalized and teased, then drew away again and moved on to offer another pleasure.

With hands and mouth he loved her, withholding the final union for so long that Nicole thought she might die for want of him. Never had she been loved like this! Never had she dreamed the pleasure would be so intense, so mind-shattering. He brought her close to the edge, then pulled back, heightening her desire, her need to a fever pitch. Stroking her breasts, her firm, flat belly, he dipped his hand to the softness between her thighs and found the moist core of her womanhood.

She moved restlessly against the pressure, wanting it to go on forever, but when she realized how close she was to that final pleasure, she tried to pull away.

"No, Theron, please, come to me," she gasped.

"Shh..." He quieted her with a sensual, tongue-tangling kiss, still stroking the most intimate part of her. "It's all right, Nicole. Relax...let it happen..."

And all reason slipped away. His words soothed, his touch and kiss intoxicated, and she felt great waves of pleasure shudder through her. Clutching his shoulders, she arched back on the bed, moaning softly.

"Now, we go together," he whispered against her mouth, and as he entered her, filling her, the world spun away.

She was the leaper, he the catcher, and they soared together in perfect synchronization, flying into paradise as one, then falling back through the clouds of ecstasy, sated and drained, to lie side-by-side in a tangle of damp limbs. It was a long time before either of them could speak.

"I think I'm going to like that lusty libido of yours," she murmured sleepily, her head on his chest.

"I think I'm going to need it where you're concerned." He kissed her damp forehead. "I do love you, Nicole," he said, but she didn't hear, for she was already asleep. Holding her close to him, he wondered if maybe it was for the best that she hadn't, for he remembered the strength of her reaction the last time, and God knew, he didn't want to chase her away again.

Closing his eyes, he slipped into a deep sleep, waking late in the afternoon, groaning with pleasure. Glancing up, he saw Nicole sitting on the edge of the bed next to him looking impossibly sexy in his shirt. She was smiling, her eyes soft and warm, as she ran her hand over his chest and down to his flat, hard stomach.

"You really are a beautiful man, Theron," she said quietly and kissed him. "And exciting...and sexy..." She punctuated each word with a touch here, a kiss there. "And I don't think I want you to leave this house, or even this bed, for a long time." She grinned mischievously. "So... I've brought you nourishment. Food and drink to keep up your strength."

"That is a hell of a way to wake a man, Nicole," he growled. Ignoring the sandwiches and champagne that she'd placed on the nightstand, he pulled her on top of him. "You could get yourself into serious trouble, you know."

"I'm counting on it."

"What kind of a monster have I created?"

She showed him, and if she wondered why he withheld the three precious words that she now longed to hear, she didn't dwell on it, for he proved with his body and eyes how much he did love her.

They stayed in the cottage for two days, and only then did they venture out because the cupboards were bare, and they'd shared the last of the apricot nectar.

Chapter Ten

Theron sat at his typewriter unable to concentrate, unable to get into the heads of his characters. For some reason, they were balking, refusing to do what he was asking of them. It was odd, he thought, that there were times when the words flowed as naturally as if they were writing themselves and other times when finding the right turn of phrase seemed as difficult as pulling an elephant's tooth.

This was one of the other times, yet he couldn't classify it as a conventional case of writer's block. Somewhere in the last page or two, something had gone wrong, something he couldn't pinpoint, and until he did, he was stuck.

He picked up the manuscript pages and reread them, wondering if perhaps the trouble stemmed from the major changes he'd made in a scene that Jess had particularly liked. He thought not. He thought the trouble was more directly linked to his preoccupation with Nicole.

He set the pages aside, reached for his pipe, cleaned and filled the bowl, and lighting it, he looked at the empty space on a shelf once occupied by a framed photograph of Jess, but he felt no pain, no sadness. When, he wondered, had he finally put Jess to rest? The day he told Nicole about the accident? Or later, during that hectic week when he hadn't seen Nicole, yet hadn't been able to get his mind off her? Or later still, on the day Nicole flew home from Atlanta?

It hadn't been a conscious thing. Though he'd loved Jess and she'd always have a place in his heart, she'd slipped away. But he thought of her now. *I love Nicole, Jess. She's good for me and the kids, and if I can make it happen, I'm going to marry her.*

Rising, he went to the windows and looked across the lawn and creek to the gatehouse. Where the devil had the past three weeks gone? It seemed like only yesterday that Nicole had come to him, filling his senses in a way he'd not imagined possible, making him want and need and take and give more fully than he'd ever done before.

Oh, hell, maybe that was his problem now. For three weeks he and Nicole had set their own pace. Theron had fallen easily into her schedule—working from four in the morning until they went on their morning ride. He worked when she went to the winter quarters, then they lunched together in the privacy of the gatehouse. He smiled thinking about those lunches. Most of them were enjoyed in the privacy of her bedroom; most having nothing to do with food.

There'd been times when he was on a roll and worked on *Images* while Nicole sat curled up on his dark brown leather couch reading. They had been times of quiet intimacy, times when he'd look up and watch the expressions chase across her face as she read. Often she seemed to sense his gaze upon her, for she'd turn green eyes, soft and warm, on him, and she'd smile a smile that was utterly beautiful; a smile that made him love her all the more.

As December marched along, they'd gone shopping, buying gifts and tree decorations. Nicole had insisted on outside lights, and they'd spent hours draping trees and lining the eaves of the house with them. Somehow, she'd managed to talk him into two trees, one for the living room, which they'd decorated last night, and a massive tree for the family room for the children to decorate when they arrived.

And there were the nights that he spent with Nicole. Long, lazy nights when they'd climb the stairs to his bedroom after Tag and Gladys had left. Nights filled with the ecstasy of lovemaking and the joy of sleeping with her body curled against him. But those nights were followed by a flurry of activity in the morning as they scurried around dressing, then bounded down the stairs so that they were sitting at the kitchen table nonchalantly drinking coffee when Tag arrived. Theron grinned. Somehow he didn't think they'd fooled the old man one bit.

Three weeks of loving, and now it was about to change. It had to. They were losing their privacy. The children would arrive tomorrow. Gladys had given up her apartment in Jacksonville Beach and had moved into the large downstairs guest room. Circus Royale had pulled into town for the winter, and Nicole was anxious to spend more time with her family—a family whom Theron had met and liked immensely.

Frowning, he drew deeply on his pipe, not wanting to think of the long, lonely nights that lay ahead. Nights of lying in his bed, aching, wanting, needing Nicole, while she slept in the gatehouse. Perhaps needing him, as well? But they had no choice. Not with the children in the house.

There were other changes brewing, as well, and a strange sense of foreboding stalked the corners of his mind as he thought of Jenny's evaluation, which was scheduled for the day after Christmas, and of Julie's coolness toward Nicole. He thought of March, and how empty his life would become when Nicole boarded that train. He wondered briefly if he could stop her from going.

He was thinking about these things when Nicole walked into the room and saw him standing by the window, the sun spilling over him, touching his hair with golden rays. He was wearing his glasses, standing in his studious pose, his pipe clamped between his teeth while he relit it. A cloud of smoke swirled around his head. Her heart skipped a beat, and she let her eyes linger on the breadth of his shoulders under the off-white turtleneck sweater he wore, and the way his navy-blue trousers hung in a clean line to plain black boots.

"Well, I've finally caught you in the act of being a *real* writer," she said quietly, unable to drag her eyes away from him.

When he turned, and she saw the intensity of his gaze, her breath caught in her lungs. There was an unfamiliar quietness in his voice. "Why? Because of the glasses?"

"No. Because you're staring out the window," she told him as she crossed the room. "Aren't writers famous for staring out of windows?"

"Sometimes it's the best way there is of working through a problem," he replied, drawing on his pipe. His eyes roamed over her appreciatively. She was wearing an emerald-green dress that skimmed the curves he knew, oh, so well. Her hair was hanging loose, spilling over her shoulders and down her back in a thick river of honey blond. "You look very beautiful, Nicole."

"You look pretty terrific yourself." Absently, she stopped at his desk and picked up the manuscript pages he'd been working on.

"Snooping again?" he asked. It was back . . . the quietness, the huskiness that made his voice crack.

"No. You said I couldn't take your work out of this room," she managed lightly. "You didn't say I couldn't read it. Is this the scene you're having trouble with?"

"It's giving me a few problems," he admitted, his eyes steady on her as she read.

"I can see why. It's powerful, but I feel sorry for poor Roger."

He narrowed his eyes. "Oh?"

"Yes. He's being too nice. If it were me, I'd take that glass of booze away from Katherine and sling it across the room." She put the pages back where she had found them. "But that's me, and I'm not Roger—and I'm definitely not a writer."

He smiled at her. "Why would you have Roger do that?"

"Because I think Katherine really loves him. She's just not thinking too clearly right now." Remembering the horrible fight between Theron and herself, Nicole shivered. "Sometimes it takes a little passionate anger to shake a person up enough so he or she will listen."

"And you think Katherine will respond to that?" he asked softly.

Nicole's mouth went dry. "I think she will. If she loves him enough. He certainly loves her, or he wouldn't've put up with the grief."

Theron's jaw clenched as he moved away from the window and stopped a few inches from her. "He hasn't told her he loves her. Not in a very long time."

"May...maybe he should," Nicole whispered. They were no longer talking about the characters in *Images*. The conversation had turned far more personal.

"What if he isn't really sure about how she feels?" he said huskily, his hands going to Nicole's shoulders. "What if he's hesitant about telling her because it chased her away once and he doesn't want to lose her again?"

"Oh, he couldn't lose her," Nicole assured him, her heart pounding furiously. "It might be just what she needs to hear."

A muscle in his jaw jumped as he gazed down at her. "It might be what he needs to hear, as well."

"I'll . . . She'll tell him. She's wanted to for a long time." Nicole rested her hands on the chest of the man whom she loved with all of her heart, and felt his heart thump erratically beneath her palms.

"When?" He lowered his head, brushing his lips across hers, wanting more—much more.

"Soon." She trembled at the light touch, wondering if she'd ever get enough of him. "But I don't remember this part of the play."

"It's a different script," he told her, touching her cheek. "And you're going to help me write the lines."

Reaching behind her for the phone, he sandwiched Nicole firmly between the desk and his body. Heat shot through her when her hips met his thighs, and she felt him stir with awareness. She pressed closer to him, heard him suck in his breath as he dialed, and while he waited for his party to answer, he savored the taste of her mouth. When he lifted his head, his eyes remained steady on her as he spoke.

"Yes, this is Theron Donahue. I'd like to cancel my lunch reservation for today," he told the maître d' at the Ocean Club, then dropped the receiver back into the cradle. Wrapping his arms around Nicole, he pulled her close. "This may be the last day we have to ourselves, Nicole, and I'm too damned selfish to share you with anyone. You don't mind, do you?"

She buried her face in the crook of his neck. "I don't mind, at all," she said, then, "Oh, God, I love you so much it almost hurts, Theron Donahue."

A great sigh shuddered from him, and she felt him tremble. Cupping her face in his hands, he looked at her tenderly. "I've been waiting a long time to hear you say those words, Nicole. Such a very, very long time." He kissed her gently. "I've wanted to tell you that I love you." He smiled. "In fact, I did. Every night, while you were sleeping in my arms, I'd tell you over and over."

"What did you say?" she asked tremulously, wanting to know.

"That I love you more than I thought a man could love a woman. That I don't want to lose you. That I want you to be a part of me forever." Desire shot through him. "Now, I'm telling you that if we don't get the hell out of here soon, I'm going to lock the door and make love with you right here."

"Gatehouse?" She grinned.

"Gatehouse," he agreed. "Is Gladys still baking?"

"She's made enough Christmas cookies to open her own bakery." Nicole laughed.

"They say sugar gives energy. Being as we're going to need all of that we can get, grab what cookies you can on the way past the counter. But be damned careful," he warned as they headed for the kitchen. "She's lethal with her spatula."

Laughing, their faces flushed, they hurried into the aromatic kitchen, and while Gladys and Tag looked on in surprise, Theron headed for the macaroons, Nicole, the sugar cookies, and with hands stuffed, they ducked out of the French doors.

After they left, Gladys turned to Tag. "Sure is good to see those two so happy. It's going to be a fine Christmas, Graham. A mighty fine Christmas."

"Yup, that it is, Gladys." He pulled off his cap. "Reckon we won't be seein' 'em till mornin', heh?"

"Probably not."

"Well, then, Gladys, how's 'bout you and me grabbin' a bite to eat. Get you outta this kitchen for a spell, heh?" Tag nervously twisted the cap in his hand. "Maybe even rent a movie for tonight. Somethin' with John Wayne, though. None of that mushy stuff."

"I'd like that, Graham." Gladys smiled. "I'd like that."

Nicole wakened the following morning wrapped in Theron's arms, the heat of his body seeping through her pores. She stretched luxuriously, memories of the long afternoon and night of loving still fresh in her mind. Sighing, she nuzzled his neck and closed her eyes dreamily.

Love. What a powerful love flowed between them, filling them until they could take no more, then filling them again. They'd talked and laughed and played and made love until the wee hours of the morning, and only then had sleep reluctantly claimed them.

And now came the changes, she thought, nestling closer to him, kissing his cheek, feeling him stir beside her. How, she wondered, was it possible for him to have become such an important part of her life as quickly as he had? How was she to bear not going to him at will? She shivered at that, and at another thought that skittered across her mind; an unbidden thought of March, of saying goodbye to Theron for nine long months. It was something she hadn't allowed herself to dwell on during the past three weeks, and she certainly didn't want to think about it now. Not when she was fairly bursting with joy and love for him.

She sighed heavily. Wasn't this exactly what she'd been afraid would happen? She'd known immediately that he was a man for whom she could care deeply. And she did. She loved him desperately, completely, and because of that, she was torn between Theron and performing.

Beside her, Theron rolled over and gathered her close, his eyes drowsy upon her. "Morning, funny face. What time is it?"

"Eight."

"Hmm. Three hours of sleep," he murmured, dropping a delicious kiss on her mouth. "You're going to make me old before my time."

She grinned. "I'm doing my very best."

"Thank God for Gladys's cookies." He ran his hand along the smooth length of her body. "You know, don't you, that when we get up, we have to do all the things we were going to do yesterday." Kissing her languidly, he felt her shiver, then grow pliant in his arms. "The last of the shopping..." He cupped a breast in his hand. She moaned. "Wrap gifts..." He nibbled her neck. "Pick up the kids..."

"Maybe you should go to the airport alone," she whispered, dipping her fingers into his hair.

"Oh, no. Not this time." He looked at her, his eyes warm with love. "I want you by my side, and I want them to get used to seeing you there. It's where you belong."

His words swirled through her. Perhaps he was right. Perhaps this was her destiny: loving him, being a part of his life. She ran her hands over his shoulders and down his back to his firm buttocks, heard his groan of pleasure, felt his desire pulse against her.

"I'm going to miss you. Not being able to go to you, to touch you..." She held him tightly, her body arching to his.

"The kids have to sleep sometime...oh, God, woman, do you have any idea of what you do to me?" he said thickly.

"Show me. Fly with me, Theron. Love me."

"Oh, Nicole, I love you...." he murmured, and taking her to him, they flew together.

Late that afternoon, Nicole stood beside Theron, her heart hammering as the jet carrying the children taxied toward the gate. Unconsciously, she clasped his hand in a death grip.

Surprised, he glanced at her. "Are you nervous?"

"Incredibly," she admitted.

"Why? You've already met them. They adore you."

"I wouldn't go so far as to say adore," she replied with a smile. Yes, she'd met them. Yes, an instant rapport had developed between herself and Rusty and Jenny. Julie, however, was another matter. But something else nagged at Nicole, and a chill shivered along her spine. Oh, God, this whole thing smacked of commitment, of permanence, and while she loved Theron with all her heart, she wasn't sure she was ready for that commitment. She shrugged and said quietly, "It's different this time."

"Ah, I think I'm beginning to understand." Looping his arm around her shoulders, he pulled her to his side. "You're afraid they'll know that you've spent the past three weeks wantonly seducing poor old helpless Dad with that luscious body of yours."

"Stop it!" she hissed, blushing hotly. A crowd of people milled around them, and she looked around anxiously to see if anyone had heard, but he'd spoken for her ears only. Looking at him, she grinned. "Poor old helpless Dad? You are about as helpless as a charging bull!"

He laughed and dropped a kiss on the top of her head. "I'll let that one pass for now," he told her, squeezing her gently. "Don't worry about the kids, sweetheart. Everything will be just fine."

But he wondered about that when the children he loved so dearly appeared on the ramp; Rusty, tightly clutching Jenny's hand, their faces wreathed in smiles; Julie, her smile fading the instant she saw Nicole at her father's side. He was going to have to have a long talk with his older daughter, he decided as he and Nicole made their way through the crowd toward the children.

"I don't know if anyone else is hungry or not, but Nicole and I worked up a good appetite today," Theron said an hour later when they were in the car heading home. Beside him, Nicole fidgeted uncomfortably on the seat. Theron grinned. "How about if we stop for pizza?"

"Pizza?" came Julie's surprised exclamation. "You never eat pizza, Dad. You've always said it was junk food."

Theron laughed. "I've learned differently. Real junk is blueberry fudge. Well?"

"But pizza?" Julie mumbled, shaking her head.

"Are you complaining, Julie?" Rusty glared at his sister. "No!"

"Then shut up before he changes his mind and we end up at some stuffy restaurant shoving raw oysters down Jenny's throat," he told her.

"Ee-yuk!" Jenny wrinkled her nose in distaste.

The easy banter filling the car stayed with them when they stopped at a pizza parlor and hungrily devoured two large pizza supremes.

Theron listened to the flow of conversation around the table. Jenny plied Nicole with an endless stream of questions regarding the trapeze, and Rusty and Julie vied for the opportunity of telling him about the weekend trip to Vermont that Aunt Shel and her husband had taken them on. The chatter was nonstop, punctuated with laughter, yet Theron was keenly aware of Julie's reticence toward Nicole. Though his daughter was polite, she remained cool and alert to every touch or look that passed between Theron and Nicole.

It troubled him, that resentment, and he could only hope it wasn't as obvious to Nicole as it was to him. As they left the restaurant and started home again, he pondered the reason for Julie's actions. Ever since her mother's death, she had resented every woman her father came in contact with. It was almost as if she expected Theron to live out his life on memories alone. But he needed so much more, so many things that Julie was too young to understand.

Yes, he needed his children, but he also needed the vibrant, warm woman sitting on the seat beside him. He needed all that she so spontaneously and lovingly brought to his life, filling it to the brim.

Glancing at her, their eyes met briefly, then Theron turned his attention back to driving, listening absently to the oohs and aahs of the children when they passed between the gates of the estate and drove into the wonderland that he and Nicole had created with such painstaking care. Multitudes of lights shimmered in the trees and on the house. There was the sleigh that Tag had built and light posts looking like enormous candy canes flanking the sidewalk.

As they walked through the front door, arms laden with luggage, the fresh scent of pine and pungent bayberry permeated the air. Setting the luggage down, the children gaped in delight. There were wreaths and holly and pine boughs. Lights twinkled everywhere, giving the rooms a warm, inviting look that wasn't lost on any of them.

"This is great, Dad," Rusty enthused, peeking into the living room on one side of the stairs and into the family room on the other. "Two trees, no less."

"It's going to be a real Christmas this year, isn't it, Daddy?" Jenny commented softly, her eyes wide and shining.

"Wow, Dad! Thanks!" Julie beamed at her father.

"It wasn't my doing," Theron told her, and curving his arm around Nicole's shoulder, he drew her to his side. "This is the lady you have to thank. I just followed directions."

While Jenny and Rusty were enthusiastic with praise of the atmosphere Nicole had created, Julie merely shrugged. "Well...thanks," she said quietly.

"It wouldn't be Christmas without lots of decorations," Nicole said with a smile, but Julie had already grabbed her suitcase and was heading up the stairs. Nicole let out a shaky sigh and glanced up to see Theron, his jaw clenched, staring after his daughter. "It's new to her. Give her time, Theron."

"Yeah," he grumbled. Picking up a load of suitcases, he started up the stairs. "I'll be back in a few minutes."

Nervous and suddenly unsure of herself, Nicole ducked into the kitchen to help Gladys carry trays of cookies and eggnog into the large, warm family room where Tag had a fire roaring on the hearth. That done, she dragged out the boxes of decorations for the twelve-foot tree and stood quietly looking around, indecision weighing heavily on her mind. Sighing, knowing she didn't belong here on this, the children's first night home, she grabbed her purse and was on her way out the French doors when Theron caught her.

"Where do you think you're going?" he demanded, clasping her arm, swinging her around to face him.

"Home."

"Why?"

"Because I've done all I can here," she said, not daring to meet his eyes. "Gladys and Tag have everything else under control."

Theron captured her shoulders in strong hands. "Not everything." He touched her with his wonderful blue-green eyes. "I want you to stay. I *need* you."

Her eyes clouded. "It's not a good idea tonight, Theron. The kids need to spend some time alone with you."

"I see. That's why Jenny is upstairs picking out photos she wants to show you, and Rusty is tuning his guitar in order to give you a Christmas concert." He smiled and tilted her chin up so she had to look at him. Brushing a strand of hair away from her face, he dropped a light kiss on her mouth, frowning when she lowered her head and grew very still. "Nicole?"

"Please . . . this isn't the time."

"You're worried about Julie," he stated simply, regarding her for a long moment. "Let's set the record straight right now, Nicole. I love my children very much, but I will not allow any one of them to dictate the terms of my relationship with you."

"Julie sees me as a *threat*, Theron! She's been away for months. Now all of a sudden she comes home to find you involved with a woman she barely knows?" Nicole countered. "She needs time to get used to this!"

"What she *needs*, Nicole, is a heart-to-heart with dear, old Dad," Theron said, knowing his daughter well enough to know that she would push him to the limit if he allowed it. "What are you going to do tomorrow if she still hasn't accepted this new situation? Cancel out Christmas Eve at Annabel's? And what about Christmas? You and your mother and Gladys have spent hours planning the dinner. Are you going to call your family and tell them Christmas Day has been canceled?" he insisted gently. "Well?"

She couldn't deny that he had a point. "Your daughter's insecure about this."

"Then we have to make her feel secure, but we have to do it together. We sure as hell won't accomplish anything if you go running off into the night."

"Dad! Gladys needs the nutmeg and Rusty wants..." Julie's voice trailed off as she walked into the kitchen and saw her father and Nicole. Her smile faded, and she tossed her head, sending her curly light-brown hair floating around her face. Eyes so like her father's rested on Nicole, then moved to Theron. "Excuse me. I thought she'd gone home a long time ago," Julie said and turned to leave.

"Hold it right there, young lady! I want to talk to you," Theron ordered firmly, determined to put a stop to this nonsense before it got out of hand. "Nicole, if you'd take Gladys what she needs, Julie and I will be along in a few minutes."

When Nicole left the room, Julie looked apprehensively at her father, her lower lip quivering. "You're mad at me."

"No, honey, I'm not mad at you. But I am disappointed."

"Well, I don't care! Why does she have to be here? This isn't her house! Why can't she just go home and leave us alone?" Julie blurted angrily.

"I will *not* tolerate this behavior from you, Julie," Theron warned. "Come over here and sit down." When she stubbornly hesitated, he commanded, "Now, Julie Anne!"

As she walked slowly into the breakfast nook, Theron pulled out two chairs, positioning them so that they were facing each other. Julie settled into one. Theron sat on the other and leaned forward, resting his forearms on his knees. He sat quietly for a moment, and when he finally spoke, he chose his words carefully.

"Nicole's being here in no way changes the way that I feel about you or Rusty or Jenny. The three of you are the light of my life, Julie. I couldn't make it without any of you. I love all of you very, very much." Reaching out, he brushed a tear from her cheeks, then tilted her chin up so she was looking at him. "It's important that you understand that, angel. I do love you."

"I know." She sniffed. "I love you, too, Daddy."

"I know you do." He paused. "You asked me why Nicole is here. She's here because I care very deeply for her. I want her here. She's become an important part of my life. She's not any more important or any less important than you three. She's important in a different kind of way, a way that you'll understand when you get a little older."

"What about Mother?" Julie asked accusingly. "Don't you still love her?"

Theron felt a sharp pang in his heart. "I will always love your mother. But, Julie, your mother's been gone for three years," he said huskily, hoping that he could get through to her. "Losing her created an emptiness in my life. Sometimes I got pretty lonely," he explained, and she looked at him in surprise, as if she'd never considered that her father could get lonely. Theron continued. "I don't feel that way any more. Not since meeting Nicole. And it's nice, Julie, to be able to smile again and laugh and be happy."

"I want you to be happy," Julie whispered, "but Nicole will never be my mother."

"She's not trying to take your mother's place," Theron assured her. "I'm not even sure which way the relationship is going, because it's still very new. But I'd be willing to bet that, whatever happens, if you gave her half a chance she could be a good friend to you." He grinned and shrugged. "Hey, she can't be all bad. She got me eating pizza again."

Julie smiled back. "Well . . . maybe she's all right. She seems nice. She laughs a lot."

Theron's next words were difficult, but they needed to be said. "My seeing Nicole doesn't depend on your approval, Julie. I want you to understand that. You can make this as easy or as difficult on yourself as you choose. You don't have to like her, but I won't have you being rude to her, either. Okay?" He watched her nod. "Good. I love you very much, and I'm hoping that we can work through this together." Theron kissed her forehead. "All I'm asking is that you give her a fair shake before you make up your mind about her."

"I'll try, Daddy."

"That's my girl." Standing, he held out his hand for her. "Now, then, if we don't get in there and help decorate that tree, they'll have it finished already."

"I'm glad you got real trees this year."

"You have to thank Nicole for that. If it hadn't been for her, we might not have had any." Theron chuckled.

Walking into the family room, Julie stopped and looked up at her father. "I guess I was pretty awful to her, wasn't I?"

"Yes, you were."

"I'm sorry."

"Aren't you telling the wrong person?" he said, knowing that she was still hesitant, but she left his side and walked across the room to Nicole. It was a small gesture on Julie's part, but it was a beginning, and as the evening progressed and they strung the lights, hung the bulbs and added a shimmering touch of tinsel to the tree, the tension eased.

It was close to midnight before Theron climbed the ladder and topped the tree with a delicately painted porcelain clown. He smiled at Nicole. "You have no idea of the hell I went through to find this."

When he climbed down from the ladder and saw the tears glistening in Nicole's eyes, he gathered her close to him, holding her tightly. Behind Nicole, he saw that damnable flash of resentment flare in Julie's eyes, so he held out his hand for her, and moments later, they all stood in a circle by the tree—Rusty, Julie, Jenny, Tag, Gladys, Theron and Nicole—and toasted the Christmas season.

It was an evening Theron knew he'd long remember, as were the two days that followed—Christmas Eve at Annabel's; Christmas Day at home, with Annabel and her family, and Nicole's parents and brothers and sisters all filling the house with laughter.

More and more, during those days, Theron's thoughts focused on Nicole and the part she played in his life, the part he wanted her to play. The part of his wife.

Perhaps he would have asked her to marry him on Christmas Day after everyone left and they were alone. But he didn't. He couldn't, for Nicole's father brought him back to reality as the Rossinis said their goodbyes and prepared to leave.

They were standing outside the front door when Gabe reached down and tapped Jenny on the nose. "You be sure to get some sleep tonight, young lady. You need to be rested for tomorrow," he told her, then offered his hand to Theron and smiled. "If Jenny is as good as Gina has said, we could both have our girls flying soon. I don't know about Jenny, yet, but I know that's where Nick belongs. Thank you for a wonderful Christmas, Theron. Good night."

Late that night, Theron stood looking out of his bedroom window toward the gatehouse, a strange sense of loss working around his heart, and he suddenly had to see Nicole. Grabbing a jacket, he tore out of the house to his car and braked in front of the cottage moments later.

Inside, Luke barked a greeting, and when Theron opened the door, he coaxed the big dog out. "Sorry, fella, but you're staying out here for a while," he said and shut the door behind him.

Walking into the living room, he saw Nicole curled up on the couch. She was staring into the fire that burned brightly on the hearth. In her lap was the porcelain carousel horse Theron had given her for Christmas.

"I was hoping you'd come down tonight," she said, and he heard the tears in her voice. Setting the horse down, she rose and turned to him. "I was just . . . wishing that Christmas didn't have to end. It's been so perfect. And now. . . . Oh, God, Theron, please hold me! I need you so much."

He crossed the room in two strides and pulled her so tightly to him that their hearts joined. "It's all right, sweetheart. I'm here. I love you . . . God . . . how I love you."

He captured her mouth in a sense-shattering kiss and lowered her to the floor. They made love in front of the fire until both of them were weak and exhausted. Then they held each other until dawn broke in the east and Theron had to go home.

Chapter Eleven

Well, kiddo, are you ready for today?'' Nicole asked a beaming Jenny Donahue, when Theron and the children arrived at the gatehouse at eight—only a few hours after he'd held her close, then left her alone.

"I'm ready," Jenny exclaimed, excitement in her voice.

"Okay." Nicole smiled and looked from Jenny to Theron. His features were tense, drawn. "We're going to work out at the bar and on the mats for an hour, so if there's something else that you and Rusty and Julie have to do...?"

"I think we'd just as soon stick around, if you don't mind," he told her, and the five of them trouped through the gatehouse to the screened-in porch where Rusty and Julie settled cross-legged on the floor and Theron leaned against a window frame, shivering. "It must get damn uncomfortable back here during the winter months."

"It does," Nicole agreed, and Theron made a mental note to have the porch glassed in and fitted with central air and heat for her. Then he turned his attention to what she was telling Jenny. "There are a series of exercises that I want you to start doing every day, Jenny. It's going to be hard to fit them in, what with your ballet, gymnastics, training at the winter quarters and school, but you're going to have to find the time."

"I know," Jenny said eagerly.

"It won't leave you much playtime," Nicole warned, almost as if she were trying to dissuade the child.

"Dad said that you're working out by four-thirty almost every morning," Jenny commented, her wide brown eyes serious. "Would you mind if I rode my bike down here and worked out with you? Before school? Maybe about five or so?" She shrugged and smiled a smile that drew Nicole in completely. "I'll just have to make sure I'm in bed early every night."

Nicole heard the determination in the child's voice, saw the commitment in her eyes, felt the desire to perform emanating from every pore of her young, lithe body. It was a powerful thing that reached out to her, to Rusty and Julie, to Theron, and Nicole thought that perhaps this was the first time the girl's father truly realized the forces that drove Jenny, for his eyes narrowed fractionally.

"That would be fine. Well, then, let's get to work," Nicole said, and for the next hour, she was the teacher, Jenny the student.

Theron watched them together: the woman in a black leotard and leg warmers whose hair was drawn into a knot at the nape of her neck and the child in a green leotard and leg warmers whose auburn hair was fashioned in exactly the same style. Both were supple, graceful. He was familiar with that in Nicole, but for some reason, it was the first time he'd noticed just how beautifully his daughter moved. No longer was she the animated, impish ten-year-old. *Imp* and *twirp* didn't fit the poised girl at the ballet bar and on the mats. In front of his eyes, Jenny seemed to grow in stature and display a maturity beyond her years.

Pride welled in Theron. Uneasiness churned through his stomach. Had he really been so blind to Jenny's determination, to her talent? he wondered, as they piled into his car after the workout and made the short drive to the winter quarters. Yet here he was parking in front of the aerialists' center, possibly on the brink of missing out on a large part of her childhood, possibly facing the reality of turning her over to a trainer who would nurture not only her professional growth, but who would have to be responsible for her emotional growth, as well.

Once inside the building, there was no time for pondering, no time for anything other than watching, feeling, reacting.

One moment, Theron was surrounded by Lawrence and by Nicole's family—Gabriel and Simone, David and Adam, Margo and Cherie. Nicole and Jenny stood at his side, Rusty and Julie in front of him.

The next moment, he'd told Jenny he loved her, then stood watching, his heart in his throat as his young daughter walked toward the net with the Rossinis. His two oldest children had settled on the floor to watch. Lawrence was talking with Simone. A few feet in front of him, Nicole paced, her eyes anxiously fixed on Jenny as the child climbed up to the pedestal.

Standing alone, his heart pounding, Theron desperately wanted to climb the web himself and bring his daughter down again. She was too young, too small to be doing something like this, something unutterably dangerous. She was his *little girl*, for God's sake!

But it was too late to do anything now. Adam secured the safety mechanic around Jenny's small waist. Gabe sat on one of the two catcher's trapeze bars that were part of the Rossinis' rigging. He talked to Jenny. Jenny nodded. Below, Theron swallowed. In front of him, Nicole stopped, her hands balled into fists.

After what seemed at once an eternity and an instant, Jenny Donahue left the pedestal, swinging out with an ease that captured the attention of everyone below, and Theron realized instantly that he'd lost his daughter to the small piece of tubing that was suspended by ropes.

She wasn't flawless, for she made mistakes as Gabe methodically put her through her paces. She wasn't a mature performer, for she didn't perform even the simplest of movements with the polish of an experienced performer.

Yet it was there. The potential. The promise. The future. Jenny Donahue, the ten-year-old daughter of a playwright, the girl who was the offspring of a nonperforming family, was gifted. Unaccountably, beautifully gifted.

The enormous significance of the moment drew those watching from below together. Rusty and Julie stood up and crowded close to their father, their eyes steady on their little sister. Lawrence and Simone positioned themselves just behind Theron, and Nicole came to him, standing close to him, seeking the comfort of his warmth.

"You tried to warn me about this," Theron said quietly to Nicole. "I should have listened."

Feeling the depth of his emotion radiate out to her, she wrapped her arm around his waist and rested her head in the crook of his shoulder. "We still wouldn't have known how good she really was until now," she said, her eyes steady on the child, her heart aching for the loss the father would suffer.

Though Nicole fully realized Theron's emotional dilemma—his pride in Jenny, his apprehension because of her success—she couldn't drag her eyes or attention away from the child long enough to offer him the support he sorely needed. She was concentrating on every move Jenny made— the right ones, the wrong ones. And, when Jenny missed a cue and fell, bobbing around at the end of the safety line, Nicole's heart lurched. Without thinking, she tore away from Theron and ran to the net, to the web.

A great knot formed in the pit of Theron's stomach, and he started after her, wanting to stop her from doing this. He was losing his daughter. He didn't want to be reminded that soon he would lose Nicole, as well.

"No, Theron. If you love her, let her go," Lawrence said quietly, stopping him. "Jenny might be exactly who Nicole needs right now."

"He's right, Theron." Simone Rossini placed her hand gently on Theron's arm. She looked up at him, green eyes filled with understanding. "It's a lot to ask of someone— that they let go of the person they love—but you have to try to find the strength to do this for her."

"Do I have a choice, Simone?" Theron muttered thickly as he glanced down at the older version of Nicole who stood at his side. Dread cinched his heart.

"No, you don't," Simone replied, her voice soft and lilting, but still failing to lessen the impact of her words. "She will never be happy if she doesn't do this, and I think you know it."

He knew. Oh, God, how well he knew! As he stood there watching Nicole's oldest brother, David, take his position on the second catcher's trapeze, a riot of emotions worked through him, tormenting him. Anticipation and apprehension, hope and fear, respect for Nicole and Jenny's talent and resentment because of it. Underlying it all was his great love for both of them and the gnawing realization that the chasm between them would soon become impossible to bridge. He was, quite simply, going to lose them both, and there wasn't a damn thing he could do about it.

A thick pall of tension hung over the center. Laughter and conversation stopped. Other aerialists gathered around to watch. All eyes turned up curiously, hopefully. Theron knew that everyone present was aware of the rumors going around about Nicole. Rumors that she'd lost her nerve, that her permanent retirement was close at hand. Yet, there she stood on the pedestal, thirty feet above the net, her expression animated, as she coached the little newcomer.

Theron's heart slammed against his ribs, and his stomach rolled when Adam handed Nicole the fly bar and, still talking to Jenny, she swung easily off the pedestal, high, then higher, her line fluid and graceful.

From their perch on the catcher's trapeze bars, Nicole's father and brother watched her, smiling at each other in approval. Below them, Theron watched the woman he loved, knowing he was losing her.

Then Adam was reaching out to help Nicole back onto the pedestal, back to where Jenny was nodding her head eagerly. Cherie handed the child a fly bar. Nicole firmly gripped the bar of hers once again. Woman and child carefully positioned themselves precariously on the edge of the narrow pedestal.

Theron stood silently, his jaw clenched, blood thrumming in his ears. It'd grown so quiet he could almost hear the beads of perspiration popping out on his forehead as he watched Gabe and David nod, then swing out and lower themselves into position, their legs wrapped securely around the ropes.

An eternity passed. A moment. An idiotic sense of being in a dream made Theron blink.

Gabe cued. Theron jumped. Nicole and Jenny left the platform, bodies arched, then tucked as they swung in an arc. High, higher, building momentum.

Gabe cued again. Goose bumps broke out on Theron's flesh as he watched Nicole and Jenny let go of the bars and hurl through that great void of emptiness above the net, hands and wrists of catchers and leapers locking, the woman and child swinging below the two men.

Gabe issued one last cue. Theron sucked in his breath so rapidly that his chest hurt as, high above and in near perfect synchronization, Nicole and Jenny were airborne once again. Rotating their bodies, their fingers closed around empty, swinging fly bars.

Only when they were safely back on the pedestal did Theron let out his breath in a long, heavy rush, his eyes steady on Nicole. If a part of him had believed that he could share her with the trapeze, it quickly died, for he saw the elation, the pure joy on her face. She glowed with a happiness that he'd never seen before. She'd let go, at long last. She was free to fly again, to soar. And it was a beautiful sight to see. Far too beautiful to ever consider clipping her wings. Doing that would kill her, he realized as he watched the remainder of the session.

When it was over, when Jenny and Nicole had made their exit falls, one at a time, into the net, Theron lowered his head. His eyes felt oddly moist, but he knew he wasn't alone. On one side, Simone stood crying great tears of happiness for her daughter. On the other, Julie leaned against him, her eyes moist with pride for Jenny.

"Wow, that was really something," Julie commented quietly, thoroughly awed by what she'd witnessed.

Rusty shook his head, staring at his little sister as Margo helped her down from the net. "I didn't think the little twirp had it in her. Guess I was wrong, huh?" He shook his head. "And Nicole? She was great! Did you see her, Dad?"

"I saw her, son," Theron replied, his voice husky with emotion.

Close to the net, Jenny appeared from the midst of the backslapping, cheering, laughing crowd and rushed to her father, grinning from ear to ear.

"Well? Whatcha think? Can I train, Daddy?" she asked, excitement shining in her brown eyes.

Theron scooped her into his arms. "I think that you were wonderful, Jenny." He kissed the top of her head, his eyes moving to Nicole, who was still caught up in the rush of well-wishers. "I'll talk to Nicole about it later."

"Does that mean you're really going to let me do it?" Jenny prodded anxiously, holding her breath, crossing her fingers.

Do I have a choice?... No, Theron, you don't. Simone's words applied to Jenny as well as Nicole, Theron thought heavily. Looking down at the little girl who'd needed him so much until now, he felt a deep sadness well in him. "Yes, sweetheart, it means that I'm going to let you train," he said and knelt down to hold her close.

One heartbreak at a time, he thought, wondering if the pain would ever ease.

Nicole stood shakily in the midst of family and friends, the import of what had just happened slowly sinking in. The world seemed to be spinning crazily out of control. Just a few short days ago, she'd almost convinced herself that flying wasn't for her, that her destiny lay with Theron. And now? Now her future with the show was locked solidly in place.

Here she was, surrounded by her family and Lawrence and Ralph and Gus and several of the aerialists from the show, all laughing and congratulating her, welcoming her back into the fold again, for she was one of them. This is where she belonged.

One day you'll fly again ... and you probably won't even realize that you've let go until it's over and the applause begins. Annabel's words came back in a rush. Nicole swallowed against the lump in her throat. Annabel had certainly called it. Nicole had been so involved with Jenny that she hadn't given her own fears a second thought. Letting go had come naturally and, oh, Lord, how wonderful it had been!

She'd felt weightless as she'd broken the shackles of the past and soared into the future.

She'd done it! She'd conquered! She was *free*! And as she made her way through the crowd of people, her mind whirled with plans. It'd take every minute of the coming months to regain the poise she'd once had, to polish the technique that had once been second nature. Then there was Jenny, and fitting in training sessions with the talented, promising little girl. And there'd be costumes to make, and hours of work still ahead on the rings . . .

And, there was Theron—the man she loved—standing not ten feet in front of her, his eyes steady on her. Nicole stopped in her tracks, for the first time realizing the potential price attached to her success.

Her heart pounded, and she wondered if she could really make a commitment to flying, or if she should give up the idea now and, instead, stay with this man who filled her with such joy. Oh, God, why couldn't he be one of us? she thought miserably. Why couldn't he be the type of man who could pick up and leave Jacksonville when the train pulled out? The type of man who could easily become a part of what she wanted so desperately to do?

He walked away from the children toward her, his long legs carrying him slowly, the expression in his eyes mirroring pride and love and sadness.

"You did it," he said simply, touching her only with his gaze.

"It sure looks that way," she replied, her eyes wide and green and soft.

"You were absolutely beautiful up there, Nicole." He cupped her cheek and smiled. "Well...maybe a little rusty."

She laughed softly. "It's going to take some time to get back in form again, but oh, Theron, it was the most *incredible* feeling that I've ever had!" she admitted, pressing her cheek deeper into his palm, drowning in his warmth.

"I could see it on your face," he told her, knowing he'd never forget her almost rapturous joy. But it was gone now, replaced by concern, by the weighty decisions that were dragging her down. Knowing that he'd become one of her problems, the pain of loving her knifed through him. He gathered her close and held her for several long moments, wanting to tell her how much he did love her but not daring to. Not now. Maybe never again. "Everything's going to be all right, Nicole."

"Is it, Theron? I wonder sometimes." Looking from him to the trapeze rigging, then back again, she felt as if she were being torn apart, for she wanted what she couldn't have. She wanted both.

"Of course it is," he assured her with more confidence than he felt. "You've been through one hell of an emotional trauma this morning. It's going to take time to absorb all of it, to catch your breath and set your direction." He kissed her lightly. "It might be a good idea if you were to get your mind off things for a while. Why don't we load up the kids and take them to St. Augustine? Have a nice, long lunch. Go to the fort." He chuckled. "I might even break down and try a piece of that ridiculous blueberry fudge."

"Now, *that's* worth making the trip for in itself. Don't let me forget to pick up my camera."

"Then you'll go?"

"If the kids are game, yes. I'd like that very much, Theron," she whispered and wrapped her arms around him, adoring the feel of his solid strength close to her. Though love flowed between them, they withheld the words, and Nicole couldn't help being uncertain over what the future might hold for them.

Flopping down on one of the overstuffed couches in the family room, Nicole leaned back and closed her eyes, wondering where the day had gone, wondering about Theron's quiet intensity during their busy afternoon in St. Augustine. But then, she hadn't been a great conversationalist, either, not with memories of the morning crowding her mind.

She sighed. If it hadn't been for the children racing here, there, everywhere, peeking into every doorway in town and chattering their way through lunch, it would have been an uncommonly quiet afternoon. Through it all, Nicole couldn't call up a single moment when Theron hadn't been at her side, firmly clasping her hand in his. There hadn't been a time when she'd looked at him that he hadn't been watching her, his eyes clouded.

Raising her head again, she curled her feet under her and glanced around this warm, inviting room with its walls of wood and plaster and brick. The only lights came from those on the Christmas tree and from the fireplace. Shadows danced in the room. Logs crackled and hissed on the hearth. The aroma of pine and burning wood permeated the air.

How I love this place, she mused as she listened to the sounds filtering through the house—the comforting sounds of a family in its home. From the kitchen came the clatter of dishes as Gladys cleaned up after the family's late dinner of turkey sandwiches. Nicole heard Tag's gravelly voice as he tried to give Gladys directions on how to properly accomplish a task that they'd been arguing about for the last hour.

From upstairs, Nicole heard the blast of a stereo, then Theron's reprimand, followed by a much lower volume. There was the sound of a girl's voice, determined and slightly defiant, and the stern response of her father, and Nicole knew that Julie's resentment had flared up again.

Then came another voice, and Nicole glanced up to the open-railed hall that bridged the family room and receiving hall and saw Jenny peeking down at her.

"I have to go to bed now," said the girl. "Are we working out in the morning?"

A premonition nudged Nicole's heart. "Not in the morning, Jenny. Maybe later in the day," she replied, thinking of Theron and all the things they had to sort through. She wanted no commitments at five in the morning. "But I will be talking to your father tonight about your training. As soon as I've worked out a schedule, we'll get started on a daily basis. Okay?"

"Yeah." Jenny was beaming. "I really like your dad, and all, but I'm glad that you're going to be coaching me, too."

"So am I . . ." Nicole paused. " . . . even if you are going to take over my spotlight someday."

"Oh, wow, I could never do that!"

Nicole chuckled. "We'll see."

"Are you going riding with us in the morning?"

"I'm planning on it."

"Yippee!" Jenny had turned into a little girl again. "Nicole?"

"What, honey?"

"I'm glad that you live here," Jenny told her shyly. "And I'm even gladder that my dad likes you so much."

Tears welled in Nicole's eyes.

Theron suddenly appeared in the hall, his eyes moving from Jenny to Nicole, then back again. "I thought you were already in bed, Cinderella."

"I had to say goodnight to Nicole."

"Have you?" Theron asked. When Jenny nodded, he kissed her. "Off with you, then. If you don't get some sleep, you won't be up in time to go riding," Theron told her and, turning, he ran down the stairs, through the receiving hall and into the family room. "Sorry that took so long, but those kids are wired tonight."

"It's been a big day for them."

"For all of us," he corrected, drawing her into his arms. He was just about to kiss her when Rusty ambled into the room. Shaking his head, Theron released Nicole. "What is it, son?"

"I've finally figured out what I'm doing wrong on that Springsteen song," Rusty said, smiling his winning smile. "I'd like to try it out."

"It's almost ten, Russell. There are people in this house trying to sleep or carry on a quiet conversation, and they don't want to do it with a drum-solo background," he told the boy.

"Gladys and Tag'll be playing gin rummy until midnight. Julie's reading. The twirp's room is too far away for her to hear anything," Rusty rationalized and shrugged. "Besides, I thought you and Nicole were going down to the dock."

"And if we were?" Theron asked, narrowing his eyes.

Rusty flipped his drumsticks. "Hey, Dad, think of the atmosphere. A full moon, a good solid drumbeat for a background. Might be just the thing to set the perfect mood for a romantic interlude."

Rusty grinned, Nicole chuckled, and Theron's mouth twitched. "You've got exactly half an hour on those drums, Russell, and please, do us a favor and close the garage doors while you practice and after you're finished," Theron relented, and watching his son leave the room, he muttered, "Kid's only fifteen, and already his hormones are kicking in. Romantic interlude?"

"Hey, come on, you were only three years older than Rusty when you married Jess," Nicole reminded him.

"You're a big help," Theron grumbled. "If we want any privacy at all, we'd better get out of here."

They left the house and walked across the lawn toward the dock. The night was cool and crisp and clear. A huge moon hung above the treetops in a velvet-black, star-sprinkled sky. The lazy water of the canal lapped against the shore and the pilings. The muffled beat of drums reached them, and sitting down on the wood planks of the dock, they smiled at each other, then grew quiet.

Theron leaned against a piling and wrapped his arm around Nicole, pulling her to him, sighing deeply. "Well, I can't put this off any longer," he commented reluctantly. "I told Jenny that she could go ahead with a training program. What exactly are we looking at?"

"It isn't going to be easy for you, Theron." A profound sense of sadness wrapped around her heart.

"I know it isn't," he said quietly, adding, "Things seem to have gotten completely out of my control today, and I'm not sure that I like any of it, but what the hell choice do I have?"

Nicole froze. There it was again. The intensity, the finality in his voice. That nagging sense of impending doom. Of loss. She swallowed, and began to outline Jenny's future: ballet and gymnastics for at least another year, training sessions at the winter quarters every day after school, spending summers traveling with the show, training, always training.

"At least I'll have her home for a while yet." Theron stared over the water, frowning. "But for how long, Nicole? How long before I pack her bags and lose her for a season?"

"You saw her potential," Nicole replied evasively, unwilling to throw everything at him at once.

"You didn't answer my question."

"It depends on her progress," she told him, and when he turned insistent eyes on her, she averted hers and laced her fingers together. "Probably within the next eighteen months. Two years at the outside."

Theron thought about that, a dull ache growing in the pit of his stomach. Two years would put Jenny on the road roughly at the age of twelve. Still far too young, he reasoned, but what was he to do? Hold back his talented daughter?

"Damn it, sometimes I wish I'd never heard of Circus Royale or the trapeze or any of the rest of it," he muttered tersely, and rising, he walked to the edge of the dock. Standing with his back to her, he gazed at the stars, and only after a very long time did he turn back to her. "Who exactly is going to raise my daughter, Nicole? What about school? What happens when she's a teenager and falls in love for the first time? Who in the hell is going to be there for her? To dry her tears and laugh with her? And who's going to take responsibility for her moral development?" he demanded. "I need to have some answers!"

Her heart lurched. "Jenny will be staying either with me or with my parents. Whichever you prefer. Mom and Dad are wonderful people, Theron. They'll love Jenny and care for her as if she were one of their own. My mother is a fabulous tutor. It might take Jenny a few months longer to graduate than it would if she were on the outside, but education is a top priority." The anguish in his eyes brought tears to hers. Wanting to do something to make it easier for him, she rose and went to him. Placing her hands on his chest, she felt his heat surge through her. "She'll be surrounded by people who love her. And Dad's a real stickler when it comes to dating. He'll probably give Jenny the same advice that he gave me when I was growing up."

"What was that?"

"Never date a townie."

"A what?"

"Someone who's not a part of the circus life."

Theron looked at her for a long, quiet moment. "You should have listened to him," he observed, and uneasiness rolled through Nicole. He sighed. "I do trust you and your parents. I guess this whole mess is just going to take some getting used to." Another pause. "What will happen with you now? And Rossles?"

"Oh, God, Theron, I don't know. Everything is so mixed up," she admitted softly. "One minute I can't wait to get back to work and the next..." Her eyes were moist when they met his. "...I don't want to leave here. This is *home*! Everything I love is here. The idea of leaving it all behind, of packing Rossles away in a musty, old trunk..." Her voice trailed off, and she drew in a shaky breath. "Things used to be so simple. My goals. My life. Now, I feel as if I'm being pulled apart, and I'm not sure what to do about it."

He gazed upon her with eyes that were dark, then pulled her roughly into his arms. "Oh, hell, maybe we should get married right now and forget about all this other nonsense."

Surprised, her heart somersaulted, and she stared at him, not completely sure that her ears hadn't deceived her. Her knees turned to jelly, and she wondered what her answer would be if he did propose to her. She loved him more than she'd ever dreamed it was possible to love a man, but she loved performing, as well. If only there were some way of having both. Knowing it wasn't possible, she feared the reality of having to choose between Theron and her career.

"Nicole—"

"No, Theron, please...no more talking tonight." Winding her arms around his neck, she kissed him. "Make love with me."

A husky groan rumbled through his chest as she traced the outline of his lips with her tongue. Her hands dipped into his hair. Her body strained against his, knowing exactly the right moves to light the flames of desire. Oh, but she'd learned him well, he thought, feeling the ache of need flare in his loins.

Tangling his hands in her hair, he claimed her mouth urgently, deeply. "Let's go home."

Home had become the intimacy of the gatehouse, and it was there that they went. There'd be no fire on the hearth tonight. There'd be no laughter, no conversation. There'd be nothing but touching and holding and loving, with a slow, savoring deliberation, each of them lingering over the other as if imprinting every sensation, every contour and curve, every hard angle and corded muscle, on their minds forever.

They were trembling as they removed each other's clothing. They stood quietly, moonlight streaming over their bodies, afraid to move, afraid to breathe, afraid the night would pass too quickly.

They loved silently, touching each other with a warm look, a light touch. Mouths tenderly tasted, lingered. Hearts pounded. Bodies yearned for the closeness the final contact would bring, yet they held back, as an odd sense of finality gripped them both with a heart-wrenching force that was unbearable to face.

Theron gently lowered her onto the bed, drinking in the sight of her lying there, her honey-blond hair fanned over the pillow, her luscious body bathed in silver moonlight. His jaw clenched. He swallowed and let out a sigh, wishing it could be different for them, wishing he could make her his for life.

Nicole accepted his weight willingly, lovingly, adoring the feel of his body pressed close to hers. Oh, God, don't let this be the last time, she pleaded silently, wanting him desperately, never wanting to lose him.

But she had him now, tonight, and he was loving her quietly, thoroughly, powerfully. She responded with body, soul and mind, knowing that the memory of this night would stay in her heart for the rest of her life, no matter what happened.

Slowly he took her, stopping now and again to prolong the moment, until, unable to hold back any longer, he filled himself with her, and they found release together. Clutching her close, he held her as if he never wanted to let her go.

It was a long time before he raised his head to gaze upon her. When he did, he saw tears roll down her cheeks to disappear in her thick, tangled hair. Tenderly, wordlessly, he brushed them away, kissed her, then drew her into his arms, where he held her long into the night, long after she fell asleep.

Lying there, indecision weighed heavily in his mind. *You have to find the strength to do this for her... If you love her, let her go.* Simone and Lawrence's words echoed heavily in his mind.

If he loved her? There wasn't a woman in the world he could love more. Letting his eyes linger on her as she slept curled next to him, her features soft and beautiful in repose, he dropped a kiss on the mouth he so adored, climbed out of bed, quietly dressed and went home, his heart aching.

Chapter Twelve

Nicole wakened slowly, savoring the cozy warmth of her bed and the feeling of contentment that coursed through her. Stretching lazily, she burrowed her head deep into the pillow that still bore Theron's musky, enticing scent, aching to reach out and find him there, aching to love him again as she had so many times before. But he was gone.

Gone. The word pounded forebodingly through her drowsy mind, and a vague sense of uneasiness stalked her. Though she tried to banish the feeling, vivid memories of the previous day held her fast: the pride and sadness in Theron's eyes when she'd come down from the trapeze, his quiet intensity, his comment about marriage, and the strong sense of finality when, later, they made love.

Sighing, she crawled out of bed and showered, hoping that the niggle of apprehension was nothing more than the working of an overactive imagination or, maybe, the result of the changes they faced because of yesterday's triumphs.

Surely they'd be able to work through these problems together, to find solutions, she reasoned as she dressed for riding and left the house, her Doberman close at her heels. The love between them was strong and binding. But was it strong enough to weather this storm? She shivered, wondering again what her answer would be if he did ask her to marry him? There was nothing that she wanted more than to belong to him. Except performing, she amended silently, miserably, as she walked to her car. Oh, Lord, there *had* to be a solution somewhere! There simply had to be a way of combining life-styles! Somehow. Some way! Even if it meant giving up a portion of what they wanted.

Yet, even as the thought skittered through her mind, she realized how absurd it was. Who would give up what? Certainly Theron wouldn't leave his children. Nor could she ask that of him. That left her, and while the pull to stay with him was strong, so was the pull to perform again.

One thought cheered her up as she climbed into her car and sped toward the estate and the barn. Time was on their side. They had two months in which to make a decision of any kind regarding the future. With that thought firmly entrenched in her mind, she parked, walked into the barn, and collided smartly with Julie.

"Oops, I didn't see you," Julie apologized. "You're early."

"I thought I'd spend a little time with Pockets before we ride," Nicole told the girl, wondering if Julie would ever warm to her. Going to her horse's stall, she stroked the animal's silky neck and smiled at Julie who was busy grooming the big gray mare in the adjoining stall. "What about you? What brings you down here so early?"

"I haven't had much of a chance to do anything with Cantata since I got down here." Julie stood on tiptoes to brush the rump of the horse. "Besides, Dad's not in a very good mood today, so I got out of the house pretty fast."

"Oh?" Nicole glanced up curiously.

"Yeah. I hate it when he gets like this."

"Like what, Julie?" Nicole asked as she slipped a halter on Pockets.

Julie shrugged. "Cranky. Like he's going to bite off our heads if we do the least little thing wrong."

"Well, honey, everyone gets in a bad mood once in a while. Even your dad," Nicole replied, her eyes steady on the girl. "Sometimes it's best to do what you did. Just kind of move out of the way until it blows over."

"Don't tell me about my father, Nicole. You don't know anything about him! It's your fault that he's in this mood!" Julie whirled around and glared at Nicole. "And don't try to tell me what to do! You're not my mother!"

Stunned, Nicole gaped at her. "I wasn't telling you what to do, and I'm not trying to be a mother to you, Julie."

"Oh, no?" the girl challenged defiantly. "I saw you and Dad on the dock last night! I know what you're trying to do, and it won't work! My dad loved my mother and he's *never* going to get married again!" The words burst from her in an angry torrent. "He has Rusty and Jenny and me! He doesn't need anyone else! Not you, not *anyone*!" Tears welled in her eyes. "I will be so glad when the show leaves in March and you finally leave us alone!"

Nicole reeled against the attack, feeling as if someone had dealt her a physical blow that stripped the air from her lungs. It took a moment to digest all that Julie had hurled out, and it was only with a great deal of effort that Nicole was able to walk to the partition separating them.

"You are worrying about something that isn't going to happen, Julie," she said in a moderately calm voice, the words tearing through her.

"What do you mean?" Julie demanded.

"Your father and I aren't going to get married." Sadness wound around Nicole's heart as she realized the painful truth of the statement. "Hey, come on, Julie. Think about it, okay? What kind of a marriage would it be, with me gone nine months out of the year?''

"A pretty lousy one," Julie agreed, her voice softening.

"Yes, it would." Nicole took a deep breath. "But, honey, you've got to realize that one day someone is going to come along that your father may want to share his life with."

"No! My father will *never*—"

"Your father will never what, Julie?" Theron interrupted tersely, his eyes moving from his daughter to Nicole, as he approached the stalls. "Well?"

Julie's eyes, wide as saucers, shot to Nicole. Time stood still, stretched out interminably. Julie held her breath. Nicole's mind raced. Theron stood stiffly, waiting for his daughter to answer.

"Julie and I were talking about riding on the beach," Nicole said quietly, her eyes steady on the girl. "She's afraid that you won't allow her to ride over there and back, and I was just about to suggest that perhaps Tag could trailer Cantata for her." Turning to Theron, she forced a smile. "That's all."

"Are you sure that's all there is to it?" Theron demanded, looking from one to the other, knowing there was much more involved. He could tell from the panic and tears in Julie's eyes. He saw it on Nicole's pinched features, but she stood her ground.

"That's all, Theron," she said, and busied herself with grooming her horse. "Hadn't you best get Thor ready?"

"Thanks," Julie whispered, as she and Nicole led their mounts out of the barn a half an hour later.

Nicole turned to her. "I will not do that for you again, Julie. And I want you to think about what I said."

Julie swallowed. "I will, Nicole. Promise."

"That's all I ask. Your father has just as much right to be happy as anyone else. Now, do you need a leg up?" she offered, and when Julie nodded, Nicole cupped her hands together and helped the girl mount the seventeen-hand horse.

Seconds later, Theron, Rusty and Jenny joined them, and they rode away from the barn. Though the morning was cool and fresh and beautiful, a strange tension, thick and oppressive, hung over them. A tension so heavy that not even the friendly squeaking of leather or the muffled sound of horses' hooves on the turf could alleviate it. The children bickered amongst themselves more than usual, then fell into complete silence, with Julie riding ahead, Rusty flanking his father and Jenny crowding her horse close to Nicole.

Nicole glanced uneasily at Theron, her heart heavy. Tired and haggard, he looked as if the weight of the world had dropped on his shoulders. His brow was deeply furrowed. The lines bracketing his mouth were more pronounced than she'd seen in a long time. His eyes were clouded, distant. He listened to Jenny's chatter about the circus and trapeze, but Nicole thought it was only with half an ear, for he seemed greatly preoccupied.

"Hey, Dad," Rusty said, breaking a long silent spell. "I think I've figured out a way to solve the drum problem."

"The problem is already solved," Theron replied.

"But—"

"It's not open for discussion, son. If you want to practice your drums, then you'll do it early in the evening."

"But—"

"That's enough, Russell," Theron interrupted tersely. "It isn't up for debate. You know the rules for the practice sessions. Now then, you can either adhere to them, or we'll dismantle the set. Is that clear?"

"Yes, sir," Rusty told him, and after they'd ridden a short distance farther, he spoke again. "Dad, can we go back? I don't feel much like riding today."

"Neither do I," Julie agreed.

"I do," Jenny piped up.

"Then ride alone, twirp. I'm so sick of hearing about the trapeze, I could throw up," Rusty countered. "That's all you've talked about this morning."

"Leave her alone, Rusty! She's got a right to be excited!" Julie defended in a burst of sisterly love. "You're just mad cuz of your drums, and cuz Dad made you turn down your stereo this morning."

"He probably wouldn't've even heard it if you hadn't gone blabbing to him. It wasn't on that loud!" Rusty shook his head. "Jeez, sisters!"

"Shut up, Rusty," Jenny tossed out indignantly.

Nicole watched as Theron reined in Thor and rounded on his children. "Enough! I am thoroughly fed up with the three of you being at each others' throats! You started the minute you got up this morning, and it hasn't let up since," he clipped, his patience wearing thin. "If you can't speak civilly to each other, then I don't want to hear another word from any of you. Do you understand?" He looked at each of them in turn, and when they nodded, he relaxed in the saddle again. "Good. I'm glad we agree on that, because if I hear one more dig or jab, you'll spend the rest of the day in your rooms." He paused. "If you want to, go on back to the house. Nicole and I will be along in a little while."

"Hey, why don't we watch the new video Nicole's parents gave me for Christmas?" Jenny suggested, and the three children turned their mounts toward home. Laughing, they rode away leaving Theron and Nicole alone.

"Amazing!" Theron grinned as he watched them. "Five minutes ago they were ready to kill each other."

Thinking of her own childhood, Nicole smiled. "They'll probably commiserate with each other all the way home, then start bickering again. Only they'll do it out of earshot, so they won't end up grounded."

"You're absolutely right," he agreed. Turning his gaze on her, he wished to God he didn't have to face what lay ahead. "Why don't we rest for a few minutes?"

Something in his eyes and manner caused Nicole's heart to lurch. Her mouth went dry. She watched as he dismounted and looped Thor's reins around the branch of a scrub oak. That done, he walked over to stand next to her horse.

"I'm not tired," she said softly.

"We have to talk, Nicole. Now. It can't wait." His tone had grown serious and deep, his eyes somber and intent.

Nicole wasn't at all sure that she wanted to hear what he had to say. Not now. Not this afternoon. *Not ever.* "Does this have to do with Julie or Jenny?"

"It's about us," he said, trying to find the words that would make this as easy as possible on both of them, when, in fact, it was killing him. But he had no other choice. He'd sat up for hours last night after leaving her, trying to find a solution to their love, to their lives. There was none to be had. "I'm leaving for New York in the morning."

She slipped off her horse and tied the animal next to Thor. Warily, she looked at Theron. "For how long?"

"A few days. I'll spend New Year's Eve with Shelly and Joe, and fly back on the first."

"What about the kids?"

"Rusty and Julie can come with me if they'd like. Jenny will be staying here. She's anxious to start training," he told her. "Gladys will be taking care of her, but I thought perhaps she could ride to and from the winter quarters with you. If you don't mind, that is?"

"No...no, of course I don't mind." Her voice sounded strained, small. "You said this was about us."

He was silent for a long moment, cursing the fates for having brought them together, then leaving them stranded with no place to go, with no future. One more heartbreak, he thought. One more damned heartbreak.

"It's not going to work between us, Nicole," he said finally, the stricken expression on her features ripping through him.

"I don't understand," she whispered, the color vanishing from her world. The hard blue of the sky faded to milky white. The sun lost its brilliance. Life stopped in that one numbing instant, as all her fears turned into brutal reality.

"It's over," he said simply.

"No, Theron . . . please . . ." Tears sprang to her eyes.

He sighed. "As far as you staying in the gatehouse, it's yours, whether you're here for the winter or on the road. There's no reason for you to have to move." The words sounded empty, wooden. "Pockets can stay where she is. She'll be well cared for. As for Luke, confining him to the train wouldn't be fair after he's had two years of freedom."

Dumbfounded, Nicole stared at him for a long moment before turning away to look over a beautiful landscape that had suddenly turned bleak and barren. Last night he'd mentioned marriage. Now he was talking of ending the relationship? She couldn't help but shiver at the calm, organized manner in which he was breaking her heart.

"You seem to have thought this through very carefully," she observed, then whirled around to face him. "And what about me? What about how I feel? What if I told you I don't *want* this to happen, Theron? That I might not go back on the road?"

"Damn it, Nicole, I want that more than anything, and if I thought for a minute that you meant it, that you'd be happy, we wouldn't be having this conversation!" he countered. "But I can't let you do it!"

"Why?" she whispered, searching his eyes for the answers she so desperately needed. "I *love* you, Theron!"

"I know you do, Nicole, and I love you! That's what's making this so hard! I don't want to lose you, but what the hell kind of life would we have with you gone for months at a time?" Frustration laced his words. "I would like nothing more than having you with me from now into eternity, but it isn't going to happen. Can't you see that?'' His eyes were clouded with pain. ''How the hell do you think I'd feel a month or a year down the road, knowing that I'd held you back from doing something you love? And don't you dare try to tell me you wouldn't miss performing! I know how hard you've worked in order to fly again! I've seen the joy on your face when you're up there! I hear the excitement in your voice when you talk about it! It's where you belong.''

''Is it?'' she asked tremulously.

''You know it is.'' Going to her, he wrapped his arms around her and pulled her close. ''If you're honest with yourself, you'll know I'm right.''

They stood quietly, bound by the enormity of the situation, both loving, both regretting, both mourning the loss of their love.

Nicole stood in the circle of his arms, wondering if, perhaps, he was right. Hadn't she feared this from the very beginning? Yet she'd pushed reality far from her mind and had hoped against hope that they could find a way to make the impossible possible. Her heart rejected the idea of losing him.

''Oh, God, I don't want this to happen!'' she cried softly, feeling his hard, warm strength against her, wondering how she would ever survive without him.

''And you think I do?''

''I don't know. I think if we tried, we could find a way of making this work!''

''How? Can you tell me that?'' he demanded. ''We don't have a choice, Nicole. We're moving in two different directions. I can't be a part of your life any more than you can be a part of mine,'' he told her, a great ache growing inside. ''Oh, hell, we both know the best we can hope for is salvaging the friendship when you come off the road. And we've damn well got to do that, for Jenny's sake.'' A heavy sigh tore from him. ''When she joins the show, I'm naming you her legal guardian.''

Nicole trembled in his arms. Oh, dear Lord, she'd have the daughter but not the father. "I'm not sure I can handle that."

"You're going to have to. I'm not turning her over to anyone else, Nicole."

Her world collapsing, she looked up at him, tears shimmering in her eyes. "It really is over, isn't it?" The statement hung between them.

"I'm sorry." A muscle in his jaw jumped as he gazed upon the woman he loved with heart and soul.

"There's nothing we can do?"

"I wish there were. You've given me so much. I'll never forget that." He brushed a tendril of hair away from her face, wondering if he'd ever be able to shake the overwhelming sense of grief that cinched his heart. "Our needs are different. I want—*need*—a wife, Nicole. A woman who's going to be there for me. A woman the kids can depend on." Seeing her shattered expression, he added, "I need those things in the same way you need a man who can share your life on the road. We can't change who we are. No matter how much we'd like to, we just can't do it."

Because he needed one last taste of her, he lowered his head and kissed her lightly. Because he desired so much more, he turned suddenly and strode to his horse, swinging easily into the saddle.

"I'll be making regular trips to New York during the next few months. When I am home, I'll be tied up with *Images*," he said. "But I'll be sure to make the financial arrangements for Jenny before I leave. If she needs anything at all your father can call me." He paused. "I'll tell Jenny that we've decided to hold off on her workout program until tomorrow."

"Thank you," Nicole replied numbly.

He looked on her one last time. "Take care of yourself, funny face."

"You, too," she whispered through the tightness in her throat, but he was already gone, already cantering across the clearing. Through eyes blurred with tears, she watched the man on the powerful black gelding disappear among the pine trees.

Moments later, Nicole vaulted onto the back of her horse, glad that she'd chosen to ride bareback this morning. Kicking the mare into a canter, she turned away from the house and leaning low over the animal's neck, she cried, her tears lost in the wind-whipped mane blowing across her face.

It was well past eleven that night when Theron heard the door to his study open. Looking up, he saw Julie's silhouette in the opening.

"What are you doing up so late?" he asked, taking a long pull on his pipe.

"I couldn't sleep." She stood stock-still. "Why are you sitting in the dark?"

"I guess because I've got a lot on my mind."

"Can I come in?" she asked hesitantly.

"Of course you can." Reaching out, Theron turned on the lamp on the end table next to the leather couch and motioned his daughter over to him. Studying her, he saw that she was troubled. "What's the matter, Julie?"

She sat down next to him. "Nicole."

"What about Nicole?" he asked quietly.

"She didn't come back from riding until this afternoon, and she looked awful, Dad. Like she'd been crying," Julie said, her lip quivering. "And you've been really sad today. What happened? Did you get in a fight?"

Theron leaned forward and rested his forearms on his knees. Lowering his head, he closed his eyes a moment, his heart wrenching. When he looked at his daughter, his eyes were filled with pain. He reached out and took her small hand in his.

"Nicole and I won't be seeing each other anymore," he said.

Julie's eyes widened in alarm. "Because of me?"

"No, angel, not because of you." He smiled at her. "Nicole and I are...different. She's a performer, and she needs to have the freedom to pursue her career without feeling guilty about leaving us. It's best that we handle it this way."

"You really love her, don't you, Daddy?" Big tears trembled on Julie's lashes.

"Yes, honey, I do."

"Were you going to marry her?"

"I wanted that very much, Julie," he told her. "Now, then, if you're going to be up and ready to go in the morning, hadn't you best get some sleep?"

Julie fidgeted, and turned wide blue-green eyes on her father. "Would you be mad if I stayed here instead of going to New York with you?"

"No, of course not, but I'd like to know what changed your mind."

"Rusty and I talked about it, and we both want to stay here—just in case someone needs us," she said softly, and Theron watched her lower her eyes and chew on her lower lip, a sure sign that she felt guilty about something.

"I see," he said thoughtfully. "Does this have anything to do with Nicole?"

"Kind of," she admitted. "I made her feel bad this morning, and now I kind of feel awful about it."

"Then maybe you should talk to her in the morning," Theron suggested.

"I will. I'm going to bed now." Julie kissed his cheek. "Thanks, Daddy. I love you."

"I love you, too, angel." He watched as Julie left the room, thinking it ironic that his daughter should accept Nicole now—when it was too late.

Leaning back on the couch, he relit his pipe, knowing that he should go to bed, as well. But it was going to be a long time before he enjoyed a peaceful night's sleep.

Nicole stood in the middle of her living room and looked around, her emotions in turmoil. Where, she wondered, had the past two months gone? They'd seemingly flown by, and here it was, March, and she was ready to board the train for a new season on the road. Most of her belongings were already in her stateroom on the train, the last of her luggage was stacked by the front door of the cottage, and any minute Tag, Gladys, Rusty, Julie and Jenny would arrive to drive her to the winter quarters. Within a few hours, the train would pull out of Jacksonville.

In one way, she was happy to finally be leaving, for the strain of living close to Theron had taken its toll. Her only salvation had been a workload that kept her busy from dawn to midnight, and the way the Donahue children had rallied around her, and the fact that Theron had been true to his word, spending much of his time either in New York or locked in his study, working. Had she run into him constantly, she couldn't have survived.

While the days were relatively free of pain, the nights were the opposite. They were long, lonely times, when she tossed restlessly while thoughts of Theron ran up and down her mind. They were the times when she ached to feel his warm embrace, to taste his kiss, to fly with him.

She sighed. Whoever it was who said time heals all wounds didn't know what the hell he was talking about. The only thing time did was numb one's heart enough to allow for a dull acceptance of something one hadn't wanted to happen in the first place.

Maybe being out of this house and living on the train would make things easier. Maybe she'd find a way to heal the pain in her heart and get on with her life. After all, wasn't she embarking on a dream? Wasn't this what she'd longed for, what she'd worked so terribly hard for during the past two years? So why had some of the gloss worn off? Where was the excitement?

Hearing a car horn outside, she took one last look around, then opened the door for Tag. Within minutes, her luggage was loaded into the back of Gladys's station wagon and they were driving away, the children chattering non-stop, Luke sitting in the back, Tag assuring Nicole that he'd look after her horse, dog, plants and house.

Only Theron was missing. But he was in New York, and Nicole knew there'd be no hope of seeing him until June—when he accompanied Jenny to Seattle, where they'd meet the show. Perhaps it was for the best that he was gone, she mused, but her heart ached, nevertheless, for one last glimpse of him. June seemed a lifetime away.

At the winter quarters, excitement charged the air as last-minute preparations were made for the train's departure. All around them, people milled and bustled about as they loaded the last of their luggage aboard the Pullman cars. Farther back, animals were led into specially equipped boxcars. Laughter rang out. Anticipation and impatience and excitement were the order of the day as the performers and crew waited for the final boarding call. Circus Royale was ready to pull out for another season on the road.

Standing near her car, Nicole turned to the friends she loved so dearly, and amidst a barrage of hugs and kisses and tears, she bade goodbye to each of them before turning to board the train on legs that were shaky, then suddenly felt like jelly as she heard a familiar voice call out her name.

"Nicole!"

Stunned, she turned around and saw Theron running toward her, the wind whipping his hair, tearing at the front of his tan cashmere topcoat. Her heart slammed against her ribs when he stopped in front of her.

"I thought you were in New York," she whispered, drinking in the glorious sight of him.

"I was. I caught a flight out this morning. The damned thing was late." He touched her cheek lightly. "I don't think there's a traffic law on the books that I didn't break between the airport and here, but there's something I want you to have," he said and handed her a box.

"What is it?"

"You'll see," he told her, gazing at her intently.

From somewhere in the distance, Nicole thought she heard the final boarding call, but she couldn't be sure, for he suddenly pulled her into his arms and lowered his head to her, kissing her soundly, thoroughly. In his arms, she felt safe. In his kiss, she felt desire and...love. In her heart, she felt a great sense of loss.

Releasing her again, he smiled wearily. "You'd best get on board or they're going to leave without their star performer," he said gruffly. "Good luck, funny face."

As she boarded, Nicole turned back for one last glimpse of the people she loved, but it was Theron's expression that she'd never forget, for she thought his eyes were wet. Still, it could have been merely a reflection of the tears that were streaming from hers.

In her stateroom, Nicole opened the box Theron had given her. Inside she found a leather-bound copy of *Images*. Running her hand over the soft, smooth leather, she opened it and read the dedication: "For Nicole, who gave me so much."

"Oh, God, I love him," she cried, tears running down her cheeks, and as the train pulled out of Jacksonville and headed west, Nicole Ross clutched the manuscript to her breast and cried herself to sleep, her dreams haunted by the face of the only man she'd ever love—a man she couldn't have.

Chapter Thirteen

As Circus Royale moved from New Orleans to Houston and Dallas, then crossed the beautiful desert southwest en route to Los Angeles and San Francisco, March slid into April, then May, and, finally, June.

Shortly before one in the morning on the first Monday in June, as the train rumbled along the tracks south of Eugene, Oregon, Nicole tossed restlessly in her bed, wishing the soothing motion and sounds would lull her to sleep. But it wasn't going to happen. Not yet, for too many emotions roiled inside of her, too many doubts and fears and apprehensions. And excitement, she admitted, listening as a long, wailing blast from the whistle sounded a warning at a country intersection.

What would the morrow bring? she wondered. Theron and Jenny were due to meet the show in Seattle sometime during the day. Exactly when, she wasn't sure. Theron had scrawled a short note to her, stating the date of their arrival but not the time. *We've all missed you. See you soon,* he'd written, then added the words that threw her into turmoil. *I love you, Nicole. We have to talk.*

Shivering, she pulled the covers up to her chin and stared into the darkness, thinking it ironic how his hint at reconciliation had filled her with sadness rather than joy. But he'd been right that day in the glade when he'd ended their affair, hadn't he? She'd reluctantly accepted the pain in her heart as her constant companion, simply because she knew that he and the children needed a woman—a wife, a mother—on a full-time basis. Though his words had hurt her, they'd come as no surprise. Not really. It was exactly what she'd feared from the very beginning.

But she understood something else, as well. As soon as the show returned to Jacksonville for the winter, she was going to move out of the gatehouse. She had no choice, for while their love was doomed, she could no more sit by and watch Theron find and fall in love with another woman than she could throw herself in front of a train.

I love you, Nicole. We have to talk. His words pounded through her mind. But love couldn't work for them, she agonized. The only connection between them now was Jenny. Unshed tears stinging her eyes, she rolled over, clutched her pillow, and slept fitfully, Theron's image haunting her dreams.

Theron sat at the kitchen table next to Tag, watching his three bleary-eyed children stumble into the breakfast nook and slump into their chairs. Glancing at his watch, he grinned. It was four a.m. It'd only taken him half an hour to get them up and ride herd over them until they were dressed. All that remained now was keeping them awake long enough to eat the breakfast of bacon, eggs and hash browns Gladys had insisted on preparing.

Jenny was the only one displaying signs of life. "What time are we leaving, Daddy?" she asked as she gulped down a glass of orange juice.

"As soon as we finish breakfast," Theron replied, leaning back to allow Gladys room to set the platters of food on the table. Tag, Jenny and Theron dug in. Julie and Rusty eyed the food distastefully. "Come on, kids. You've got to have something to eat."

"This is totally unnatural, Dad. It's not even daylight, yet," Julie grumbled.

"Reckon gettin' up this early is a shock to your system, heh, Julie? But your father's right. You're gonna be glad you ate this 'fore the day's out." Tag dumped two eggs and a spoonful of hash browns on the girl's plate. "There you go, heh?"

"Come on you guys! Hurry up!" Jenny exclaimed impatiently.

"You know, squirt, you're giving childhood a bad name," Rusty accused as he grabbed a piece of toast.

"I am not!" came Jenny's protest.

"Oh, yeah? Well, let me remind you that *normal* kids don't like to get up this early. Normal kids don't smile when someone shakes them out of bed at three-thirty in the morning." He shook his head. "You are *weird*!"

"I am not weird!" Jenny countered.

"Settle down. All of you," Theron ordered quietly.

"But I haven't said a word yet!" Julie protested.

"If anyone in this house is weird, Daddy, it's Rusty," Jenny pushed. "He walks around all day wearing that goofy headset, groovin' to the music, and if Julie and me don't get out of his way, he uses our heads for drums."

"Only because they're hollow." Rusty laughed.

"They are not!" Julie rounded on her brother, glaring at him when he tapped her forehead with a knuckle and made a hollow, popping sound with his mouth. She looked at Theron. "Dad!"

"Don't even start," Theron warned. "Let me remind you that you picked this flight. All three of you wanted to leave as early as possible. Now, you've got exactly twenty minutes to finish your breakfast, help Gladys clear the table and get to the car, or we're going to be late."

"Dad?"

"What, Julie?"

"Why can't we stay in Seattle a couple of days, instead of flying to New York tomorrow?"

Theron frowned. "Because I have a production meeting for *Images* and because Aunt Shel is expecting you tomorrow."

"Aunt Shel would understand if we stayed in Seattle a while. Especially if you and Nicole got married," Julie said, and the room fell silent with five pairs of eyes turning to Theron.

"Where, in heaven's name, did that come from?" Astounded, Theron stared at his daughter.

"Oh, honestly, Dad! I'm almost fourteen. A woman knows these things," Julie replied indignantly. "Besides, you told me you wanted to marry her."

"It's not that simple, Julie," Theron told her, a smile tugging his mouth. *A woman knows these things*? He shook his head. Hell, she was right. Marriage was exactly what he intended on proposing to Nicole—if she'd listen to him.

"We're going to the Space Needle tonight, aren't we, Daddy?" Jenny asked.

"Yes. Lawrence is making our dinner reservations." Theron pushed away from the table. "Get a move on it, kids. It's almost time to go."

An hour and a half later, when their flight was called, Theron dropped a kiss on Gladys's forehead and firmly gripped Tag's hand. "I want both of you to take some time off while we're gone."

"Yup, reckon you can count on that," Tag said. "Good luck to you, son. I hope everything works out 'tween you and little Nikki."

"So do I, Tag. So do I." If it did, it would put an end to the unspeakable loneliness Theron had lived with for the past five months. If not . . . it would be the beginning of a lifetime of hell, he thought, as he ushered the children along the ramp to the plane.

"Dad, Nicole won't mind that Rusty and I are coming, too, will she?" Julie asked, as she settled back in her seat and buckled the seat belt.

"No, angel, it'll be a nice surprise for her. She loves all of you very much," he assured Julie. That Nicole cared deeply for the children had been clearly evident in the stream of postcards and letters coming in from the various cities in which the show had appeared. And, of course, she'd kept up a constant dialogue with Ralph regarding Jenny's progress in training.

What he couldn't anticipate were her feelings toward him, and the thought that he'd lost her love tore through him. Frowning, he looked out the window, absently watching as the jet rolled away from the terminal, lumbered to takeoff position, then roared down the runway and left the ground.

The first leg of the journey had begun. What lay ahead? he wondered, silently praying that she'd be willing to listen to him, that it wasn't too late for them.

He missed her. He needed her. And, oh, God, how he loved her! So much that he was sure, no matter what obstacles cluttered their path, they could work through them together—if she could forgive him the terrible mistake he'd made when, thinking there was no alternative, he'd set her free to pursue her dreams unencumbered by complications.

The love had been very much alive when the train pulled out in March. He'd seen it in her eyes, felt it in her kiss. It had hit him so hard that there'd been a wild moment when he'd been tempted to pick her up and take her home, or climb onto the train with her—anything not to lose her.

But that was in March. Three months ago. And, while he had reason to suspect that she was as miserable as he, there was the very real possibility that she'd turn him away. He fervently hoped that wouldn't be the case, but if it was, he had no one to blame but himself.

The moment the train rolled to a stop at the King Street Station in Seattle for its two-week stay, a flurry of activity began, as nearly two hundred performers, animal trainers, handlers and workhands prepared costumes, equipment and animals for the move to the Coliseum a few miles away.

In her stateroom in Car Twenty-nine, Nicole dragged out a trunk filled with costumes and makeup and pulled it to the door. Suddenly someone knocked. Her heart in her throat, she moved toward the door. Oh, God! Theron? Already? Wide-eyed, her mouth bone-dry, she took a deep breath and closed her hand over the latch. Panic swept through her, then excitement, then disappointment as she pulled it open.

"Oh, it's you," she said when seeing her oldest brother.

"Good morning to you, too." David laughed.

"Sorry, I seem to be a little on edge today."

"Today? You've been looking over your shoulder for the past week, Nick. Ever since you got the letter from Theron," David commented. "What are you going to do if he wants to get back together with you?"

Nicole looked up at the tall, dark-haired, green-eyed hunk of a man who was her brother, and sighed. "Why would he do that? Nothing's changed. It's over, David."

"I don't buy that for a minute, and neither do you," he told her. "I saw the two of you together before you split, remember? When you were both happy? But afterward, God, I don't think I've ever seen two more miserable people in my life!" He paused. "He loves you. You love him. Isn't that what really matters?"

Her shoulders sagged. "Oh, David, sometimes all the love in the world doesn't help."

"How do you know that unless you try?" he countered, shaking his head. "I don't understand this at all. Here I am—twenty-eight—and looking forward to the day when that special someone walks into my life, and when she does, I don't care if she's a townie or with the show. I'll fight through hell and back to make it work, because in the end, Nick, it's the relationship that counts." His eyes swept the plush stateroom. "All of this is nothing more than temporary trappings. We won't be in the spotlight forever, and you sure as hell can't take the trapeze and rings to bed with you at night and expect them to keep you warm."

"And what exactly are you going to do, David, if your special someone has three kids, a stable home and a mortgage?" Nicole demanded. "Are you going to tear her away from that home to follow you around the country? Or are you planning to kiss her goodbye, tell the kids to be good, and live separate lives for nine months?" She let out a deep breath. "That's *not* what love and marriage are about—in case you hadn't noticed!"

"There's got to be a solution, Nick!" he persisted. "Maybe you and Theron just haven't looked hard enough."

"There isn't. So drop it, okay?"

"I'm not trying to badger you, sis. But I love you, and I hate to see you hurting like this." His voice softened. "Please, just think about what I said."

"Hey, you guys, what's the holdup? We're ready to go!" Cherie bounded into the room, followed closely by Adam. "Jeez, it's going to take all day to set up if you don't move it!"

"We're coming," Nicole told Cherie, then turned back to David. "I'll think about it."

She had no choice but to think about David's words. They hammered through her mind during the ride through the sun-washed day to the Coliseum. They plagued her until she thought she might go crazy, as she and her family carried in costumes and equipment and began setting up—David and Nicole working on her Roman rings, while Gabe, Adam, Margo and Cherie unpacked coils of guy wires, ropes and pulley blocks for the trapeze rigging and Simone unpacked and hung costumes in their dressing rooms.

What if David was right? What if Theron wanted to put the relationship back on track again? But how would that be possible, when she faced six more months on the road? she wondered as she climbed the rope to her rings and took a couple of practice swings high over what would become center ring. Satisfied with the tension of the rings, she slid down the rope again and moved to help with the trapeze rigging, while a stream of *what-if's* stalked her.

But she was absolutely sure of one thing, she discovered with a jolt. Sensing someone watching her, she looked over her shoulder and saw Theron standing on the sidelines, out of the way of the organized chaos that marked set-up day. There was no doubt in Nicole's mind that it would be a very long time before she could ever think of him as a friend in the platonic sense.

Her heart whapped against her ribs, her mouth went dry, her hands turned clammy. She stared at him, all resolve and bravado slipping away, and for a moment, she felt as if she were in a tailspin.

Lord, but he cut a handsome figure, standing there tall and proud, his blue-green eyes steady on her. Memories scorched her mind. Memories of lovemaking, of sharing laughter and dreams and long, intimate conversations. Memories of the way he'd once smiled at her, held her, comforted her. All of it came rushing back, swirling around her, overwhelming her.

Oh, God, what now? She wanted to run to him, away from him. But he'd said she had courage, and if ever there was a time to live up to that, it was now. Feeling as if she might collapse in a heap on the canvas-covered floor, she walked slowly toward him, toward the center of her universe.

"Hi," she said as she ducked under a guy wire to stand in front of him. Damn, why did she have to sound so breathless?

"Hi, yourself," he replied, his gaze intent upon her.

"Where's Jenny?" Soft. Her voice was so soft it was almost inaudible.

"With Lawrence." He placed a warm, strong hand on her cheek, his heart thudding heavily when she closed her eyes and a single tear rolled into his palm. Love welling in him, needing to hold her, he pulled her into his arms and cradled her close. Burying his face in her wealth of hair, he felt her body mold to his and her arms go around his neck. "I've missed you, Nicole. More than words can say."

She knew he meant it. She felt it in his embrace, heard the ragged emotion in his voice. Unwilling to let go of him, she held him tightly. "I've missed you, too, Theron," she whispered against his neck, then raising her head, she looked at him and smiled hesitantly. "I guess it's going to take a while to get over some of the feelings."

"We have to talk about that, Nicole." He studied her for a long time, looking into her heart and soul, in search of the love she'd once given so freely. What he found was caution and wariness, but there was a softness, as well; an expectancy that gave him hope.

"The last time you wanted to talk, I didn't particularly like what you had to say," she reminded him.

"I made a mistake. A terrible mistake," he admitted. "And I've paid dearly for it, but I thought at the time that it was the only solution—one that was right for both of us. I was wrong."

"No, Theron. You weren't," she said, tears shimmering in her eyes. "It was the only thing you could have done."

"Was it, Nicole?" He looked doubtful. "Then why do I feel like hell, day in and day out? Why is it that every day a funny-faced little clown pops into my mind, teasing me with laughter and paper roses?" He smiled when his comment prompted a little laugh from her; then his eyes turned serious again, and he wiped a tear from her cheek. "And why is it that you've spent the last three months closed up in your stateroom when you aren't working?" She shot him a questioning glance. He shrugged. "Hey, don't forget— Lawrence and I are old friends. He's been worried about you."

"Lawrence has a big mouth," she told him, lowering her eyes. Oh, Lord, the love was still there! She felt it flow strong and warm between them. But what could come of it? "All right. We can talk. How long will you be here?"

Theron let out a deep sigh of relief and felt some of the tension drain from his body. "We may leave in the morning. It depends."

"On what?"

"On us. You and me."

"But there is no us—" Alarmed, she broke off mid-sentence and stared at him. "What do you mean by *we*?"

"*We* as in Rusty, Julie and I. Jenny will be staying."

"All the kids are here? Why didn't you tell me?" she whooped, her eyes soft and shining with happiness—an expression that tangled around his heart.

"Oh...I guess I just wanted to spend a few minutes alone with you." But he wanted so much more than that. He wanted to savor the curvy body hidden beneath the tank top and frayed denim cutoffs. He wanted to feel her long, silky legs wrapped around him and hear her murmured words of love. But more than anything, Theron wanted to have her by his side for life. "Listen, Lawrence and I are taking the kids to the Space Needle tonight. Why don't you join us, and after dinner we'll have some time and privacy."

She sighed, wondering if she'd survive being alone with him, doubting it. A panicky feeling swept through her. She was doing it again—setting herself up for a heartbreak. "What time should I be ready?"

* * *

As it turned out, Nicole couldn't have begged her way out of having dinner with Theron, the kids and Lawrence, if she'd wanted to. Julie and Jenny were at her side from the moment they were reunited, the girls fussing over Nicole as she carefully dressed for the evening.

"Wow! Dad's really going to flip *out* when he sees you in that!" Julie exclaimed, when Nicole emerged in a simple strapless, knee-length creation with deep rose-and-green flowers on a white background. "If that doesn't put him in a good mood, nothing will!"

Buoyed by the presence of the children, Nicole felt relaxed and happy. She smiled brightly. "You think so, huh?"

"I know so!" Julie assured her.

But what it did, apparently, was put Theron Donahue in an uncomfortably lusty mood. "You're determined not to make this easy on me, aren't you?" he muttered. His eyes swept over her—that wonderful tumble of honey-blond hair falling over her shoulders, the fullness of her soft breasts, the way the dress skimmed her luscious body, her long legs, the white pumps she wore—and an ache of desire burned in his loins.

"Not if I can help it."

His eyes were smoky and intense. "You have the kids as a buffer now, but what about later—when you find yourself alone with a man who's been sorely deprived of certain pleasures for the past five months?" His words made her swallow, made her body heat, made his voice seem far away, as he summoned his daughters out of Nicole's bedroom. "Girls, if we don't get out of here now, I might change my mind about dinner tonight!"

"Aw, Daddy, you wouldn't do that!" Jenny laughed.

Theron glanced at Nicole again. "Don't bet on it, kid," he commented dryly. "Let's go. Lawrence and Rusty are waiting."

Dinner atop the Space Needle was one of the happiest events that Nicole had experienced in months. The panoramic vista drew exclamations from adults and children alike, as the restaurant slowly revolved and the jewellike city unveiled herself: the city skyline, and to the west, Elliot Bay, which flowed into the sparkling water of Puget Sound, the jagged peaks of the Olympic Mountains, then around to Lakes Union and Washington and the Cascade Mountains; and farther south, Mount Rainier rose majestically, its snow-capped peak misty in the early twilight.

While the conversation around the table was lively and punctuated with laughter, Nicole became increasingly more aware of Theron. It seemed as if every time she looked up he was watching her, his eyes warm but so intense that they unnerved her. But she was sitting across the table from him. She was safe.

All too soon they were filing out of the restaurant, taking the elevator down, and the touching began—Theron's hand on the small of her back, on her bare shoulder, on her arm. Brief contact, high voltage. Her flesh burned. Her pulse throbbed.

It was worse when they climbed into Theron's rental car for the drive back to the train. The children, subdued and yawning, rode in the backseat, while Nicole sat between Theron and Lawrence in the front. She almost cried out when Theron shifted behind the wheel and she felt the heat of his thigh pressing against her leg. Fear and excitement washed through her when he took her hand in his and placed it palm down on his leg. Feeling the tautness of his body, the tension, she raised her eyes to his.

We're going to make love, he seemed to be saying, and her heart caromed wildly. *I know,* came her silent reply, and she looked away—quickly, before his eyes burned her.

"Well, I'm sure the two of you have plans for the rest of the evening," Lawrence said when they arrived back at the King Street Station. "If you have no objections, I'll take the kids back to my Pullman."

"You've got yourself a deal," Theron replied without hesitation, then turned to kiss the girls goodnight and clamp a hand on Rusty's shoulder. "Sleep well. I'll see you in the morning."

Nicole's knees felt like rubber as Lawrence and the children walked away, leaving her alone with Theron for the first time that day. For a moment, she wanted to bolt and run from the man whose mere presence reduced her to a quivering mass of jelly. Being alone with him was sheer madness! Yet, here she was, walking beside him to her stateroom, opening the door, entering the dark room.

"Would you like some coffee?" she asked, dismayed when her voice cracked. Needing to put some space between them, she flipped on a light, then tried to duck around him. But he caught her wrist and swung her back to face him.

"I don't want coffee," he told her, his gaze moving from her lovely features to the cleft of her breasts.

Dizzy, her senses reeling, Nicole swallowed. She'd always sensed that there was a dangerous element in Theron, one that he kept in close check. Tonight it was surfacing. She saw it in his smoldering gaze, felt it in the strength of the hand clamped around her wrist. Raw need emanated from every pore of his body, and though she knew she should run before it was too late, she stood mesmerized, desperately wanting to feel the full power of his passion.

"What, then?" she asked, her voice a whisper.

"What we've both wanted from the very beginning," he told her, desire burning through him. Watching her intently, he trailed the tip of a finger over the softness of her breasts just above the strapless top of her dress, the ache in him growing when he saw her draw in a sharp, swift, little breath. "To hold...to touch...to taste."

"It'll only make things worse when you leave, Theron," she murmured, feeling as if she were about to collapse in his arms. She saw the familiar twitch of a muscle in his jaw. His features were set with determination. His eyes raked over her, and Nicole knew instantly that his need would not be denied. The realization both thrilled and terrified her.

"We'll talk about that later," he told her, tangling his hands in her hair. "Right now, I can barely think." A husky groan rumbled in his chest. "God, but you are beautiful!"

His words swirling around her, she flew into his arms, casting aside the past, not thinking of the future. Nothing mattered but the man in whose arms she stood, the man whose mouth claimed hers urgently, insistently. Against her, his body was hot and deliciously hard. On her flesh, his hands were demanding. Holding him tightly, Nicole matched him kiss for kiss, touch for touch, desire making her tremble.

Months of repressed passion surged. Mouths clung feverishly, hands impatiently discarded clothing, then touched and stroked. Nicole took him to her bed, marveling at the feel of the body she knew and loved so well pressed close to her. Urgently, they came together, each of them greedily taking, then giving back again, needing more. Every touch, every movement crashed through their senses until finally Theron took them flying, spinning over the edge and into paradise, great shuddering waves of pleasure racking through them.

Still entwined, they fell back on the bed. Hearts pounded. Breathing was ragged. Bodies glistened with a sheen of perspiration. But when Theron tried to ease his weight off her, she held him tightly.

"No, don't move," she whispered, pressing her mouth to his damp shoulder. "I love the feel of your body. I wish it could always be like this for us."

"It can," he said, kissing her temple. A shaft of light from the living room spilled over them, and he saw the love in her eyes. "We can put an end to all this craziness and start a life together if you'll marry me. Here. In Seattle."

Her eyes flew to his. "What?"

"I love you, Nicole. I'm asking you to marry me." He kissed her tenderly. "I've been going crazy without you in my life."

"It's what you wanted," she reminded him softly.

"No, it's not what I *wanted*." He rolled onto his side, pulling her with him. "I've never wanted to be without you."

"Yes, but marriage, Theron?" Frowning, she sat up. Leaning against the headboard, she unconsciously drew the sheet up to cover bared breasts. She looked at him, her eyes moist. "Nothing has changed between us."

His stomach knotted. While he anticipated her hesitation, her withdrawal, he wasn't fully prepared for the actuality. He sat up next to her.

"Do you love me, Nicole?" he asked, and when she turned away, he cupped her cheek, forcing her eyes back to him. Seeing big tears shimmering on her lashes, his heart stopped. "Do you?"

"Yes, I love you. Sometimes so much I think I might die if I can't see you," she admitted, a profound sadness winding around her heart. "But we're still the same people we were five months ago. Our lives are still moving in different directions. Look at us, Theron! You and the kids in Florida, and me nomading it around the country? What kind of a marriage could we possibly have?"

"One that's based on love."

"That's not enough for us!" If only it could be, she thought. "Maybe it would be different if I was ready to leave the show, but I'm not."

"Sweetheart, I'm not asking you to leave the show! I would never stand in the way of you doing something that you love," he assured her and smiled. "In case you haven't heard, there's an invention called a jet. The amazing thing is, it can get you anywhere in the country in a matter of a few hours. And don't forget about the three months you'd be home during the off-season, and another three months during the summer when the kids and I could travel with the show."

"What about your writing?"

"I can do that anywhere."

"And what about the other six months, Theron? All those months when you and the kids would be alone? What about the long, lonely nights when you need someone with you?"

"Like I said before, flying in to meet you would be no problem," he told her.

"Right. Like today? Fly in, have dinner, come back here for a wild night of lovemaking, then poof!—you're gone again? We don't need a marriage license for that!" she countered, her words hitting him like a slap in the face. Seeing the hurt she'd inflicted, and the anger, she swallowed. "I'm sorry. I didn't mean it the way it sounded, Theron."

"Didn't you?" he asked, his voice ominously quiet.

"All right, maybe this is all we're supposed to have!"

Stunned, he stared at her. "Is that what you think this is about? *Sex*?" he grated and shook his head. "Hell, I'll be the first to admit that we're good together in bed, but I've always thought it was because we loved each other."

"I do love you, Theron."

"You've got a damned strange way of showing it." Swinging his legs off the bed, he reached for his clothes. As he slipped into jockey shorts and trousers, his anger and frustration grew. When he looked down at her, his eyes were hard. "At least I finally know what you want from me."

Seeing his rage, she stiffened. "What do you mean?"

"Come on, Nicole, cut the bull." He slipped his arms into his shirtsleeves. "The most you're willing to commit yourself to is an affair. From the very beginning you've backed away from anything that smacked of permanence, of commitment." Angrily, he tucked in his shirt and buckled his belt. "Well, I'm sorry, lady, an affair might be good enough for you, but it won't cut it for me. I don't need or want a mistress."

"I don't want an affair!"

"Then marry me!"

"Why do we have to decide this now?"

"You just don't get it, do you?" He regarded her for a long moment, then sighed in exasperation. "Relationships evolve, Nicole. They move from one plateau to the next— unless one of the partners involved refuses to take the next step." His voice grew husky. "I'm ready for that final plateau. The commitment. You're obviously not." When she opened her mouth to protest, he cut her off. "We have gone beyond sneaking down to the gatehouse to make love and hiding from the kids when we shouldn't have to! I'm ready for more than that! I want you in my life!"

"Marrying you wouldn't be fair to any of us!" she exclaimed softly. "Not to you or me or the kids!"

"I don't know what's fair for you anymore, but for the kids and me, *fair* is having the person we love as a part of our lives." He shrugged into his suit coat and looped his tie around his neck, letting it hang loose. "Love is made of compromises, Nicole. No one can have it all his way. Not you. Not me. Not the kids. Not unless we live in an emotional vacuum." Reaching into his breast pocket, he pulled out an envelope and dropped it on the bedside table. "I was hoping I wouldn't have to give this to you."

"What is it?" she croaked through an incredibly tight throat.

"Everything you need to know about Jenny. Medical information, a release that allows you to seek treatment if an emergency should arise," he said. "There are a couple of documents that need your signature. When you've looked them over and signed them, mail them directly to my attorney."

A sick feeling rolled through Nicole's stomach. "Why can't I give them to you when you bring Jenny down in the morning?"

"I won't be bringing Jenny down. Lawrence will." He rubbed the bridge of his nose wearily, then quietly, regretfully, he delivered the final blow. "From now on you'll be dealing directly with my attorney, as far as Jenny is concerned. There'll be no reason for you to call the house."

"Why are you doing this? Why the *hell* are you pushing me, Theron?" she exploded angrily. "I don't want to lose you, but I need some time, damn it!"

He pinned her with steady, achingly beautiful eyes. "How much time do you need? A month? Six?" he asked, then rounded on her. "I don't want to lose you, either, Nicole, but you want it both ways!" His voice softened. "Sweetheart, if you can't say yes now, what makes you think you're going to change your mind later? I know you well enough to understand how stubborn and determined you can be when you set your mind for or against something." He sighed. "Some people can rock along indefinitely in a relationship that isn't going anywhere. I can't. I didn't think you could, either. Apparently, I was wrong again."

"Theron, please, this isn't fair!"

"I've got to get out of here, Nicole. If you should need me for anything...I'll be in Lawrence's Pullman until seven or so in the morning. If I don't see you, then I'll know how things stand between us. We both will." He looked at her for a long time, his eyes clouded. "Goodbye, funny face."

Nicole flinched when she heard the soft click of the door as he walked out of the stateroom and her life. For a long time she stared at the place where he'd been standing, struggling with her emotions while Theron's words ran up and down her mind.

Theron lay on the couch staring at the ceiling, starting at every sound. But there was no sign of her—not during the night, not in the morning—and a heavy sense of loss fell over him as he said goodbye to Jenny and Lawrence, then climbed into the car with Rusty and Julie for the drive to the airport.

Chapter Fourteen

Oh, my God, no!'' Nicole cried the instant she opened her eyes and saw the time. It was almost seven! Scrambling off the couch, she bolted for the door, panic choking her. "Please...please, don't let me be too late! Please...let him still be there!''

Hurrying out of her stateroom, she ran along the side of the train toward Lawrence's car. She barely noticed the steady rain that soaked her, for her mind was on Theron. She'd wanted this to be so right! He hadn't been gone more than an hour the previous night before she fully realized the terrible mistake it would be to throw their love away. She'd showered immediately and dressed, then paced her small living quarters, praying that the long, dark night would quickly pass. Twice she'd started out of the door to go to him. Both times the lateness of the hour stopped her. She remembered sitting on the couch at four-thirty, watching the hands on the clock slowly tick off the minutes....

Now, here it was, seven in the morning, and her life was nearly in ruins because of her own stupidity and blindness.

He'd offered her everything but the moon, and she'd turned him down because of some crazy idea she had about what a family should be, rather than the reality of the very special family who needed her. She'd thought of the negative aspects, blithely discarding the positive elements. And oh, God, she'd thrown the most precious gift of all right back in his face—his love.

She knew that marrying him wouldn't solve their problems. It would create a raft of new ones, but together she and Theron could work through them, and with that knowledge curling around her heart, all fears of making a commitment fell away. Losing him was a far more terrifying prospect.

But what if she was too late? Her heart racing, her legs shaking, rain pelting her, she pounded once on Lawrence's door, then impatiently tried it, and finding it unlocked, she stepped inside. A sharp pain knifed through her when she saw Jenny standing in the middle of the plush living room, her eyes tear-streaked and accusing.

Nicole's blood turned to ice. "Jenny, what's wrong? Where's your father?"

"He's gone." The child's mouth quivered. "My Daddy wanted to marry you. Why don't you want to? Don't you like him?"

"Oh, Jenny, no! I love your father very much!"

"Then is it because you don't like Rusty, Julie and me?" Jenny sobbed.

Going to the child, Nicole knelt down and scooped her close, her own tears flowing freely. "No, honey. It's nothing like that! I love all of you so very, very much!" Nicole said, feeling hesitant small arms go around her neck, then cling to her tightly. Nicole leaned back and looked at Jenny. "That's why I have to know how long ago he left. Jenny, I've got to talk to him before he gets on that plane." Dear

Lord, while trying to protect the children she loved so dearly from possible pain, she'd almost alienated them completely. "Honey, where's Lawrence?"

"Right here, Nick." Lawrence walked out of the kitchen from where he'd been watching. "If we leave now, we might make it. I'll drive you."

Running through a rain as cold as the dread in Nicole's heart, they scrambled into one of the small vans that traveled with the show and set off through the slick streets of Seattle, Nicole tense and nervous, Lawrence concentrating on driving, Jenny fidgeting on the seat between them.

"Are you going to marry Daddy?" she asked quietly.

Nicole sighed. "If he'll still have me."

"Why didn't you want to before?" the child persisted.

"It's not that I didn't want to, honey. Sometimes grown-ups aren't as smart as they think. Sometimes they can be pretty dumb," she said as they sped up a ramp and joined the southbound traffic on Interstate 5. Nicole looked idly at the sea of bright yellow blooms of the Scotch broom that blanketed the grassy roadside, wishing their beauty would ease the ache in her heart. "How much farther?"

"Fifteen, twenty minutes," Lawrence replied, glancing at Nicole. "You're serious about this, aren't you?"

"I've never been more serious about anything in my life."

"We're going to miss you."

"Why? I'm not going anywhere."

"Maybe not this season, but I wouldn't place any bets on next."

She hadn't thought that far ahead. She couldn't. "How much farther?"

"We're about three minutes closer than we were the last time you asked." Lawrence grinned, and a tension-filled silence marked the remainder of the drive to Seattle-Tacoma International Airport. It was broken only when Lawrence stopped outside of the lower level of the main terminal. "You've got about fifteen minutes, Nick. Be sure to go down the escalator for the north satellite and take the subway to the gates. We'll meet you in a few minutes.''

Nicole bolted out of the van and into the building, desperately trying to get her bearings. Oh, God, she was never going to make it! Not through this unfamiliar maze, and the people milling around. She wanted to run but couldn't. Her eyes burned; her stomach rolled. Fear clawing at her, she froze.

Had Lawrence said the north or south satellite? Heading for the south, she stopped suddenly and turned back. *North.* He'd said north—she hoped. She rode the escalator down and passed through security, frantically trying to catch the subway car, but it was too late. She missed it. Impatient, wanting to scream, she waited for another, her heart pounding out the seconds, minutes.

"No, please, this can't happen," she cried softly, tears brimming her eyes. *Time.* She was running out of time! Hours passed. Days. A lifetime! Or was it only a moment? She wasn't sure of anything anymore, only that she was suddenly walking through a doorway, sitting down, riding through a tunnel somewhere under SeaTac, surrounded by strangers while panic played havoc with her nerves.

Panic turned to desperation the instant Nicole rode the escalator up again in the north satellite and saw the reader board. She had less than five minutes to catch Theron, to tell him how much she did love him, or she'd lose him forever. The thought was unbearable. She hurried through the crowd, half running, half walking, to the closest departure gate and cut into the front of the line. She'd never cut in front of anyone in line in her life! Tears trembled on her lashes, and she bit her lip to keep from breaking down completely.

"Please... I need help," she implored the young woman behind the counter.

Seeing Nicole's distraught condition, the woman took her aside. "How can I help you?"

"It's urgent that I get a message to a passenger on the New York flight, but he's probably already boarded. Can you do that?"

"Yes, we can do that for you," said the woman. "I'll need his name."

Nicole gave her Theron's name, then smiled shakily. "Tell him...tell him that there's a clown here who desperately wants to marry him as soon as possible."

The young woman looked up questioningly, smiled and made the call. "It's done. Good luck."

"Thank you. I need it," Nicole replied and hurried toward the departure gate, feeling hopeful for the first time in hours. But the instant she saw the large, empty waiting area, the realization that she'd really lost him hit her with a devastating impact. There was no sign of Theron, or the kids.

Dear God, what now? she prayed silently. Her legs numb, she walked to the wall of windows and stared at the jet that was backing away from the gate, pivoting for its long taxi to takeoff position; the jet that carried the people she loved more than life itself.

She didn't want to cry. Not here. Not now. Not when Jenny and Lawrence would be coming for her soon. But she couldn't help it. Her heart was crying—mourning the loss of the sun and laughter and all the good things Theron had put back in her life.

Looking one last time at the departing plane, she wiped away her tears, turned to leave and suddenly felt her knees buckle as the door to the loading ramp opened and Theron walked out, followed closely by Julie and Rusty. Nicole stood riveted to the spot, her heart racing. She blinked once to be sure it was really him.

"I thought you'd gone!" she exclaimed softly, her eyes steady on him as he walked away from the children to her.

"I thought so, too. You cut it pretty damned close, Nicole. I was worried." His voice was husky with emotion.

"That was the last thing I meant to do. I wanted to talk to you last night, but I was afraid of waking everyone else up," she said, aching to be in his arms. "I dozed off on the couch."

He looked at her for a long, silent moment, his jaw clenching, relaxing, clenching again. "Are you very sure about this?"

"Oh, yes, Theron."

A great sigh shuddered through him, and he thought his heart might burst. Blue-green eyes sought hers. "It's not going to be easy for us, Nicole," he reminded her. "We'll have to work at it a lot harder than most people."

"I know. But I'm not afraid any more. The important thing is that we have each other and the children," she whispered. "Oh, God, Theron, I love you so much, and when I think of how close I came to losing you . . ."

"Shh..." He silenced her with a warm kiss. "You'll never lose me. You never have. You never will." Cupping her face in trembling hands, he lowered his head once again and claimed her mouth fully, tenderly. A husky groan rumbled through his chest, and needing to hold her, he drew her close, loving the feel of her supple body molding to his. Emotions, strong and poignant, made his eyes mist and his voice crack. "I love you, Nicole. More than you'll ever know, and I meant what I said about getting married here. In Seattle."

Nicole smiled up at him, her heart singing. "The show is dark on Monday."

"I knew this wouldn't be easy." He grinned. "Monday, it is."

"Hey, Dad, we gotta go shopping today!" Julie announced happily.

"Why's that, Julie?" Theron asked.

"Because our luggage just took off for New York." She laughed.

"Shelly's going to love this." Theron smiled, making a mental note to alert his sister-in-law of the change in plans and to reschedule the production meeting. But for now, he placed his arm around Nicole's shoulder, and they turned to face the children. "How would you like to go to a wedding on Monday?"

Nicole and Theron were married six days later on a bright, jewellike afternoon, exchanging their vows before family and friends in a beautiful, huge traditional old church whose gray steeples rose heavenward toward a hard blue sky. From its commanding position on Capitol Hill, the church overlooked the city and the sparkling water of Elliot Bay.

Everyone they loved flew in for the wedding: Annabel and her four children, and Tag and Gladys came from Florida, Shelly and Joe Ballinger from New York. They sat at the front of the enormous church with Nicole's family, Lawrence and a few close friends from the show. When the music began, all eyes turned toward the back to watch as Nicole and Theron came in from opposite sides, met at the aisle and linked arms for the walk to the altar, where Rusty, Julie and Jenny waited.

"You are absolutely beautiful, Nicole," he breathed softly, when seeing her in the ivory silk dress with its layers of chiffon swirling around her knees. Her hair fell in a deep gold cascade of curls down her back. Emerald eyes shone with love.

"You're pretty breathtaking yourself," she replied, loving him in the black that he wore so well. Feeling his warm strength beside her, she walked with him toward her new life, tears of happiness springing to her eyes as they pledged their love before God and the others present.

"By the power vested in me, I now pronounce you husband and wife," the pastor proclaimed. "You may kiss your bride."

Theron gazed down at Nicole. Lovingly, he touched her cheek, then lowered his head to kiss his wife. And she was in his arms, holding him close, committing herself to the man whom she loved with all her heart.

The remainder of the day passed in a blur of congratulations and celebration, with a round of picture-taking followed by an early dinner. The sun had set in the west when Nicole and Theron left the children with Lawrence and drove to the hotel where Theron had booked a suite high above the city.

"Oh, Theron, this is forever, isn't it?" Nicole whispered when they were alone. Lifting her left hand, she looked at the emerald-and-diamond engagement ring he'd slipped on her finger a few days ago and the simple gold band he'd added today.

"It's forever, Nicole."

"I love you."

"I love you, too, sweetheart."

She looked at him shyly. "Will you make love with me?"

"Will I?" He cocked an eyebrow and laughed. "I don't know. I may have to think about it a while."

He pondered the idea for all of five seconds, then scooping her close, Theron Donahue made love to his wife—tenderly, reverently, completely—for the first of many times that followed during the unconventional three months they spent together.

There were things they would have liked to change. The living arrangements fell short of perfection, with Theron moving into Nicole's stateroom while the children quite happily stayed with Lawrence. There were times, at night, when Theron missed looking in on his children; times, during the day, when Nicole wished she could go with Theron and the kids when they took sight-seeing trips around the various cities in which they stopped—Boise, Salt Lake City, Denver, Kansas City. There were times when she longed for the room to move about and the freedom to interact as a family rather than being so confined in train cars. Then she'd look at Theron hard at work at the typewriter he'd purchased in Seattle, and with love welling in her, she thanked God she had him.

Twice, she and the children saw him off at airports, and Nicole had spent long, lonely nights sleeping alone while he was in New York on business. But he was never gone more than a day or two....

Until late August when he could no longer put off leaving the train. It was time to end the idyllic summer. Time to go back to Florida. Time for the children to get ready for another school year.

Nicole stood at the windows of the departure gate at the Minneapolis-St. Paul International Airport, staring into the heavens long after Theron and the children's plane had disappeared, the first twinge of anxiety eating at her. But as she walked out of the terminal with Lawrence, she held fast to Theron's promise of meeting the show in Chicago in two weeks.

It didn't happen, for the first of many obstacles suddenly loomed before them. Theron's work demanded he make several trips to New York. The kids had been sick. And, as always, the circus had to go on. While she and Theron enjoyed long, daily phone conversations, the calls couldn't make up for the loneliness she experienced every night when she crawled into bed.

Weeks passed, then months, and by the end of October, she felt the distance growing between them and began to wonder if the summer had been nothing more than a dream.

The final blow came in November when *Images* opened to rave reviews on Broadway on the very same night that Circus Royale opened in Atlanta.

It isn't going to work this way, Nicole thought late that night as she lay in her bed staring into the darkness. *It just isn't going to work.*

* * *

Theron was frowning when he turned off the Palm Valley road and started down the lane toward home. He was worried, had been for several weeks, and he rued the day that he'd left Nicole in Minneapolis with the promise to meet her in Chicago—a promise he couldn't keep. It was the first of many cancelled rendezvous. But, hell, the events of the past four months made Murphy's Law seem optimistic: a round of bad colds and flu with the kids, the constant trips to New York as the opening night for *Images* drew near, the death of a friend. On those occasions when he had met Nicole, they'd been quick trips, often in and out on the same day. He grimaced. The one weekend he'd managed to spend with her had fallen far short of ideal, as that was her busiest time, doing six shows—three on both Saturday and Sunday.

He'd known, going into the marriage, that it wouldn't be easy, but he certainly hadn't bargained for the unexpected obstacles they'd been faced with, and he knew Nicole hadn't, either. That's what worried him, he thought, as he parked the Seville in the driveway and walked into the dark, quiet house. He sensed the distance growing between them. He heard it in her voice, felt it in her embrace on those few, brief occasions when he'd seen her, and he couldn't help but wonder if she was about to bolt and run from the extreme pressure of a long-distance marriage. He hoped not, thought not, and prayed that tomorrow, when the train pulled into Jacksonville for the show's final appearance of the season, they could put their marriage and their lives back on solid ground.

Looking at his watch, he grimaced. It was after midnight. He'd stayed at Annabel's far too late. Taking the stairs two at a time, he checked in on his sleeping children, then strode down the hall to his bedroom, his heart thundering in his chest when he walked in and saw her standing by the window bathed in moonlight.

"Nicole?" He started across the room to her, stopping the instant he saw the expression in her eyes. "Sweetheart, why didn't you let me know you were coming in early?"

"I didn't know myself until I boarded the plane in Atlanta," she told him softly, her eyes brimming with tears. "We have to talk, Theron."

Dread cinched his heart. "That sounds ominous."

She lowered her eyes. "Are you happy?"

"It is ominous." He sighed heavily. "I love you very much, Nicole. I'm happy that we have each other, but I sure as hell won't lie and say that the past few months have been easy. They've been pure hell."

"For me, too."

"Honey, we both knew going in what it would be like." His chest tightened in apprehension.

"No. Neither of us realized exactly what it would be like. Neither of us had any idea that the kids would get sick, or that *Images* would take up so much of your time, or that I'd have to miss that very special opening night with you." She fought a losing battle with her tears. "It isn't working this way, Theron."

"Nick, don't do this to us. My God, we haven't had a chance to make it work."

"Please, Theron, hear me out." She paused, and shook her head as if to clear her mind. "I've been thinking a lot about my life—our life together—and the things that are most important."

"And?" He watched her intently, dreading what was coming.

She took a deep breath and smiled shakily. "And...I didn't renew my contract for next season. It was sitting right in front of me, but all I could think about were you and the kids, and how much I've already missed in your lives." She burst into tears. "I even missed your birthday!"

A tidal wave of relief washing through Theron, he crossed the room to her and pulled her into his arms. "You just shaved five years off my life to tell me that you've missed me and want to stay at home?'' Picking her up, he laughed, then kissed her soundly. "Oh, how I love you, Nicole. So much. So very, very much.''

''I wasn't sure what you'd think about my decision. You were so set against me leaving the show—''

"Not about you leaving the show," he interrupted. "I wanted you to make that decision on your own, with no influence from me.'' Thinking of Nicole's mother, Theron smiled. "A very wise woman taught me a lesson in finding the strength to let go, to give those you love their freedom." He paused a moment. "But I've got to admit I took her too literally at first. The point is that it was your decision to make. Not mine.''

''Then you don't mind?''

''There is nothing in the world that I want more than to share my life with you," he said quietly, a huskiness creeping into his voice. "The past few months haven't been easy, Nicole. Not for any of us. I've missed you next to me at night....'' He kissed her cheeks, her chin, her eyes, her nose, then slowly, deliciously brought his lips to hers, and the world seemed to tremble. "Do you realize how long it's been since we've made love?''

''Two months, five days.'' She pressed close to him, desire heating her at the feel of his hard body and that part of him that she longed to take deep within her. "It's been far too long. Make love with me, Theron.''

Tenderly, he carried her to the bed, and, while outside a full moon silvered the landscape and a yacht moved south on the waterway, sounding its horn for the drawbridge, a man and woman made love from the depths of their hearts and souls. It was the final commitment.

Theron held her quietly for a long time afterward, marveling at the profound sense of peace winding through and around him. Loving the feel of her skin, he lazily ran his hand up and down her arm, leaning down now and again to kiss her gently.

"I love you, you know," he told her, smiling into her eyes.

"I love you, too." She kissed his shoulder.

"What are you going to do now?"

She grinned at him. "Keep you in bed as long as possible."

"I like the sound of that, but what about later? I can't imagine you being idle."

Nicole rolled over and flopped her arm across his chest. "Well...with Gus quitting, Ralph is going to need help when the show leaves in March. We'll team up to work with Jenny. And..." She twirled the tip of a finger through his chest hair. "...Gina called while I was in New York. She's sending a girl down here who wants to train on the rings."

"What about Rossles?"

"Oh, she's coming out of the trunk. I spent a lot of time in Clown Alley after you and the kids left." She smiled warmly. "And of course I want to take care of my very special family."

"You'll have Gladys."

"Gladys needs some time off now and then." Her eyes clouded suddenly, and she pursed her lips. There was something else that she wanted, as well, but now that the time had come to bring it up, uneasiness rolled through her.

"Sweetheart, what's wrong?" Concerned, he tilted her head back, searching the green eyes he loved so much.

She let out her breath in a long rush. "Do you remember the night we talked about babies and adoption?"

He grinned. "How could I ever forget? That was the night of the lusty libido."

She hesitated a moment. "Were you serious? Did you mean what you said about adoption?"

He narrowed his eyes on her, the familiar muscle in his jaw tightening. "What are you trying to say, Nicole?"

"That we do it. I would love to be able to have your child, Theron, but I can't—"

His hand trembling, he touched a finger to her lips to silence her, his heart brimming with love. "It will be ours. Yours and mine. And it'll be ours in a very special way, Nicole." Lowering his head, he kissed her, desire for this woman leaping through him. "I think it's a wonderful idea."

Nicole wrapped her arms around him, going to him eagerly, happily. She'd come home, at long last, and nothing would ever stand between them again.

*   *   *   *   *

#583 TAMING NATASHA—Nora Roberts
Natasha Stanislaski was a pussycat with Spence Kimball's little girl, but to Spence himself she was as ornery as a caged tiger. Would some cautious loving sheath her claws and free her heart from captivity?

#584 WILLING PARTNERS—Tracy Sinclair
Taking up residence in the fabled Dunsmuir mansion, wedding the handsome Dunsmuir heir and assuming instant "motherhood" surpassed secretary Jessica Lawrence's wildest dreams. But had Blade Dunsmuir wooed her for money...or love?

#585 PRIVATE WAGERS—Betsy Johnson
Rugged Steven Merrick deemed JoAnna Stowe a mere bit of fluff—until the incredibly close quarters of a grueling motorcycle trek revealed her fortitude *and* her womanly form, severely straining *his* manly stamina!

#586 A GUILTY PASSION—Laurey Bright
Ethan Ryland condemned his stepbrother's widow for her husband's untimely death. Still, he was reluctantly, obsessively drawn to the fragile-looking Celeste...and he feared she shared his damnable passion.

#587 HOOPS—Patricia McLinn
Though urged to give teamwork the old college try, marble-cool professor Carolyn Trent and casual coach C. J. Draper soon collided in a stubborn tug-of-war between duty...and desire.

#588 SUMMER'S FREEDOM—Ruth Wind
Brawny Joel Summer had gently liberated man-shy Maggie Henderson...body and soul. But could her love unchain him from the dark, secret past that shadowed their sunlit days of loving?

AVAILABLE THIS MONTH:

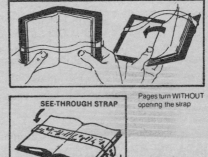
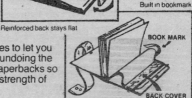

At long last, the books you've been waiting for
by one of America's top romance authors!

DIANA PALMER

DUETS

Ten years ago Diana Palmer published her very first
romances. Powerful and dramatic, these gripping tales
of love are everything you have come to expect from
Diana Palmer.

In March, some of these titles will be available again in
DIANA PALMER DUETS—a special three-book collec-
tion. Each book will have two wonderful stories plus an
introduction by the author. You won't want to miss them!

Book 1
SWEET ENEMY
LOVE ON TRIAL

Book 2
STORM OVER THE LAKE
TO LOVE AND CHERISH

Book 3
IF WINTER COMES
NOW AND FOREVER